slammed

Also by Colleen Hoover

Point of Retreat

slammed

A Novel

Colleen Hoover

ATRIA PAPERBACK

NEW YORK   LONDON   TORONTO   SYDNEY   NEW DELHI

ATRIA PAPERBACK
A Division of Simon & Schuster, Inc.
1230 Avenue of the Americas
New York, NY 10020

First Atria Paperback edition September 2012

ATRIA PAPERBACK and colophon are trademarks of Simon & Schuster, Inc.

The author and publisher gratefully acknowledge permission from the following source to reprint material in their control: Portions of song lyrics from the Avett Brothers. Reprint permission granted by the Avett Brothers.

For information about special discounts for bulk purchases, please contact Simon & Schuster Special Sales at 1-866-506-1949 or business@simonandschuster.com.

The Simon & Schuster Speakers Bureau can bring authors to your live event. For more information or to book an event, contact the Simon & Schuster Speakers Bureau at 1-866-248-3049 or visit our website at www.simonspeakers.com.

Designed by Suet Y. Chong

Manufactured in the United States of America

10 9 8 7 6 5 4 3 2 1

Library of Congress Cataloging-in-Publication Data is available.

ISBN 978-1-4767-1590-2
ISBN 978-1-4767-1591-9 (ebook)

This book is dedicated to the Avett Brothers, for giving me the motivation to "decide what to be, and go be it."

part one

1.

I'm as nowhere as I can be,
Could you add some somewhere to me?

—THE AVETT BROTHERS, "SALINA"

KEL AND I LOAD THE LAST TWO BOXES INTO THE U-HAUL.
I slide the door down and pull the latch shut, locking up eighteen years of memories, all of which include my dad.

It's been six months since he passed away. Long enough that my nine-year-old brother, Kel, doesn't cry every time we talk about him, but recent enough that we're being forced to accept the financial aftermath that comes to a newly single-parented household. A household that can't afford to remain in Texas and in the only home I've ever known.

"Lake, stop being such a downer," my mom says, handing me the keys to the house. "I think you'll love Michigan."

She never calls me by the name she legally gave me. She and my dad argued for nine months over what I would be named. She loved the name Layla, after the Eric Clapton song. Dad loved the name Kennedy, after a Kennedy. "It doesn't matter which Kennedy," he would say. "I love them all!"

I was almost three days old before the hospital forced them to decide. They agreed to take the first three letters of both names and compromised on Layken, but neither of them has ever once referred to me as such.

I mimic my mother's tone, "Mom, stop being such an *upper*! I'm going to *hate* Michigan."

My mother has always had an ability to deliver an entire lecture with a single glance. I get the glance.

I walk up the porch steps and head inside the house to make a walk-through before the final turn of the key. All of the rooms are eerily empty. It doesn't seem as though I'm walking through the house where I've lived since the day I was born. These last six months have been a whirlwind of emotions, all of them bad. Moving out of this home was inevitable—I realize that. I just expected it to happen after the *end* of my senior year.

I'm standing in what is no longer our kitchen when I catch a glimpse of a purple plastic hair clip under the cabinet in the space where the refrigerator once stood. I pick it up, wipe the dust off of it, and run it back and forth between my fingers.

"It'll grow back," Dad said.

I was five years old, and my mother had left her trimming scissors on the bathroom counter. Apparently, I had done what most kids of that age do. I cut my own hair.

"Mommy's going to be so mad at me," I cried. I thought that if I cut my hair, it would immediately grow back, and no one would notice. I cut a pretty wide chunk out of my bangs and sat in front of the mirror for probably an hour, waiting for the hair to grow back. I picked the straight brown strands up off the floor and held them in my hand, contemplating how I could secure them back to my head, when I began to cry.

When Dad walked into the bathroom and saw what I had done, he just laughed and scooped me up, then positioned me on the countertop. "Mommy's not going to notice, Lake," he promised as he removed something out of the bathroom cabinet. "I just happen to have a piece of magic right here." He opened up his palm and revealed the purple clip. "As long as you have this in your hair, Mommy will never know." He brushed the remaining strands of hair across and secured the clip in place. He then turned me around to face the mirror. "See? Good as new!"

I looked at our reflection in the mirror and felt like the luckiest girl in the world. I didn't know of any other dad who had magic clips.

I wore that clip in my hair every day for two months, and my mother never once mentioned it. Now that I look back on it, I realize he probably told her what I had done. But when I was five, I believed in his magic.

I look more like my mother than like him. Mom and I are both of average height. After having two kids, she can't really fit into my jeans, but we're pretty good at sharing everything else. We both have brown hair that, depending on the weather, is either straight or wavy. Her eyes are a deeper emerald than mine, although it could be that the paleness of her skin just makes them more prominent.

I favor my dad in all the ways that count. We had the same dry sense of humor, the same personality, the same love of music, the same laugh. Kel is a different story. He takes after our dad physically with his dirty-blond hair and soft features. He's on the small side for nine years old, but his personality makes up for what he lacks in size.

I walk to the sink and turn it on, rubbing my thumb over the thirteen years of grime collected on the hair clip. Kel walks backward into the kitchen just as I'm drying my hands on my jeans. He's a strange kid, but I couldn't love him more. He has a game he likes to play that he calls "backward day," in which he spends most of the time walking everywhere backward, talking backward, and even requesting dessert first. I guess with such a big age difference between him and me and no other siblings, he has to find a way to entertain himself somehow.

"Hurry to says Mom Layken!" he says, backward.

I place the hair clip in the pocket of my jeans and head back out the door, locking up my home for the very last time.

* * *

OVER THE NEXT few days, my mother and I alternate driving my Jeep and the U-Haul, stopping only twice at hotels to sleep. Kel switches between Mom and me, riding the final day with me in the U-Haul. We complete the last exhausting nine-hour stretch through the night, only stopping once for a short break. As we close in on our new town of Ypsilanti, I take in my surroundings and the fact that it's September but my heater is on. I'll definitely need a new wardrobe.

As I make a final right-hand turn onto our street, my GPS informs me that I've "reached my destination."

"My destination," I laugh aloud to myself. My GPS doesn't know squat.

The cul-de-sac is not very long, lined with about eight single-story brick houses on each side of the street. There's a basketball goal in one of the driveways, which gives me hope that Kel might have someone to play with. Honestly, it looks like a decent neighborhood. The lawns are manicured, the sidewalks are clean, but there's too much concrete. Way too much concrete. I already miss home.

Our new landlord emailed us pictures of the house, so I immediately spot which one is ours. It's small. It's *really* small. We had a ranch-style home on several acres of land in Texas. The minuscule amount of land surrounding *this* home is almost nothing but concrete and garden gnomes. The front door is propped open, and I see an older man who I assume is our new landlord come outside and wave.

I drive about fifty yards past the house so that I can

back into the driveway, where the rear of the U-Haul will face the front door. Before I put the gearshift in reverse, I reach over and shake Kel awake. He's been passed out since Indiana.

"Kel, wake up," I whisper. "We've reached our *destination*."

He stretches his legs out and yawns, then leans his forehead against the window to get a look at our new house. "Hey, there's a kid in the yard!" Kel says. "Do you think he lives in our house, too?"

"He better not," I reply. "But he's probably a neighbor. Hop out and go introduce yourself while I back up."

When the U-Haul is successfully backed in, I put the gearshift in park, roll down the windows, and kill the engine. My mother pulls in beside me in my Jeep and I watch as she gets out and greets the landlord. I crouch down a few inches in the seat and prop my foot against the dash, watching Kel and his new friend sword fight with imaginary swords in the street. I'm jealous of him. Jealous of the fact that he can accept the move so easily, and I'm stuck being the angry, bitter child.

He was upset when Mom first decided on the move. Mostly because he was in the middle of his Little League season. He had friends he would miss, but at the age of nine your best friend is usually imaginary, and transatlantic. Mom subdued him pretty easily by promising he could sign up for hockey, something he wanted to do in Texas. It was a hard sport to come by in the rural south. After she agreed to that, he was pretty upbeat, if not stoked, about Michigan.

I understand why we had to move. Dad had made a respectable living managing a paint store. Mom worked PRN as a nurse when she needed to, but mostly tended to the house and to us. About a month after he died, she was able to find a full-time job. I could see the stress of my father's death taking its toll on her, along with being the new head of household.

One night over dinner, she explained to us that she wasn't left with enough income to continue paying all the bills and the mortgage. She said there was a job that could pay her more, but we would have to move. She was offered a job by her old high-school friend Brenda. They grew up together in my mother's hometown of Ypsilanti, right outside of Detroit. It paid more than anything she could find in Texas, so she had no choice but to accept. I don't blame her for the move. My grandparents are deceased, and she has no one to help her. I understand why we had to do it, but understanding a situation doesn't always make it easier.

"Layken, you're dead!" Kel shouts through the open window, thrusting his imaginary sword into my neck. He waits for me to slump over, but I just roll my eyes at him. "I stabbed you. You're supposed to die!" he says.

"Believe me, I'm already dead," I mumble as I open the door and climb out. Kel's shoulders are slumped forward and he's staring down at the concrete, his imaginary sword limp by his side. Kel's new friend stands behind him looking just as defeated, causing me immediately to regret the transference of my bad mood.

"I'm already dead," I say in my best monster voice, "because I'm a *zombie*!"

They start screaming as I stretch my arms out in front of me, cock my head to the side, and make a gurgling sound. "Brains!" I grumble, walking stiff-legged after them around the U-Haul. "Brains!"

I slowly round the front of the U-Haul, holding my arms out in front of me, when I notice someone grasping my brother and his new friend by the collars of their shirts.

"Get 'em!" The stranger yells as he holds the two screaming boys.

He looks a couple of years older than me and quite a bit taller. "Hot" would be how most girls would describe him, but I'm not most girls. The boys are flailing around, and his muscles flex under his shirt as he tries hard to maintain his grip on them.

Unlike Kel and me, these two are unmistakably siblings. Aside from the obvious age difference, they're identical. They both have the same smooth olive skin, the same jet-black hair, even the same cropped hairstyle. He's laughing as Kel breaks free and starts slicing at him with his "sword." He looks up at me and mouths "Help," when I realize I'm still frozen in my zombie pose.

My first instinct is to crawl back inside the U-Haul and hide on the floorboard for the remainder of my life.

Instead, I yell "Brains" once more and lunge forward, pretending to bite the younger boy on top of his head. I grab Kel and his new friend and start tickling them until they melt into heaps on the concrete driveway.

As I straighten up, the older brother extends his hand. "Hey, I'm Will. We live across the street," he says, pointing to the house directly across from ours.

I reciprocate his handshake. "I'm Layken. I guess I live here," I say as I glance toward the house behind me.

He smiles. Our handshake lingers as neither one of us says anything. I hate awkward moments.

"Well, welcome to Ypsilanti," he says. He pulls his hand from mine and puts it in his jacket pocket. "Where are you guys moving here from?"

"Texas?" I reply. I'm not sure why the tail end of my reply comes out like a question. I'm not sure why I'm even analyzing why it came out like a question. I'm not sure why I'm analyzing the reason why I'm analyzing—I'm flustered. It must be the lack of sleep I've gotten over the past three days.

"Texas, huh?" he says. He's rocking back and forth on his heels. The awkwardness intensifies when I fail to respond. He glances down at his brother and bends over, grabbing him by the ankles. "I've got to get this little guy to school," he says as he swings his brother up and over his shoulders. "There's a cold front coming through tonight. You should try to get as much unloaded today as you can. It's supposed to last a few days, so if you guys need help unloading this afternoon, let me know. We should be home around four."

"Sure, thanks," I say. They head across the street, and I'm still watching them when Kel stabs me in my lower back. I drop to my knees and clutch at my stomach, crouching forward as Kel climbs on top of me and finishes me off. I glance across the street again and see Will watching us. He shuts his brother's car door, walks around to the driver's-side door, and waves goodbye.

IT TAKES US most of the day to unload all of the boxes and furniture. Our landlord helps move the larger items that Mom and I can't lift on our own. We're too tired to get to the boxes inside the Jeep and agree to put it off until tomorrow. I'm a little disappointed when the U-Haul is finally empty; I no longer have an excuse to solicit Will's help.

As soon as my bed is put together, I start grabbing boxes with my name on them from the hallway. I get most of them unpacked and my bed made, when I notice the furniture in my bedroom casting shadows across the walls. I look out my window, and the sun is setting. Either the days are a lot shorter here, or I've lost track of time.

In the kitchen, I find Mom and Kel unloading dishes into the cabinets. I climb into one of the six tall chairs at the bar, which also doubles as the dining room table because of the lack of dining room. There isn't much to this house. When you walk through the front door, there's a small entryway followed by the living room. The living room is separated from the kitchen by nothing more than a hallway to the left and a window to the right. The living room's beige carpet is edged by hardwood that leads throughout the rest of the house.

"Everything is so clean here," my mother says as she continues putting away dishes. "I haven't seen a single insect."

Texas has more insects than blades of grass. If you aren't swatting flies, you're killing wasps.

"That's one good thing about Michigan, I guess," I reply. I open up a box of pizza in front of me and eye the selection.

"*One* good thing?" She winks at me as she leans across the bar, grabs a pepperoni, and pops it into her mouth. "I'd think that would be at least *two* good things."

I pretend I'm not following.

"I saw you talking to that boy this morning," she says with a smile.

"Oh, please, Mom," I reply as indifferently as I can get away with. "I'm pretty positive we'll find it no surprise that Texas isn't the only state inhabited by the male species." I walk to the refrigerator and grab a soda.

"What's anabited?" Kel asks.

"Inhabited," I correct him. "It means to occupy, dwell, reside, populate, squat, *live*." My SAT prep courses are paying off.

"Oh, kinda like how we anabited Ypsilanti?" he says.

"Inhabited," I correct him again. I finish my slice of pizza and take another sip of the soda. "I'm beat, guys. I'm going to bed."

"You mean you're going to *inhabit* your bedroom?" Kel says.

"You're a quick learner, young grasshopper." I bend and kiss the top of his head and retreat to my room.

It feels so good to crawl under the covers. At least my bed is familiar. I close my eyes and try to imagine that I'm in my old bedroom. My old, *warm* bedroom. My sheets and pillow are ice cold, so I pull the covers over my head to generate some heat. Note to self: Locate the thermostat first thing in the morning.

AND THAT'S EXACTLY what I set out to do as soon as I crawl out of bed and my bare feet meet the ice-cold floor beneath them. I grab a sweater out of my closet and throw it on over my pajamas while I search for socks. It's a futile attempt. I quietly tiptoe down the hallway, trying not to wake anyone while at the same time attempting to expose the least possible amount of foot to the coldness of the hardwood. As I pass Kel's room, I spot his Darth Vader house shoes on the floor. I sneak in and slip them on, finally finding some relief as I head into the kitchen.

I look around for the coffeepot but don't find it. I remember packing it in the Jeep, which is unfortunate since the Jeep is parked outside. Outside in this absurdly cold weather.

The jackets are nowhere to be found. Septembers in Texas rarely call for jackets. I grab the keys and decide I'll just have to make a mad dash to the Jeep. I open the front door and some sort of white substance is all over the yard. It takes me a second to realize what it is. Snow? In September? I bend down and scoop some up in my hands and examine it. It doesn't snow that often in Texas, but when it does it isn't *this* kind of snow. Texas snow is more like minuscule pieces of rock-hard hail. Michigan snow is just how I imagined real snow would be: fluffy, soft, and *cold*! I quickly drop the snow and dry my hands on my sweatshirt as I head toward the Jeep.

I don't make it far. The second those Darth Vader house shoes meet the snow-dusted concrete, I'm no longer looking at the Jeep in front of me. I'm flat on my back, staring up at the clear blue sky. I immediately feel the pain in my right shoulder and realize I've landed on something hard. I reach around and pull a concrete garden gnome out from beneath me, half of his red hat broken off and shattered into pieces. He's smirking at me. I groan and raise the gnome with my good arm and pull it back, preparing to chuck the thing, when someone stops me.

"That's not a good idea!"

I immediately recognize Will's voice. The sound of it is smooth and soothing like my father's was, but at the same time has an authoritative edge to it. I sit upright and see him walking up the driveway toward me.

"Are you okay?" he laughs.

"I'll feel a lot better after I bust this damn thing," I say, trying to pull myself up with no success.

"You don't want to do that: Gnomes are good luck," he says as he reaches me. He takes the gnome out of my hands and gently places it on the snow-covered grass.

"Yeah," I reply, taking in the gash on my shoulder that has now formed a bright red circle on my sweater sleeve. "*Real* good luck."

Will stops laughing when he sees the blood on my shirt. "Oh my god, I'm so sorry. I wouldn't have laughed if I knew you were hurt." He bends over and takes my un-injured arm and pulls me up. "You need to get a bandage on that."

"I wouldn't have a clue where to find one at this point," I reply, referring to the mounds of unopened boxes we have yet to unpack.

"You'll have to walk with me. There's some in our kitchen."

He removes his jacket and wraps it around my shoulders, holding on to my arm as he walks me across the street. I feel a little pathetic with him assisting me—I can walk on my own. I don't object though, and I feel like a hypocrite to the entire feminist movement. I've regressed to the damsel in distress.

I remove his jacket and lay it across the back of the

couch, then follow him into the kitchen. It's still dark inside, so I assume everyone is still asleep. His house is more spacious than ours. The open floor plans are similar, but the living room seems to be a few feet larger. A large bay window with a sitting bench and large pillows looks out over the backyard.

Several family pictures hang along the wall opposite the kitchen. Most of them are of Will and his little brother, with a few pictures that include his parents. I walk over to inspect the pictures while Will looks for a bandage. They must have gotten their genes from their dad. In one picture, which seems like the most recent but still looks a few years dated, his dad has his arms around the two boys, and he's squeezing them together for an impromptu photo. His jet-black hair is speckled with gray, and a thick black moustache outlines his huge smile. His features are identical to Will's. They both have eyes that smile when they laugh, exposing perfect white teeth.

Will's mother is breathtaking. She has long blond hair and, from the pictures at least, looks tall. I can't pick out any facial features of hers that were passed on to her boys. Maybe Will has her personality. All of the pictures on the wall prove one big difference between our houses—this one is a *home*.

I walk into the kitchen and take a seat at the bar.

"It needs to be cleaned before you put the bandage on it," he says as he rolls up his shirtsleeves and turns on the faucet. He's wearing a pale-yellow button-down collared shirt that is slightly transparent under the kitchen lights, revealing the outline of his undershirt. He has broad shoulders, and his sleeves are snug around the muscles in his arms. The top of his head meets the cabinet above him, and I estimate from the similarities in our kitchens that he stands about six inches taller than me. I'm staring at the pattern on his black tie, which is flipped over his shoulder to avoid getting it wet, when he turns the water off and walks back to the bar. I feel my face flush as I grab the wet napkin out of his hands, not proud of the amount of attention his physique is getting from me.

"It's fine," I say, pulling my sleeve down over my shoulder. "I can get it."

He opens a bandage as I wipe the blood off the wound. "So, what were you doing outside in your pajamas at seven o'clock in the morning?" he asks. "Are you guys still unloading?"

I shake my head and toss the napkin into the trash can. "Coffee."

"Oh. I guess you aren't a morning person." Will says this as more of a statement than a question.

As he moves in closer to place the bandage on my shoulder, I feel his breath on my neck. I rub my arms to hide the chills that are creeping up them. He adheres it to my shoulder and pats it.

"There. Good as new," he says.

"Thanks. And I *am* a morning person," I say. "*After* I get my coffee." I stand up and look over my shoulder, pretending to inspect the bandage as I plot my next move. I already thanked him. I could turn and walk out now, but that would seem rude after he just helped me. If I just stand here waiting on him to make more small talk, I might look stupid for *not* leaving. I don't understand why I'm even contemplating basic actions around him. He's just another inhabitant!

When I turn around, he's at the counter, pouring a cup of coffee. He walks toward me and sets it on the bar in front of me. "You want cream or sugar?"

I shake my head. "Black is fine. Thanks."

He's leaning across the bar watching me as I drink the coffee. His eyes are the exact same hue of deep green as his mother's are in the picture. I guess he did get a feature from her. He smiles and breaks our gaze by looking down at his watch. "I need to go: My brother's waiting in the car, and I've got to get to work," he says. "I'll walk you back. You can keep the cup."

I look at the cup before taking another sip and notice the big letters emblazoned on the side. World's Greatest Dad. It's exactly the same as the cup my father used to drink coffee from. "I'll be okay," I say as I head toward the front door. "I think I've got the whole walking-erect thing down now."

He follows me outside and shuts his front door behind him, insisting I take his jacket with me. I pull it on over my shoulders, thank him again, and head across the street.

"Layken!" he yells just as I'm about to walk back inside my house. I turn back toward him and he's standing in his driveway.

"May the force be with you!" He laughs and hops into his car as I stand there, staring down at the Darth Vader house shoes I'm still sporting. Classic.

THE COFFEE HELPS. I locate the thermostat, and by lunch the house has finally started to warm up. Mom and Kel have gone to the utility company to get everything switched into her name, and I'm left with the last of the boxes, if you don't count what's still in the Jeep. I get a few more things unpacked and decide it's high time for a shower. I'm pretty sure I'm closing in on day three of my granola-girl look.

I get out of the shower and wrap myself in a towel, flipping my hair forward as I brush it out and blow-dry it. When it's dry, I point the blow-dryer at the fogged up mirror, forming a clear circular area so that I can apply a little makeup. I notice my tan has started to fade. There won't be much lying-out here, so I might as well get used to a slightly paler complexion.

I brush my hair and pull it back into a ponytail and put on some lip gloss and mascara. I forgo the blush, since there no longer seems to be a need for it. Between the weather and my brief encounters with Will, my cheeks seem to stay red.

Mom and Kel have already returned and gone again while I was in the shower. There is a note from her informing me she and Kel are following her friend Brenda into the city to return the U-Haul. Three twenty-dollar bills are on the counter next to the car keys and a grocery list. I snatch them up and head to the Jeep, reaching it successfully this time.

I realize as I'm putting the car into reverse that I have absolutely no idea where I'm going. I know nothing about this town, much less whether I need to turn left or right off of my own street. Will's little brother is in their front yard, so I pull the car up parallel to their curb and roll down my passenger window.

"Hey, come here for a sec!" I yell at him.

He looks at me and hesitates. Maybe he thinks I'm going to bust out in zombie mode again. He walks toward the car, but stops three feet short of the window.

"How do I get to the closest grocery store?" I ask him.

He rolls his eyes. "Seriously? I'm nine."

Okay. So the resemblance to his brother is only skin deep.

"Well, thanks for nothing," I say. "What's your name anyway?"

He smiles at me mischievously and yells, "Darth Vader!" He's laughing as he runs in the opposite direction of the car.

Darth Vader? I realize the significance of his response. He's making a crack about the house shoes I had on this morning. Not a big deal. The big deal is that Will must have been talking about me to him. I can't help but try to imagine the conversation between them and what Will thinks about me. *If* he even thinks about me. For some reason, I've been thinking about him more than I'm comfortable with. I keep wondering how old he is, what his major is, whether he's *single*.

Luckily, I didn't leave any boyfriends behind in Texas. I haven't dated anyone in almost a year. Between high school, my part-time job, and helping out with Kel's sports, I hadn't had much time for boys. I realize it's going to be an adjustment, going from a person with absolutely no free time to a person with absolutely nothing to do.

I reach into the glove box to retrieve my GPS.

"That's not a good idea," Will says.

I look up to see him walking toward the car. I make my best attempt to stifle the smile that is trying to take over my face. "What's not a good idea?" I say as I insert the GPS into its holder and power it on.

He crosses his arms and leans in the window of the car. "There's quite a bit of construction going on right now. That thing will get you lost."

I'm about to respond when Brenda pulls up alongside me with my mother. Brenda rolls down her driver's-side window and my mother leans across the seat. "Don't forget laundry detergent—I can't remember if I put it on the list.

And cough syrup. I think I'm coming down with something," she says through the window.

Kel jumps out of the backseat, runs to Will's brother, and invites him inside to look at our house.

"Can I?" Will's brother asks him.

"Sure," Will says as he opens my passenger door. "I'll be back in a little while, Caulder. I'm riding with Layken to the store."

He is? I shoot a look in his direction and he's buckling his seat belt.

"I don't give very good verbal directions. Mind if I go with you?"

"I guess not," I laugh.

I look back toward Brenda and my mother, but they have already pulled forward into the driveway. I put the car in drive and listen as Will gives me directions out of the neighborhood. "So, Caulder is your little brother's name?" I say, making a halfhearted attempt at small talk.

"One and only. My parents tried for years to have another baby after me. They eventually had Caulder when names like 'Will' weren't that cool anymore."

"I like your name," I say. I regret saying it as soon as it comes out of my mouth. It sounds like a lame attempt at flirting.

He laughs. I like his laugh. I hate that I like his laugh.

It startles me when I feel him brush the hair off my shoulder and touch my neck. His fingers slip under the collar of my shirt and he pulls it slightly down over my shoulder. "You're going to need a new bandage soon." He pulls my shirt back up and gives it a pat. His fingers leave a streak of heat across my neck.

"Remind me to grab some at the store," I say, trying to prove that his actions and his presence have no effect on me whatsoever.

"So, Layken." He pauses as he glances past me at the boxes still piled high in the backseat. "Tell me about yourself."

"Um, no. That's so cliché," I say.

He laughs. "Fine. I'll figure you out myself." He leans forward and hits eject on my CD player. His movements are so fluid, like he's been rehearsing them for years. I envy this about him. I've never been known for my grace.

"You know, you can tell a lot about a person by their taste in music." He pulls the CD out and examines the label. " 'Layken's shit?' " he says aloud and laughs. "Is *shit* descriptive here, or possessive?"

"I don't like Kel touching my shit, okay?" I grab the CD out of his hands and insert it back into the player.

When the banjo pours out of the speakers at full volume, I'm immediately embarrassed. I'm from Texas, but I don't want him mistaking this for country music. If there's one thing I *don't* miss about Texas, it's the country music. I reach over and turn down the volume, when he grabs my hand in objection.

"Turn it back up, I know this," he says. His hand remains clasped on top of mine.

My fingers are still on the volume so I turn it back up. There's no *way* he knows this. I realize he's bluffing—his own lame attempt at flirting.

"Oh yeah?" I say. I'll call his bluff. "What's it called?"

"It's the Avett Brothers," he says. "I call it 'Gabriella,' but I think it's the end to one of their 'Pretty Girl' songs. I love the end of this one when they break out with the electric guitars."

His response to my question startles me. He really does know this. "You like the Avett Brothers?"

"I *love* them. They played in Detroit last year. Best live show I've ever seen."

A rush of adrenaline shoots through my body as I look down at his hand, still holding on to mine, still holding on to the volume button. I like it, but I'm mad at myself for liking it. Boys have given me the butterflies before, but I usually have more control over my susceptibility to such mundane movements.

He notices me noticing our hands and he lets go, rubbing his palms on his pant legs. It seems like a nervous gesture and I'm curious whether he shares my uneasiness.

I tend to listen to music that isn't mainstream. It's rare when I meet someone that has even heard of half the bands I love. The Avett Brothers are my all-time favorite.

My father and I would stay up at night and sing some of the songs together as he attempted to work out the chords on his guitar. He described them to me once. He said, "Lake, you know a band has true talent when their *imperfections* define *perfection*."

I eventually understood what he meant when I started really *listening* to them. Broken banjo strings, momentary passionate lapses of harmony, voices that go from smooth to gravelly to all-out screaming in a single verse. All these things add substance, character, and believability to their music.

After my father died, my mother gave me an early present he had intended to give me for my eighteenth birthday: a pair of Avett Brothers concert tickets. I cried when she gave them to me, thinking about how much my father was probably looking forward to giving me the gift himself. I knew he would have wanted me to use them, but I couldn't. The concert was just weeks after his death, and I knew I wouldn't be able to enjoy it. Not like I would have if he were with me.

"I love them, too," I say unsteadily.

"Have you ever seen them play live?" Will asks.

I'm not sure why, but as we talk, I tell him the entire story about my dad. He listens intently, interrupting only to instruct me when and where to turn. I tell him all about our passion for music. I tell him about how my father died suddenly and extremely unexpectedly of a heart attack. I tell him about my birthday present and the concert we never made it to. I don't know why I keep talking, but I can't seem to shut myself up. I never divulge information so freely, especially to people I barely know. Especially to *guys* I barely know. I'm still talking when I realize we've come to a stop in a grocery store parking lot.

"Wow," I say as I take in the time on the clock. "Is that the quickest way to the store? That drive took twenty minutes."

He winks at me and opens his door. "No, actually it's not."

That's *definitely* flirting. And I definitely have butterflies.

The snow flurries start to mix with sleet as we're making our way through the parking lot. "Run," he says. He takes my hand in his and pulls me faster toward the entrance.

We're out of breath and laughing when we make it inside the store, shaking the wetness from our clothes. I take my jacket off and shake it out, when his hand brushes against my face, wiping away a strand of wet hair that's stuck to my cheek. His hand is cold, but the moment his fingers graze my skin, I forget about the frigid temperature as my face grows warm. His smile fades as we both stare at each other. I'm still trying to become accustomed to the reactions I have around him. The slightest touch and simplest gestures have such an intense effect on my senses.

I clear my throat and break our stare as I grab an available cart next to us. I hand him the grocery list. "Does it always snow in September?" I ask in an attempt to appear unfazed by his touch.

"No, it won't last more than a few days, maybe a week. Most of the time the snow doesn't start until late October," he says. "You're lucky."

"Lucky?"

"Yeah. It's a pretty rare cold front. You got here right in time."

"Huh. I assumed most of y'all would hate the snow. Doesn't it snow here most of the year?"

He laughs. "*Y'all?*"

"What?"

"Nothing," he says with a smile. "I've just never heard anyone say 'y'all' in real life before. It's cute. So southern belle."

"Oh, I'm sorry," I say. "From now on I'll do like you Yankees and waste my breath by saying 'all you guys.' "

He laughs and nudges my shoulder. "Don't. I like your accent; it's perfect."

I can't believe I've actually turned into a girl who swoons over a guy. I detest it so much; I start to inspect his features more intently, trying to find a flaw. I can't. Everything about him so far is perfect.

We get the items on our list and head to the checkout. He refuses to let me put anything on the conveyor belt, so I just stand back and watch as he unloads the items from the buggy. The last item he places on the line is a box of bandages. I never even saw him grab them.

When we pull out of the grocery store, Will tells me to turn in the direction opposite to the one from which we came. We drive maybe two whole blocks when he instructs me to turn left—onto our street. The drive that took us twenty minutes on the way there takes us less than a minute on the way back.

"Nice," I say when I pull in my driveway. I realize what he's done and that the flirtation on his end is blatantly obvious.

Will has already rounded to the back of the Jeep, so I press the trunk lever for him. I get out and walk to where he is, expecting him to have an armload of groceries. Instead, he's just standing there holding the trunk up, watching me.

With my best southern belle impression, I place my hand across my chest and say, "Why! I never would have been able to find the store without your help. Thank you *so* much for your hospitality, kind sir."

I sort of expect him to laugh, but he just stands there, staring at me.

"*What?*" I say nervously.

He takes a step toward me and softly cups my chin with his free hand. I'm shocked by my own reaction, the fact that I allow it. He studies my face for a few seconds as my heart races within my chest. I think he's about to kiss me.

I attempt to calm my breathing as I stare up at him. He steps in even closer and removes his hand from my chin and places it on the back of my neck, leaning my head in toward him. His lips press gently against my forehead, lingering a few seconds before he releases his hand and steps back.

"You're so cute," he says. He reaches into the trunk and grabs four sacks with one hefty swoop. He walks toward the house and sets them outside the door.

I'm frozen, attempting to absorb the last fifteen seconds of my life. Where did that come from? Why did I just stand there and let him do that? Despite my objections I realize, almost pathetically, that I have just experienced the most passionate kiss I've ever received from a guy— and it was on the freaking forehead!

AS WILL REACHES into the trunk for another handful of groceries, Kel and Caulder run out of the house, followed by my mother. The boys dart across the street to check out Caulder's bedroom. Will politely extends his hand out to my mother when she walks toward us.

"You must be Layken and Kel's mom. I'm Will Cooper. We live across the street."

"Julia Cohen," she says. "You're Caulder's older brother?"

"Yes, ma'am," he replies. "Older by twelve years."

"So that makes you . . . twenty-one?" She glances at me and gives me a quick wink. I'm standing behind Will at this point, so I take the opportunity to reciprocate one of her infamous glares. She just smiles and turns her attention back to Will.

"Well, I'm glad Kel and Lake were able to make friends so fast," she says.

"Me too," he replies.

She turns and heads inside but purposefully nudges me with her shoulder as she passes. She doesn't speak a word but I know what she's hinting at: She's giving me her approval.

Will reaches in for the last two sacks. "*Lake*, huh? I like that." He hands me the sacks and shuts the trunk.

"*So*, Lake." He leans back against the car and crosses his arms. "Caulder and I are going to Detroit on Friday. We'll be gone until late Sunday—family stuff," he says with a dismissing wave of his hand. "I was wondering if you had any plans for tomorrow night, before I go?"

It's the first time anyone has ever called me Lake, other than my mom and dad. I like it. I lean my shoulder against the car and face him. I try to keep my cool, but inside I'm screaming with excitement.

"Are you really going to make me admit that I have absolutely no life here?" I say.

"Great! It's a date then. I'll pick you up at seven thirty." He immediately turns and heads toward his house when I realize he never actually *asked*, and I never actually *agreed*.

2.

It won't take long for me
To tell you who I am.
Well you hear this voice right now
Well that's pretty much all I am.

—THE AVETT BROTHERS,
"GIMMEAKISS"

THE NEXT AFTERNOON, I'M PICKING OUT WHAT TO WEAR but can't seem to locate any clean, weather-appropriate clothing. I don't own many winter shirts besides what I've already worn this week. I choose a purple long-sleeved shirt and smell it, deciding it's clean enough. I spray some perfume, though, just in case it isn't. I brush my teeth, touch up my makeup, brush my teeth again, and let down my ponytail. I curl a few sections of my hair and pull some silver earrings out of my drawer, when I hear a knock on the bathroom door.

My mother enters with a handful of towels. She opens the cabinet next to the shower and places them inside.

"Going somewhere?" she says. She sits down on the edge of the bathtub while I continue to get ready.

"Yeah, somewhere." I try to hide my smile as I put in my earrings. "Honestly, I'm not sure what we're doing. I really never even agreed to the date."

She stands up and walks to the door, leaning up against the frame. She watches me in the mirror. She has aged so much in the short time since my dad's death. Her bright green eyes against her smooth porcelain skin used to be breathtaking. Now, her cheekbones stand out above the hollowed shadows in her cheeks. The dark circles under her eyes overpower their emerald hue. She looks tired. And sad.

"Well, you're eighteen now. You've had enough of my dating advice for a lifetime," she says. "But I'll provide you with a quick recap just in case. Don't order anything with onion or garlic, never leave your drink unattended, and *always* use protection."

"Ugh, Mom!" I roll my eyes. "You know I know the rules, and you *know* I don't have to worry about the last one. Please don't give Will a recap of your rules. Promise?" I make her promise.

"So . . . tell me about Will. Does he work? Is he in college? What's his major? Is he a serial killer?" She says this with such sincerity.

I walk the short distance from the bathroom to my

bedroom and bend down to search through my shoes. She follows me and sits on the bed.

"Honestly, Mom, I don't know anything about him. I didn't even know how old he was until he told you."

"That's good," she says.

"Good?" I glance back at her. "How is not knowing anything about him good? I'm about to be alone with him for hours. He could be a *serial killer*." I grab my boots and walk over to the bed to slip them on.

"It'll give you plenty to talk about. That's what first dates are for."

"Good point," I say.

Growing up, my mother did give great advice. She always knew what I wanted to hear but would tell me what I *needed* to hear. My dad was her first boyfriend, so I have always wondered how she knows so much about dating, boys, and relationships. She's only been with one person, and it seems most knowledge would have to come from life experiences. She's the exception, I guess.

"Mom?" I say as I slip on my boots. "I know you were only eighteen when you met Dad. I mean, that's really young to meet the person you spend the rest of your life with. Do you ever regret it?"

She doesn't answer immediately. Instead, she lies back on my bed and clasps her hands behind her head, pondering my question.

"I've never regretted it. Questioned it? Sure. But never regretted."

"Is there a difference?" I ask.

"Absolutely. Regret is counterproductive. It's looking back on a past that you can't change. *Questioning* things as they occur can prevent regret in the future. I questioned a lot about my relationship with your father. People make spontaneous decisions based on their hearts all the time. There's *so* much more to relationships than just love."

"Is that why you always tell me to follow my head, not my heart?"

My mother sits up on the bed and takes my hands in hers. "Lake, do you want some real advice that doesn't include a list of foods you should avoid?"

Has she been holding out on me? "Of course," I reply.

She's lost the authoritative, parental edge to her voice, which makes me aware that this conversation is less mother-daughter and more woman to woman. She pulls her legs up Indian-style on the bed and faces me.

"There are three questions every woman should be able to answer yes to before she commits to a man. If you answer no to any of the three questions, run like hell."

"It's just a date," I laugh. "I doubt we'll be doing any committing."

"I know you're not, Lake. I'm serious. If you can't answer yes to these three questions, don't even waste your time on a relationship."

When I open my mouth, I feel like I'm just reinforcing the fact that I'm her child. I don't interrupt her again.

"Does he treat you with respect at all times? That's the first question. The second question is, if he is the exact same person twenty years from now that he is today, would you still want to marry him? And finally, does he inspire you to want to be a better person? You find someone you can answer yes about to all three, then you've found a good man."

I take a deep breath as I soak in even more sage advice from her. "Wow, those are some intense questions," I say. "Were you able to answer yes to all of them? When you were with Dad?"

"Absolutely," she says, without hesitation. "Every second I was with him."

A sadness enters her eyes as she finishes her sentence. She loved my dad. I immediately regret bringing it up. I put my arms around her and embrace her. It's been so long since I've hugged her, a twinge of guilt rises up inside me. She kisses my hair, then pulls away and smiles.

I stand up and run my hands down my shirt, smoothing out the folds.

"Well? How do I look?"

"Like a woman," she sighs.

It's seven thirty sharp, so I go to the living room, grab the jacket Will insisted I borrow the day before, and head to the window. He's coming out of his house, so I walk outside and stand in my driveway. He looks up and notices me as he's opening his car door.

"You ready?" he yells.

"Yes!"

"Well, come on then!"

I don't move. I just stand there and fold my arms across my chest.

"What are you doing?" He throws his hand up in defeat and laughs.

"You said you would pick me up at seven thirty! I'm waiting for you to pick me up!"

He grins and gets in the car. He backs straight out of his driveway and into mine so that the passenger door is closest to me. He hops out of the car and runs around to open it. Before I get in I give him the once-over. He's wearing loose-fitted jeans and a black long-sleeved shirt that outlines his arms. It's the defined arms that prompt me to return his jacket to him.

"That reminds me," I say, handing him his jacket. "I bought this for you."

He smiles when he takes it and slides his arms inside. "Wow, thanks," he says. "It even smells like me."

He waits until I've buckled up before he shuts the door. As he's walking around to his side, I notice the car smells like . . . cheese. Not old, stale cheese, but fresh cheese. Cheddar, maybe. My stomach growls. I'm curious where we're going to eat.

When Will gets in, he reaches into the backseat and grabs a sack. "We don't have time to eat, so I made us grilled cheese." He hands me a sandwich and a bottle of soda.

"Wow. This is a first," I say, staring at the items in my

hands. "And where exactly are we going in such a hurry?" I twist open the lid. "It's obviously not a restaurant."

He unwraps his sandwich and takes a bite. "It's a surprise," he says with a mouthful of bread. He navigates the steering wheel with his free hand as he simultaneously drives and eats. "I know a lot more about you than you know about me, so tonight I want to show you what *I'm* all about."

"Well, I'm intrigued," I say. I really *am* intrigued.

We both finish our sandwiches, and I put the trash back in the bag and place it in the backseat. I try to think of something to say to break the silence, so I ask him about his family.

"What are your parents like?"

He takes a deep breath and slowly exhales, almost like I've asked the wrong thing. "I'm not big on small talk, Lake. We can figure all that out later. Let's make this drive interesting." He winks at me and relaxes further into his seat.

Driving, no talking, keeping it interesting. I'm repeating what he said in my head and hope I'm misunderstanding his intent. He laughs when he sees the hesitation on my face and it dawns on him that I've misinterpreted what he said.

"Lake, no!" he says. "I just meant let's talk about something besides what we're *expected* to talk about."

I breathe a sigh of relief. I thought I had found his flaw. "Good."

"I know a game we can play," he says. "It's called 'would you rather.' Have you played it before?"

I shake my head. "No, but I know I would *rather* you go first."

"Okay." He clears his throat and pauses for a few seconds. "Okay, would you rather spend the *rest* of your life with *no* arms, or would you rather spend the rest of your life with arms you couldn't *control?*"

What the hell? I can honestly say this date is not going the way any of my previous dates have gone. It's pleasantly unexpected, though.

"Well . . ." I hesitate. "I guess I would rather spend the rest of my life with arms I couldn't control?"

"What? Seriously? But you wouldn't be controlling them!" he says, flapping his arms around in the car. "They could be flailing around and you'd be constantly punching yourself in the face! Or worse, you might grab a knife and stab yourself!"

I laugh. "I didn't realize there were right and wrong answers."

"You suck at this," he teases. "Your turn."

"Okay, let me think."

"You have to have one ready!" he says.

"Jeez, Will! I barely heard of this game for the first time thirty seconds ago. Give me a second to think of one."

He reaches over and squeezes my hand. "I'm teasing."

He repositions his hand underneath mine, and our fingers interlock. I like how easy the transition is, like we've been holding hands for years. So far, everything about this date has been easy. I like Will's sense of humor. I like that I find it so easy to laugh around him after having gone so many months without laughing. I like that we're holding hands. I *really* like that we're holding hands.

"Okay, I've got one," I say. "Would you rather pee on yourself once a day at random, unknown times? Or would you rather have to pee on someone *else*?"

"It depends on who I'd have to pee on. Can I pee on people I don't like? Or is it random people?"

"Random people."

"Pee on myself," he says, without hesitation. "My turn now. Would you rather be four feet tall or seven feet tall?"

"Seven feet tall," I reply.

"Why?"

"You aren't allowed to ask why," I say. "Okay, let's see. Would you rather drink an entire gallon of bacon grease for breakfast every day? Or would you rather have to eat five pounds of popcorn for supper every night?"

"Five pounds of popcorn."

I like the game we're playing. I like that he didn't worry about impressing me with dinner. I like that I have no idea where we're headed. I even like that he didn't compliment what I was wearing, which seems to be the standard opening line for dates. So far, I like everything about tonight. As far as I'm concerned, we could drive around for another two hours just playing "would you rather," and it would be the most fun I've ever had on a date.

But we don't. We eventually reach our destination, and I immediately tense up when I see the sign on the building.

Club N9NE

"Uh, Will? I don't dance." I'm hoping he'll be empathetic.

"Uh, neither do *I*."

We exit the vehicle and meet at the front of the car. I'm not sure who reaches out first, but once again our fingers find each other in the dark and he holds my hand and guides me toward the entrance. As we get closer, I notice a sign posted on the door.

Closed for Slam
Thursdays
8:00–Whenever
Admission: Free
Fee to slam: $3

Will opens the door without reading the sign. I start to inform him the club is closed, but he seems like he knows what he's doing. The silence is interrupted by the noise of a crowd as I follow him through the entryway and into the room. There is an empty stage to the right of us and tables and chairs set up all over the dance floor. The place is packed. I see what looks like a group of younger kids, around age fourteen or so, at a table toward the front.

Will turns to the left and heads to an empty booth in the back of the room.

"It's quieter back here," he says.

"How old do you have to be to get into clubs here?" I say, still observing the group of out-of-place children.

"Well, tonight it's not a club," he says as we scoot into the booth. It's a half-circle booth facing the stage, so I scoot all the way to the middle to get the best view. He moves in right beside me. "It's slam night," he says. "Every Thursday they shut the club down and people come here to compete in the slam."

"And what's a slam?" I ask.

"It's poetry." He smiles at me. "It's what I'm all about."

Is he for real? A hot guy who makes me laugh *and* loves poetry? Someone pinch me. Or not—I'd rather not wake up.

"Poetry, huh?" I say. "Do people write their own or do they recite it from other authors?"

He leans back in the booth and looks up at the stage. I see the passion in his eyes when he talks about it. "People get up there and pour their hearts out just using their words and the movement of their bodies," he says. "It's amazing. You aren't going to hear any Dickinson or Frost here."

"Is it like a competition?"

"It's complicated," he says. "It differs between every club. Normally during a slam, the judges are picked at random from the audience and they assign points to each performance. The one with the most points at the end of the night wins. That's how they do it here, anyway."

"So do you slam?"

"Sometimes. Sometimes I judge; sometimes I just watch."

"Are you performing tonight?"

"Nah. Just an observer tonight. I don't really have anything ready."

I'm disappointed. It would be amazing to see him perform onstage. I still have no idea what slam poetry is, but I'm really curious to see him do *anything* that requires a performance.

"Bummer," I say.

It's quiet for a moment while we both observe the crowd in front of us. Will nudges me with his elbow and I turn to look at him. "You want something to drink?" he says.

"Sure. I'll take some chocolate milk."

He cocks and eyebrow and grins. "Chocolate milk? *Really*?"

I nod. "With ice."

"*Okay*," he says as he slides out of the booth. "One chocolate milk on the rocks coming right up."

While he's gone, the emcee comes to the stage and attempts to pump up the crowd. No one is in the back of the room where we're seated, so I feel a little silly when I yell "Yeah!" with the rest of the crowd. I sink further into my seat and decide to just be a spectator for the remainder of the night.

The emcee announces it's time to pick the judges and the entire crowd roars, almost everyone wanting to be chosen. They pick five people at random and move them to the judging table. As Will walks toward our booth with our drinks, the emcee announces it's time for the "sac" and chooses someone at random.

"What's the sac?" I ask him.

"Sacrifice. It's what they use to prepare the judges." He slides back into the booth. Somehow, he slides even closer this time. "Someone performs something that isn't part of the competition so the judges can calibrate their scoring."

"So they can call on anyone? What if they had called on me?" I ask, suddenly nervous.

He smiles at me. "Well, I guess you should have had something ready."

He takes a sip from his drink then leans back against the booth, finding my hand in the dark. Our fingers don't interlock this time, though. Instead, he places my hand on his leg and his fingertips start to trace the outline of my wrist. He gently traces each of my fingers, following the lines and curves of my entire hand. His fingertips feel like electric pulses penetrating my skin.

"Lake," he says quietly as he continues tracing up my wrist and back to my fingertips with a fluid motion. "I don't know what it is about you . . . but I like you."

His fingers slide between mine and he takes my hand in his, turning his attention back to the stage. I inhale and reach for my chocolate milk with my free hand, downing the entire glass. The ice feels good against my lips. It cools me off.

They call on a young woman who looks to be around twenty-five. She announces she is performing a piece she wrote titled "Blue Sweater." The lights are lowered as a spotlight is positioned on her. She raises the microphone and steps forward, staring down at the floor. A hush sweeps over the audience, and the only sound in the entire room is the sound of her breath, amplified through the speakers.

She raises her hand to the microphone, still staring down to the floor. She begins to tap her finger against it in a repetitive motion, resonating the sound of a heartbeat. I realize I'm holding my own breath as she begins her piece.

Bom Bom

Bom Bom

Bom Bom

Do you *hear* that?

(Her voice lingering on the word hear.)

That's the sound of my heart beating.

(She taps the microphone again.)

Bom Bom

Bom Bom

Bom Bom

Do you *hear* that?

That's the sound of *your* heart beating.

(She begins to speak faster, much louder than before.)

It was the *first* day of October. I was wearing my *blue*
sweater, you know the one I bought at **Dillard's**? The
one with a double-knitted *hem* and *holes* in the *ends*
of the *sleeves* that I could poke my *thumbs* through
when it was cold but I didn't feel like wearing *gloves*?
It was the *same* sweater you said made my **eyes** look
like reflections of the *stars* on the *ocean*.
You promised to love me *forever* that night . . .

and *boy*

did *you*

ever.

It was the *first* day of **December** this time. I was
wearing my *blue* sweater, you know the one I bought
at *Dillard's*? The one with a double-knitted *hem* and
holes in the *ends* of the *sleeves* that I could poke my
thumbs through when it was cold but I didn't feel like
wearing *gloves*? It was the *same* sweater you said made
my *eyes* look like reflections of the *stars* on the *ocean*.
I told you I was three weeks *late.*
You *said* it was *fate.*
You promised to love me forever that night . . .
and *boy*

did *you*

ever!

It was the first day of May. I was wearing my *blue*
sweater, although *this* time the double-stitched *hem*
was *worn* and the *strength* of each thread *tested* as
they were pulled *tight* against my *growing belly*. *You*
know the one. The same one I bought at *Dillard's*?
The one with *holes* in the *ends* of the *sleeves* that I
could poke my *thumbs* through when it was cold but I
didn't feel like wearing *gloves*? It was the *same* sweater
you said made my **eyes** look like reflections of the
stars on the *ocean*.

The *SAME* sweater you *RIPPED* off of my body as
you *shoved* me to the floor,

calling me a <u>*whore*</u>,

telling me

you didn't *love* me

anymore.

Bom Bom

Bom Bom

Bom Bom

Do you *hear* that? That's the sound of my heart
beating.

Bom Bom

Bom Bom

Bom Bom

Do you *hear* that? That's the sound of *your* heart
beating.

(There is a long silence as she clasps her hands to her stomach, tears streaming down her face.)

Do you *hear* that? Of course you don't. That's the
silence of my womb.
Because you
RIPPED
OFF
MY
SWEATER!

The lights come back up and the audience roars. I take a deep breath and wipe tears from my eyes. I'm mesmerized by her ability to hypnotize an entire audience with such powerfully portrayed words. Just *words*. I'm immediately addicted and want to hear more. Will puts his arm around my shoulders and leans back into the seat with me, bringing me back to reality.

"Well?" he says.

I accept his embrace and move my head to his shoulder as we both stare out over the crowd. He rests his chin on top of my head.

"That was unbelievable," I whisper. His hand touches the side of my face, and he brushes his lips against my forehead. I close my eyes and wonder how much more my emotions can be tested. Three days ago, I was devastated, bitter, hopeless. Today I woke up feeling happy for the first time in months. I feel vulnerable. I try to mask my emotions, but I feel like everyone knows what I'm thinking and feeling, and I don't like it. I don't like being an open book. I feel like I'm up on the stage, pouring my heart out to him, and it scares the hell out of me.

We sit in the same embrace as several more people perform their pieces. The poetry is as vast and electrifying as the audience. I have never laughed and cried so much. The way these poets are able to lure you into a whole new world, viewing things from a vantage point you've never seen before. Making you feel like you are the mother who lost her baby, or the boy who killed his father, or even the man who got high for the first time and ate *five plates* of bacon. I feel a connection with these poets and their stories. What's more, I feel a deeper connection to Will. I can't imagine that he's brave enough to get up on the stage and bare his soul like these people are doing. I have to see it. I *have* to see him do this.

The emcee makes one last appeal for performers.

I turn toward him. "Will, you can't bring me here and not *perform*. Please do one? Please, please, please?"

He leans his head back against the booth. "You're killing me, Lake. Like I said, I don't really have anything new."

"Do something old then," I suggest. "Or do all these people make you *nervous?*"

He tilts his head toward me and smiles. "Not all of them. Just *one* of them."

I suddenly have the urge to kiss him. I suppress the

urge for now, and continue to plead. I clasp my hands together under my chin. "Don't make me beg," I say.

"You already *are!*" He pauses for a few seconds, then removes his arm from around my shoulders and leans forward. "All right, all right," he says. He grins at me as he reaches into his pocket. "But I'm warning you, you asked."

He pulls his wallet out just as the emcee announces the start of round two. Will stands up, holding his three dollars in the air. "I'm in!"

The emcee shields his eyes with his hand, squinting into the audience to see who spoke up. "Ladies and gentlemen, it's one of our very own, Mr. Will Cooper. So nice of you to finally join us," he teases into the microphone.

Will makes his way through the crowd and walks onto the stage and into the spotlight.

"What's the name of your piece tonight, Will?" the emcee asks.

"'Death,'" Will replies, looking past the crowd and directly at me. The smile fades from his eyes and he begins his performance.

Death. The only thing inevitable in life.
People don't like to *talk* about death because
it makes them *sad.*
They don't want to *imagine* how life will go on
without them,
all the people they love will briefly grieve
but continue to *breathe.*

They don't *want* to imagine how life will go on
without *them*,
Their children will still *grow*
Get married
Get *old* . . .
They don't want to *imagine* how life will *continue* to
go on without them,
Their material things will be *sold*
Their medical files stamped *"closed"*
Their name becoming a *memory* to everyone they
know.
They don't *want* to *imagine* how life will go on
without them, so *instead* of accepting it head *on*, they
avoid the subject *altogether*,
hoping and *praying* it will *somehow* . . .
pass them by.
Forget about them,
moving on to the *next* one in line.
No, they didn't *want* to imagine how life would
continue to go on . . .
without them.
But death
didn't
forget.
Instead they were met **head-on** by death,
disguised as an **18-wheeler**
behind a cloud of *fog.*
No.

Death didn't *forget* about *them*.
If *only* they had been *prepared*, *accepted* the
inevitable, laid out their *plans*, understood that it
wasn't just *their* lives at hand.
I may have legally been considered an adult at the age
of nineteen, but I still felt very much
all
of just nineteen.
Unprepared
and *overwhelmed*
to suddenly have the *entire life* of a seven-year-old
In my *realm*.
Death. The only thing inevitable in *life*.

Will steps out of the spotlight and off of the stage
before he even sees his scores. I find myself hoping he
gets lost on his way back to our booth so that I have time
to absorb this. I have no idea how to react. I had no idea
that this was his life. That Caulder was his *whole life*. I'm
amazed by his performance but devastated by his words.
I wipe tears away with the back of my hand. I don't know
if I'm crying for the loss of Will's parents, the responsibilities brought by that loss, or the simple fact that he
spoke the truth. He spoke about a side of death and loss
that never seems to be considered until it's too late. A
side that I'm unfortunately all too familiar with. The
Will I watched walk up to the stage is not the same Will
I'm watching walk toward me. I'm conflicted, I'm con-

fused, and most of all I'm taken aback. He was beautiful.

He notices me wiping tears from my eyes. "I warned you," he says, sliding back into the booth. He reaches for his drink and takes a sip, stirring the ice cubes with his straw. I have no idea what to say to him. He put it all out there, right in front of me.

My emotions take control over my actions. I reach forward and take his hand in mine and he sets his drink back down on the table. He turns toward me and gives me a half smile, like he's waiting for me to say something. When I don't say anything, he pulls his hand up to my face and wipes away a tear, then traces the side of my cheek with the back of his hand. I don't understand the connection I feel with him. It all seems so fast. I put my hand on top of his and pull it to my mouth, then gently kiss the inside of his palm as we hold each other's stare. We suddenly become the only two people in the entire room; all the external noise fades into the distance.

He brings his other hand to my cheek and slowly leans forward. I close my eyes and feel his breath draw closer as he pulls me toward him. His lips touch my lips, but barely. He slowly kisses my bottom lip, then my top lip. His lips are cold, still wet from his drink. I lean in further to return his kiss, but he pulls away when my mouth responds. I open my eyes and he's smiling at me, still holding my face in his hands.

"Patience," he whispers. He closes his eyes and leans in, kissing me softly on the cheek. I close my eyes and inhale, trying to calm the overwhelming impulse I have to wrap my arms around him and kiss him back. I don't know how he has so much self-control. He presses his forehead against mine and slides his hands down my arms. Our eyes lock when we open them. It's during this moment that I finally understand why my mother accepted her fate at the age of eighteen.

"Wow," I exhale.

"Yeah," he agrees. "Wow."

We hold each other's stare for a few more seconds until the audience starts to roar again. They are announcing the qualifiers for round two when Will grabs my hand and whispers, "Let's go."

As I make my way out of the booth, my entire body feels like it's about to give out on me. I've never experienced anything like what just happened. *Ever*.

We exit the booth and our hands remain locked as he navigates me through the ever-growing crowd and into the parking lot. I don't realize how warm I am until the cold Michigan air touches my skin. It feels exhilarating. Or I feel exhilarated. I can't tell which. All I know is that I wish the last two hours of my life could repeat for eternity.

"You don't want to stay?" I ask him.

"Lake, you've been moving and unpacking for days. You need sleep."

His mention of sleep induces an involuntary yawn from me. "Sleep does sound good," I say.

He opens my door, but before I get in, he wraps his

arms around me and pulls me to him in a tight embrace. Several minutes pass while we just stand there, holding on to the moment. I could get used to this, which is a completely foreign feeling. I've always been so guarded. This new side of me that Will brings out is a side of me I didn't know I had.

We eventually break apart and get into the car. As we drive away from the parking lot, I lean my head against the window and watch the club minimize in the rearview mirror.

"Will?" I whisper, without breaking my gaze from the building disappearing behind us. "Thank you for this."

He takes my hand into his, and I eventually fall asleep, smiling.

I wake up as he's opening my door and we're in my driveway. He reaches in and grabs my hand, helping me out of the car. I can't remember the last time I fell asleep in a moving vehicle. Will was right: I *am* tired. I rub my eyes and yawn again as he walks me to the front door. He wraps his arms around my waist, and I raise mine around his shoulders. Our bodies are a perfect fit. A chill runs down my body as his breath warms my neck. I can't believe we met only three days ago; it seems like we've been doing this for years.

"Just think," I say. "You'll be gone three whole days. That's the same length of time I've known you."

He laughs and pulls me even closer. "This will be the longest three days of my life," he says.

If I know my mother at all, then we've got an audience, so I'm relieved his final kiss is nothing more than a quick peck on the cheek. He slowly walks backward, his fingers sliding out of mine, eventually letting go. My arm falls limp to my side as I watch him get into his car. He cranks the engine and rolls down his window. "Lake, I've got a pretty long drive home," he says. "How about one for the road?"

I laugh, then walk to the car and lean through his window, expecting another peck. Instead, he slips his hand behind my neck and gently pulls me toward him, our lips opening when they meet. Neither of us holds back this time. I reach through the window and run my fingers through the back of his hair as we continue kissing. It takes all I have not to swing open the car door and crawl into his lap. The door between us feels more like a barricade.

We finally come to a stop. Our lips are still touching as we both hesitate to part.

"Damn," he whispers against my lips. "It gets better every time."

"I'll see you in three days," I say. "You be careful driving home tonight." I give him one final kiss and reluctantly pull away from the window.

He backs out of the driveway and again straight into his own. I'm tempted to run after him and kiss him again to prove his theory. Instead, I avoid temptation and turn to head inside.

"Lake!"

I turn around and he shuts his car door and jogs toward me. He smiles when he reaches me. "I forgot to tell you something," he says, wrapping his arms around me again. "You look beautiful tonight." He kisses me on top of my head, releases his hold, and turns back toward his house.

Maybe I was wrong earlier—about me liking the fact that he didn't compliment me. I was *definitely* wrong. When he gets to his front door, he turns around and smiles before he goes inside.

Just as I had imagined, my mother is sitting on the sofa with a book, attempting to appear uninterested when I walk through the front door. "Well, how'd it go? Is he a serial killer?" she says.

My smile is uncontrollable now. I walk to the sofa opposite her and throw myself on it like a rag doll and sigh. "You were right, Mom. I *love* Michigan."

3.

But I can tell by watching you
That there's no chance of pushing through
The odds are so against us
You know most young love, it ends like this.

—THE AVETT BROTHERS, "I WOULD BE SAD"

I'M MORE NERVOUS THAN I ANTICIPATED WHEN I WAKE UP Monday morning. My mind has been so preoccupied with all things Will I haven't had time to process my impending doom. Or rather, my first day at a brand-new school.

Mom and I finally had a chance to go shopping for weather-appropriate clothing over the weekend. I throw on what I picked out the evening before and slide on my new snow boots. I leave my hair down for the day but slide an extra band onto my wrist for when I want to pull it back, which I know I'll do.

After I finish up in the bathroom, I move to the

kitchen and grab my backpack and my class schedule off the counter. Mom began her new night shift at the hospital last night, so I agreed to take Kel to school. Back in Texas, Kel and I went to the same school. In fact, everyone in the vicinity of our town went to the same school. Here, there are so many schools I have to print out a district map just to be sure I'm taking him to the right place.

When we pull up to the elementary school, Kel immediately spots Caulder and jumps out of the car without even saying goodbye. He makes life look so easy.

Luckily, the elementary is only a few blocks from the high school. I'll have extra time to spare so that I can locate my first class. I pull into the parking lot of what I consider to be a massive high school and search for a spot. When I find one available, it's as far from the building as it could be, and there are dozens of students standing around their vehicles, chatting. I am hesitant to get out of my car, but realize when I do that no one even notices me. It's not like in the movies when the new girl steps out of her car onto the lawn of the new school, clutching her books, everyone stopping what they're doing to stare. It's not like that at all. I feel invisible and I like it.

I make it through first-period Math without being assigned homework, which is good. I plan on spending the entire evening with Will. When I went to leave this morning, there was a note on my Jeep from him. All it said was, "Can't wait to see you. I'll be back home by four."

Seven hours and three minutes to go.

History isn't any harder. The teacher is giving notes on the Punic Wars, something we had just covered in my previous school. I find it hard to focus as I literally count down the minutes. The teacher is very monotonous and mundane. If I don't find something to be interesting, my mind tends to wander. It keeps wandering to Will. I am methodically taking notes, trying my best to focus, when someone behind me pokes my back.

"Hey, let me see your schedule," the girl directs.

I inconspicuously reach for my schedule and fold it up tightly in my left hand. I raise my hand behind me and quickly drop the schedule on her desk.

"Oh, please!" she says louder. "Mr. Hanson is half blind and can barely hear. Don't worry about him."

I stifle a laugh and turn toward her while Mr. Hanson is facing the board. "I'm Layken."

"Eddie," she says.

I look at her questioningly and she rolls her eyes. "I *know*. It's a family name. But if you call me Eddie Spaghetti I'll kick your ass," she threatens mildly.

"I'll keep that in mind."

"Cool, we have the same third period," she says, inspecting my schedule. "It's a bitch to find. Stick with me after class and I'll show you where it is."

Eddie leans forward to write something down, and her slinky blond hair swings forward with her. It falls just below her chin in an asymmetrical style. Her nails are each painted a completely different color, and she has a variety of about fifteen bracelets on each of her wrists that rattle and clank every time she moves. She has a small, simple outline of a black heart tattooed on the inside of her left wrist.

When the bell rings, I stand up and Eddie passes me back the schedule. She reaches into my jacket pocket and pulls out my phone and starts punching numbers. I look at the schedule she has returned to me and it's now covered in websites and phone numbers in green ink. Eddie sees me looking and points to the first web address on the page.

"That's my Facebook page, but if you can't find me there, I'm also on Twitter. Don't ask me for my MySpace username because that shit's lame," she says, strangely serious.

She scrolls down the remaining numbers jotted on my schedule with her finger. "That's my cell phone number, that's my home phone number, and that's the number to Getty's Pizza," she says.

"Is that where you work?"

"No, they just have great pizza." She moves past me, and I start to follow her out the door, when she turns and hands me back my phone. "I just called myself so I have your number now, too. Oh, and you need to go to the office before next period."

"Why? I thought you wanted me to follow you?" I ask, feeling slightly overwhelmed by my new friend.

"They have you in B lunch. I'm in A lunch. Go switch yours to A lunch and meet me in third period."

And she's gone. Just like that.

THE ADMINISTRATION OFFICE is just two doors down. The secretary, Mrs. Alex, makes rolling her eyes a new form of art as she prints my *new* new schedule just as the second bell for third period rings.

"Do you know where this English elective is located?" I say before I leave.

She gives me somewhat lengthy and confusing directions, assuming that I know where Hall A is, and Hall D. I wait patiently until she's finished and walk out the door, more confused than before.

I wander across three different hallways, entering two wrong classrooms and one janitor's closet. I round the corner when I finally see Hall D and feel some relief. I set my backpack down on the floor and place the schedule between my lips, then pull the rubber band off my wrist. It's not even ten in the morning, and I'm already pulling my hair up. It's that kind of day already.

"Lake?"

My heart nearly jumps out of my chest when I hear his voice. I turn around and see Will standing next to me with a confused look on his face. I pull the schedule out of my mouth and smile, then instinctively wrap my arms around him. "Will! What are you doing here?"

He hugs me back, but only for a second before he wraps his hands around my wrists and removes my arms from around his neck.

"Lake," he says, shaking his head. "Where . . . what are you doing here?"

I sigh and thrust my schedule into his chest. "I'm trying to find this stupid elective but I'm lost," I whine. "Help me!"

He takes another step back against the wall. "Lake, no," he says, putting the schedule back into my hands without even looking at it.

I watch him react for a moment, and he seems almost horrified to see me. He turns away and clasps his hands behind his head. I don't understand his reaction. I stand still, waiting for some sort of explanation, when it dawns on me. He's here to see his girlfriend. The *girlfriend* that he failed to mention. I snatch my backpack up and immediately start to walk away, when he reaches out and pulls me to a stop.

"Where are you going?" he demands.

I roll my eyes and let out a short sigh. "I get it, Will. I *get* it. I'll leave you alone before your girlfriend sees us." I'm trying to hold back tears at this point, so I step out of his grasp and turn away from him.

"Girlfr—no. No, Lake. I don't think you do get it."

The faint sound of footsteps quickly becomes louder as they round the corner to Hall D. I turn to see another student barreling toward us.

"Oh man, I thought I was late," the student says when he spots us in the hallway. He comes to a stop in front of the classroom.

"You *are* late, Javier," Will replies, opening the door behind him, motioning for Javier to enter. "Javi, I'll be there in a few minutes. Let the class know they have five minutes to review before the exam."

Will closes the door behind him, and we're once again alone in the hallway. The air is all but gone from my lungs. I feel pressure building in my chest as this new realization sinks in. This can't be happening. This can't be possible. *How* is this possible?

"Will," I whisper, not able to get a full breath out. "Please don't tell me . . ."

His face is red and he has a pained look in his eyes as he bites his lower lip. He leans his head back and looks up at the ceiling, rubbing his palms on his face while he paces the length of the hallway between the lockers and the classroom door. With each step he takes, I catch a glimpse of his faculty badge as it sways back and forth from his neck.

He flattens his palms against the lockers, repeatedly tapping his forehead against the metal as I stand frozen, unable to speak. He slowly drops his hands and turns toward me. "How did I not *see* this? You're still in *high school*?"

4.

I am sick of wanting
And it's evil how it's got me
And every day is worse
Than the one before.

—THE AVETT BROTHERS, "ILL WITH WANT"

WILL LEANS WITH HIS BACK AGAINST THE LOCKERS. HIS legs are crossed at the feet and his arms are folded across his chest as he stares at the floor. The events unfolding have caught me so off guard I can barely stand. I go to the wall opposite him and lean against it for support.

"Me?" I reply. "How did the fact that you're a teacher not come up? How are you a teacher? You're only twenty-one."

"Layken, listen," he says, ignoring my questions.

He didn't call me Lake.

"There has apparently been a huge misunderstanding between the two of us." He doesn't make eye contact with me as he speaks. "We need to talk about this, but now is definitely not the right time."

"I agree," I say. I want to say more, but I can't. I'm afraid I'll cry.

The door to Will's classroom opens, and Eddie emerges. I selfishly pray that she, too, is lost. This cannot be my elective.

"Layken, I was just coming to look for you," she says. "I saved you a seat." She looks at Will, then back at me and realizes she's interrupted a conversation. "Oh, sorry, Mr. Cooper. I didn't know you were out here."

"It's fine, Eddie. I was just going over Layken's schedule with her." He says this as he walks toward the classroom and holds the door for both of us.

I reluctantly follow Eddie through the door, around Will, and to the only empty seat in the room—directly in front of the teacher's desk. I don't know how I am expected to sit through an entire hour in this classroom. The walls won't stop dancing when I try to focus, so I close my eyes. I need water.

"Who's the hottie?" asks the boy I now know as Javier.

"Shut it, Javi!" Will snaps as he walks toward his desk, picking up a stack of papers. Several students let out a small gasp at this reaction. I guess Will isn't his usual self right now, either.

"Chill out, Mr. Cooper! I was paying her a compliment. She's hot. Look at her." Javi says this as he leans back in his chair, watching me.

"Javi, get out!" Will says, pointing to the classroom door.

"Mr. Cooper! Jeez! What's with the temp? Like I said, I was just—"

"Like *I* said, get out! You will not disrespect women in my classroom!"

Javi grabs his books and snaps back. "Fine. I'll go disrespect them in the hallway!"

After the door shuts behind him, the only sound in the room is the distant second hand ticking on the clock above the blackboard. I don't turn around, but I can feel most of the eyes in the classroom on me, waiting for some sort of reaction. It's not so easy to blend in now.

"Class, we have a new student. This is Layken Cohen," Will says, attempting to break the tension. "Review is over. Put up your notes."

"You're not going to have her introduce herself?" Eddie asks.

"We'll get to that another time." Will holds up a stack of papers. "Tests."

I'm relieved Will has spared me from having to get in front of the class and speak. It's the last thing I would be able to do right now. It feels like there is a ball of cotton in my throat as I unsuccessfully try to swallow.

"Lake." Will hesitates, then clears his throat, realizing his slip. "Layken, if you have something else to work on, feel free. The class is completing a chapter test."

"I'd rather just take the test," I say. I have to focus on *something*.

Will hands me a test, and in the time it takes to complete it I do my best to focus entirely on the questions at hand, hoping I'll find momentary respite from my new reality. I finish fairly quickly, though, but keep erasing and rewriting answers just to avoid having to deal with the obvious: the fact that the boy I'm falling for is now my teacher.

When the dismissal bell rings, I watch as the rest of the class files toward Will's desk, laying their papers face down in a pile. Eddie lays hers down and walks to my desk.

"Hey, did you get your lunch switched?"

"Yeah, I did," I tell her.

"Sweet. I'll save you a seat," she says. She stops at Will's desk and he looks up at her. She removes a red tin from her purse and pulls out a small handful of mints and sets them on his desk. "Altoids," she says.

Will stares questioningly at the mints.

"I'm just making assumptions here," she whispers, loud enough that I hear her. "But I've heard Altoids work wonders on hangovers." She pushes the mints toward him.

And again, just like that, she's gone.

Will and I are the only ones left in the classroom at this point. I need to talk to him so bad. I have so many questions, but I know it's still not a good time. I grab my paper and walk over to his desk, placing it on top of the stack.

"Is my mood that obvious?" he asks. He continues to stare at the mints on his desk. I grab two of the Altoids and walk out of the room without responding.

As I navigate the halls, searching for my fourth-period class, I see a bathroom and quickly duck inside. I decide to spend the remainder of fourth period and my entire lunch in the bathroom stall. I feel guilty knowing Eddie is waiting for me, but I can't face anyone right now. Instead, I spend the entire time reading and rereading the writing on the walls of the stall, hoping to somehow make it through the rest of the day without bursting out in tears.

My last two classes are a blur. Luckily, neither of those teachers seem interested in my "about me," either. I don't speak to anyone, and no one speaks to me. I have no idea if I was ever even assigned homework. My mind is consumed by this whole situation.

I walk to my car as I search in my bag for my keys. I pull them out and fidget with the lock, but my hands are shaking so bad that I drop them. When I climb inside I don't give myself time to reflect as I throw the car in reverse and head home. The only thing I want to think about right now is my bed.

When I pull into my driveway I kill the engine and pause. I don't want to face Kel or my mother yet, so I kick my seat back and shield my eyes with my arms and begin to cry. I replay everything over and over in my head. How did I spend an entire evening with him and not know he was a teacher? How can something as big as an occupation not come up in conversation? Or better yet, how did I do so much talking and fail to mention the fact that I was still in high school? I told him so much about myself. I feel like it's what I deserve for finally letting down my walls.

I wipe at my eyes with my sleeve, trying hard to conceal my tears. I've been getting pretty good at it. Up until six months ago, I hardly had a reason to cry. My life back in Texas was simple. I had a routine, a great group of friends, a school I loved, and even a home I loved. I cried a lot in the weeks following my father's death until I realized Kel and my mother wouldn't be able to move on until I did. I started making a conscious effort to be more involved in Kel's life. Our father was also his best friend at the time, and I feel Kel lost more than any of us. I got involved in youth baseball, his karate lessons, and even Cub Scouts: all the things my dad used to do with him. It kept both Kel and me preoccupied, and the grieving eventually started to subside.

Until today.

A tap on the passenger window brings me back to reality. I don't want to acknowledge it. I don't want to see anyone, let alone speak to anyone. I look over and see someone standing there; the only thing visible is his torso . . . and faculty ID.

I flip the visor down and wipe the mascara from my eyes. I divert my gaze out the driver's-side window and press the automatic unlock button, focusing on the injured garden gnome, who is staring back at me with his smug little grin.

Will slides into the passenger seat and shuts the door. He lays the seat back a few inches and sighs, but says nothing. I don't think either of us knows what to say at this point. I glance over at him, and his foot is resting on the dash. He's stiff against the seat with his arms folded across his chest. He's staring directly at the note he wrote this morning that is still sitting on my console. I guess he made it by four o'clock after all.

"What are you thinking?" he asks.

I pull my right leg up into the seat and hug it with my arms. "I'm confused as hell, Will. I don't know what to think."

He sighs and turns to look out the passenger window. "I'm sorry. This is all my fault," he says.

"It's nobody's fault," I say. "In order for there to be fault, there has to be some sort of conscious decision. You didn't know, Will."

He sits up and turns to face me. The playful expression in his eyes that drew me to him is gone. "That's just it, Lake. I should have known. I'm in an occupation that doesn't just require ethics inside the classroom. They apply to all aspects of my life. I wasn't *aware* because I wasn't doing my job. When you told me you were eighteen, I assumed you were in college." His obvious frustration seems entirely directed toward himself.

"I've only been eighteen for two weeks," I reply.

I don't know why I felt the need to clarify that. After I say it, I realize it sounds like I'm placing blame on him. He's already blaming himself; he doesn't need me to be angry at him, too. This was an outcome that neither of us could possibly have predicted.

"I student teach," he says, in an attempt to explain. "Sort of."

"*Sort of?*"

"After my parents died, I doubled up on all my classes. I have enough credits to graduate a semester early. Since the school was so shorthanded, they offered me a one-year contract. I have three months left of student teaching. After that, I'm under contract through June of next year."

I listen and take in everything he says. Really, though, all I hear is, "*We can't be together . . . blah blah blah . . . we can't be together.*"

He looks me in the eyes. "Lake, I need this job. It's what I've been working toward for three years. We're broke. My parents left me with a mound of debt and now college tuition. I can't quit now." He breaks his gaze and leans back into the seat, running his hands through his hair.

"Will, I understand. I'd never ask you to jeopardize your career. It would be stupid if you threw that away for someone you've only known for a week."

He keeps his focus out the passenger window. "I'm not saying you *would* ask me that. I just want you to understand where I'm coming from."

"I do understand," I say. "It's ridiculous to assume we even have anything worth risking."

He glances at the note on my console again and quietly responds, "We both know it's more than that."

His words cause me to wince, because I know deep down he's right. Whatever was happening with us, it was more than just an infatuation. I can't possibly comprehend at this moment what it must be like to actually have a broken heart. If it hurts even one percent more than the pain I'm feeling now, I'll forgo love. It's not worth it.

I attempt to stop the tears from welling up again, but the effort is futile. He brings his leg off the dash and pulls me to him. I bury my face in his shirt, and he puts his arms around me and gently rubs my back.

"I'm so sorry," he says. "I wish there was something I could do to change things. I have to do this right . . . for Caulder." The physical grip he has on me seems less like a consoling hug and more like a goodbye. "I'm not sure where we go from here, or how we'll transition," he says.

" 'Transition'?" I suddenly start to panic at the thought of losing him. "But—what if you talk to the school? Tell them we didn't know. Ask them what our options are . . ." I realize as the words are coming out of my mouth that I'm grasping at straws. There is no way in which a relationship between us would be feasible at this point.

"I can't, Lake." His voice is small. "It won't work. It *can't* work."

A door slams, and Kel and Caulder come bounding down the driveway. We immediately pull apart and reposition our seats. I rest my head against the headrest and close my eyes, attempting to conjure up a loophole in our situation. There has to be one.

When the boys have crossed the street and are safely inside Will's house, he turns to me. "Layken?" he says, nervously. "There's one more thing I need to talk to you about."

Oh god, what else? What else could be relevant at this moment?

"I need you to go to administration tomorrow. I want you to withdraw from my class. I don't think we should be around each other anymore."

I feel the blood rushing from my face. My hands start to sweat, and the car is quickly becoming too small for the two of us. He really means it. Anything we had up to this point is over. He's going to shut me out of his life entirely.

"Why?" I make no effort to mask the hurt in my voice.

He clears his throat. "What we have isn't appropriate. We have to separate ourselves."

My hurt quickly succumbs to the anger building up inside of me. "Not appropriate? Separate ourselves? You live across the street from me, Will!"

He opens the door and gets out of the car. I do the same and slam my door. "We're both mature enough to know what's appropriate. You're the only person I know here. Please don't ask me to act like I don't even know you," I plead.

"Come on, Lake! You aren't being fair." He matches his tone to mine, and I know I've hit a nerve. "I can't do this. We can't *just* be friends. It's the only choice we have."

I can't help but feel like we're going through a horrible breakup, and we aren't even in a relationship. I'm angry at myself. I can't tell if I'm really just upset about what has happened today, or about my entire life this *year*.

The one thing I know for sure is that the only time I've been happy lately has been with Will. To hear him tell me that we can't even be friends hurts. It scares me that I'll go back to who I've been for the past six months, someone I'm not proud of.

I open the door to the car and grab my purse and keys. "So, you're saying it's either all or nothing, right? And since it *obviously* can't be *all*—" I slam the car door again and head toward the house, "you'll be rid of me by third period tomorrow!" I say as I purposely kick the gnome over with my boot.

I walk into the house and throw the keys toward the bar in the kitchen with such force that they glide completely across the surface and hit the floor. I step on the heel of my boot with my toe and kick it off in the entry, when my mother comes in.

"What was that all about?" she asks. "Were you just yelling?"

"Nothing," I say. "That's what it's about. Absolutely *nothing*!" I pick up my boots and walk to my room, slamming the door behind me.

I lock my bedroom door and head straight to the hamper of clothes. I pick it up and dump the contents out onto the floor, searching through them until I find what I'm looking for. My hand slides into the pocket of my jeans, and I remove the purple hair clip. I walk over to the bed, pull back the covers, and climb in. My fist tightens around the clip as I pull my hands to my face and cry myself to sleep.

When I wake up, it's midnight. I lie there a moment, hoping I'll come to the conclusion that this was all a bad dream, but the clarity never comes. When I pull back the covers, my hair clip falls from my hands and lands on the floor. This small piece of plastic, so old that it's probably covered in lead-ridden paint. I think about how I felt the day my father gave it to me, and how all the sadness and fears were eliminated as soon as he put it in my hair.

I lean forward and retrieve it from the floor, pressing down in the center so that it snaps open. I move a section of my bangs to the opposite side and secure it in place. I wait for the magic to take effect, but sure enough, everything still hurts. I pull the clip from my hair and throw it across the room and climb back into bed.

5.

MY PULSE IS POUNDING AGAINST MY TEMPLES AS I CLIMB out of bed. I'm in dire need of my own box of Altoids. My entire body is dragging from hours of alternating between crying and inadequate sleep.

I make a quick pot of coffee and sit down at the bar and drink it in silence, dreading the day that lies ahead of me. Kel eventually comes in, wearing his pajamas and Darth Vader house shoes. "Morning," he says groggily as he grabs a cup out of the dish strainer. He walks over to the coffeepot and proceeds to pour coffee into the World's Greatest Dad cup.

"What do you think you're doing?" I ask him.

"Hey, you aren't the only one who had a bad night." Kel climbs onto a stool on the opposite side of the bar. "Fourth grade is rough. I had two hours of homework," he says as he brings the cup to his mouth.

I take the coffee out of his hands and pour the contents into my own, then toss the mug into the trash can. I walk to the refrigerator, grab a juice, and place it in front of him.

Kel rolls his eyes and pokes through the hole at the top of the pouch, bringing it to his mouth. "Did you see they delivered the rest of our stuff yesterday? Mom's van finally got here. We had to unpack the whole thing by ourselves, you know," he says, obviously trying to guilt me.

"Go get dressed," I say. "We're leaving in half an hour."

IT BEGINS TO snow again after I drop Kel off at school. I hope Will is right about it being gone soon. I hate the snow. I hate *Michigan*.

When I arrive at the school, I go straight to the administration office. Mrs. Alex is powering on her computer when she notices me and shakes her head.

"Let me guess, you want C lunch now?"

I should have brought her Kel's coffee. "Actually,

I need a list of third-period electives. I want to switch classes."

She tucks her chin in and looks up at me through the top of her glasses. "Aren't you in the Poetry elective with Mr. Cooper? That's one of the more popular electives."

"That's the one," I confirm. "I'd like to withdraw."

"Well, you have until the end of the week before I submit your final schedule," she says as she grabs a sheet and hands it to me. "Which class do you prefer?"

I look over the short list of available electives.

Botany.

Russian Literature.

My options are limited.

"I'll take Russian Literature for two hundred, Alex."

She rolls her eyes and turns to enter the information into the computer. I guess she's heard that one before. She hands me yet another *new* new schedule and a yellow form.

"Have Mr. Cooper sign this, and bring it back to me before third period, and you'll be all set."

"Great," I mumble as I exit the office.

When I successfully navigate my way to Will's classroom, I'm relieved to find the door locked and the lights turned out. Seeing him again was not on my to-do list for the day, so I decide to take matters into my own hands. I reach into my backpack and retrieve a pen, press the yellow form up against the door to the classroom, and begin to forge Will's name.

"That's not a good idea."

I spin around and Will is standing behind me with a black satchel slung across his shoulder, keys in hand. My stomach flips when I look at him. He's wearing khaki slacks and a black shirt tucked in at the waist. The color of his tie matches his green eyes perfectly, making them hard to look away from. He looks so—*professional.*

I step back as he moves past me and inserts his key into the door. He enters the room and flips the light switch on, then places his satchel on the desk. I'm still standing in the doorway when he motions for me to come in.

I smack the form faceup on his desk. "Well, you weren't here yet, so I thought I'd spare you the trouble," I say, defending my actions with a defensive tone.

Will picks up the form and grimaces. "Russian Lit? *That's* what you chose?"

"It was either that or Botany," I reply evenly.

Will pulls his chair out and sits. He grabs a pen and lays the paper flat, pressing the tip of the pen on the line. He hesitates, though, and lays the pen down on the paper without signing his name.

"I thought a lot last night . . . about what you said yesterday," he says. "It's not fair of me to ask you to transfer just because it makes me uneasy. We live a hundred yards apart; our brothers are becoming best friends. If anything, this class will be good for us, help us figure out how to navigate when we're around each other. We're going to have to get used to this one way or another. Besides," he says as he pulls a paper from his satchel and shoves it forward on the desk. "You'll obviously breeze through."

I look at the test I had completed the day before, and it's marked with a 100.

"I don't mind switching," I say, even though I really *do* mind. "I understand where you're coming from."

"Thanks, but it can only get easier from here, right?"

I look up at him and nod. "Right," I lie.

He's completely wrong. Being around him every day is definitely not going to make it easier. I could move back to Texas today, and I'd still feel too close to him. However, my conscience still can't come up with a good enough argument to convince me to switch classes.

He crumples up my transfer form and chucks it toward the trash can. It misses by about two feet. I pick it up as I walk to the door and toss it in.

"I guess I'll see you third period, Mr. Cooper." I see him frown out of my peripheral vision as I exit.

I feel somewhat relieved. I hated how we had left things yesterday. Even though I would do whatever it took to rectify the awkward situation we're in, he still somehow finds a way to put me at ease.

"What happened to you yesterday?" Eddie says as we enter second period. "Get lost again?"

"Yeah, sorry about that. Issues with admin."

"You should have texted," she teases in a sarcastic tone. "I was worried about you."

"Oh, I'm sorry, dear."

"'Dear'? You tryin' to steal my girl?" A guy I have yet to meet puts his arm around Eddie and kisses her on the cheek.

"Layken, this is Gavin," she says. "Gavin, this is Layken, your competition."

Gavin has blond hair almost identical to Eddie's except in length. They could pass for brother and sister, although his eyes are chestnut while hers are blue. He is wearing a black hoodie and jeans, and when he moves his arm from Eddie's shoulder to shake my hand, I notice a tattoo of a heart on his wrist . . . the same as Eddie's.

"I've heard a lot about you," he says, extending his hand out to mine.

I eye him curiously, wondering what he could have possibly heard.

"Not really," he admits, smiling. "I haven't heard anything at all about you. That's usually just what people say when they're introduced."

He turns toward Eddie and gives her another peck on the cheek. "I'll see you next period, babe. I've got to get to class."

I envy them.

Mr. Hanson enters the room and announces there's a chapter test. I don't object when he hands me a test, and we spend the rest of the class period in silence.

* * *

AS I FOLLOW Eddie through the crowd of students, my stomach is in knots. I'm already regretting not having switched to Russian Literature. How either of us thought this would help make things easier, I don't know.

We arrive in Will's class, and he's holding the door open, greeting the students as they arrive.

"Mr. Cooper, you look a little better today. Need a mint?" Eddie says as she walks to her seat.

Javi walks in and glares at Will as he slides into his seat.

"All right, everyone," Will says, shutting the door behind him. "Good efforts on the test yesterday. 'Elements of Poetry' is a pretty mundane section, so I know you're all glad to have it out of the way. I think you'll find the performance section more interesting, which is what we'll focus on the rest of this semester.

"Performance poetry resembles traditional poetry, but with an added element: the actual *performance*."

"Performance?" Javi asks, disdained. "You mean like in that movie about the dead poets? Where they had to read crap in front of the whole class?"

"Not exactly," Will says. "That's just poetry."

"He means slamming," Gavin adds. "Like they do down at Club N9NE on Thursdays."

"What's slamming?" a girl inquires from the back of the room.

Gavin turns toward her. "It's awesome! Eddie and

I go sometimes. You have to see it to really get it," he adds.

"That's one form of it," Will says. "Has anyone else ever been to a slam?"

A couple of other students raise their hands. I don't.

"Mr. Cooper, show them. Do one of yours," Gavin says.

I can see the hesitation in Will's eyes. I know from experience he doesn't like being put on the spot.

"I'll tell you what. We'll make a deal. If I do one of my pieces, everyone has to agree to go to at least one slam this semester at Club N9NE."

No one objects. I'd like to object, but that would require raising my hand and speaking. So I don't object.

"No objections? All right, then. I'll do a short one I wrote. Remember, slam poetry is about the poetry *and* the performance."

Will stands in the front of the room and faces the students. He shakes his arms out and stretches his neck left and right in an attempt to relax himself. When he clears his throat, it's not the kind of throat clearing people do when they're nervous; it's the kind they do right before they yell.

Expectations, evaluations, internal evasions
Fly out of me like *puddles* of *blood* from a *wound*
A fetus from the *womb* of a *corpse* in a *tomb*
Withered and *strewn* like red sheets on the bed
Of an immaculate **room**.

I can't *breathe*,

I can't *win*,

From this indelible *position* I'm in

It *controls* the only *piece* of my unfortunate soul

Left to *fend* for itself in this hollowed-out hole

That I *dug* from within, like a *prisoner* in

An *unlocked* cell sitting in the deepest *pits* of hell

Unencumbered he's *not* in his sweltering spot

He could open the door 'cause he don't *need*

a damn key

But then again,

Why *would* he?

Circumlocution is *his* revolution.

The silence in the room is deafening. No one speaks, no one moves, no one claps. We are in awe. *I* am in awe. How does he expect me to transition if he keeps doing things like this?

"There you go," he says matter-of-factly as he walks back to his seat. The rest of the class period is spent talking about slam poetry. I try hard to follow along as he goes into further explanation, but the entire time I'm simply focused on the fact that he hasn't made eye contact with me. Not even once.

I CLAIM MY seat next to Eddie at lunch. I notice a guy who sits a couple of rows behind me in Will's class walking toward us. He's balancing two trays with his left arm and his backpack and a bag of chips in his right. He positions himself in the seat across from me and proceeds to combine the food onto one tray. When that task is complete, he pulls a two-liter of Coke out of his backpack and places it in front of him. He unscrews the lid and drinks directly from it. As he is chugging the soda, he looks at me then places it back down on the table, wiping his mouth.

"You gonna drink that chocolate milk, new girl?"

I nod. "That's why I got it."

"What about that roll? You gonna eat that roll?"

"Got the roll for a reason, too."

He shrugs and reaches across to Gavin's tray and takes his roll just as Gavin turns around and swipes at his hand, a moment too late.

"Dude, Nick! There's no way you're gaining ten pounds by Friday. Give it up," Gavin says.

"Nine," Nick corrects him with a mouthful of bread.

Eddie takes her roll and throws it across the table. Nick catches it midair and gives her a wink. "Your girl has faith in me," Nick says to Gavin.

"He lifts weights." Eddie is directing her comment to me. "He's got to be nine pounds heavier by Friday to compete in his weight class, and it's not looking good."

With that, I grab my roll and toss it on Nick's tray. He winks at me and dips it in a mound of butter.

I'm thankful to Eddie for accepting me into her group of friends so easily. Not that I had a choice; it was done pretty forcibly. In Texas, there were twenty-one people in my entire senior class. I had friends, but with such a limited pool to choose from, I never really considered any of them to be my best friend. I mostly hung out with my friend Kerris, but I haven't even spoken to her since the move. From what I've seen of Eddie so far, she's intriguing enough that I can't help but hope we become closer.

"So, how long have you and Gavin been dating?" I ask her.

"Since sophomore year. I hit him with my car." She looks at him and smiles. "It was love at first swipe."

"What about you?" she asks. "You got a boyfriend?"

I wish I could tell her about Will. I want to tell her about how when we met, I immediately felt something I had never felt about a guy before. I want to tell her about our first date and how the entire night seemed like we had known each other for years. I want to tell her about his poetry, our kiss, everything. Most of all, though, I want to tell her about seeing him in the hallway, when we realized our fate was not our own to decide. But I know I can't. I can't tell anyone. So I don't. I simply reply, "No."

"Really? No boyfriend? Well, we can fix that," she says.

"No need. It's not broken."

Eddie laughs and turns to Gavin, discussing possible suitors for her new, lonely friend.

* * *

THE END OF the school week finally arrives and I have never felt more relieved to pull out of a parking lot in my entire life. Even though Will lives across the street from me, I feel less vulnerable when I'm inside my house than I do two feet from him in a classroom. He successfully achieved an entire week of absolutely no eye contact. Not saying I didn't do my best to catch even a glimpse in my direction: I practically stared him down.

During the drive home, I make a detour to better formulate my plan to spend the entire weekend indoors. It's called movies and junk food.

Mom is sitting at the bar in the kitchen when I walk through the front door. I can see by the stern look on her face that she isn't particularly happy to see me. I walk into the kitchen and lay the movies and bags of junk food on the counter in front of her.

"I'm spending the weekend with Johnny Depp," I say, attempting to appear oblivious to her demeanor.

She doesn't smile. "I took Caulder home from school today," she says. "He mentioned something very interesting."

"Oh, yeah? You sound sick, Mom. Do you have a cold?" I try to sound nonchalant, but I can tell by the tone in her voice that what she's really trying to say is, "*I found out something from your little brother's friend that I should have found out from you.*"

"Anything you want to tell me?" she asks, staring daggers through me.

I sip from a bottle of water and take a seat at the bar. I had planned on talking to her about everything tonight, but it looks like it's going to happen sooner rather than later.

"Mom. I was going to talk to you about it. I swear."

"He's a teacher at your school, Lake!" She starts coughing and grabs at a Kleenex, then gets up from the bar. After she regains her composure, she lowers her voice in an attempt to avoid attracting the attention of the nine-year-olds who are somewhere within our vicinity. "Don't you think that's something you should have mentioned before I allowed you out of the house with him?"

"I didn't know! *He* didn't know!" I say in an overly defensive tone.

She cocks her head to the side and rolls her eyes as though I've insulted her. "What are you doing, Lake? Don't you realize he's raising his little brother? This can ruin his—"

Both of our eyes dart to the front door when we hear Will's car pull into his driveway. I quickly head to the front door in an attempt to block it so she'll let me explain. She beats me to it so I follow her outside, pleading.

"Mom, please. Just let me explain everything. *Please.*"

She's walking up Will's driveway when he notices us bombarding him. He smiles when he first notices my mother, but his smile fades when he sees I'm right behind her. He has surmised that this is not a friendly visit.

"Julia, please," he says. "Can we go inside to talk about this?"

She doesn't respond. She just marches toward his front door and lets herself in.

Will looks at me questioningly.

"Your brother mentioned you were a teacher. I haven't had a chance to explain anything to her," I say.

He sighs, and we reluctantly make our way inside.

It's the first time I've been inside his home since I found out about the death of his parents. Nothing has changed, yet at the same time everything has changed. That first day when I sat at his bar, I assumed that everything in the house belonged to his parents, that Will's situation was not unlike my own. Now, when I take in my surroundings, it sheds a different light on him. A light of responsibility. Maturity.

My mother is sitting stiffly on the sofa. Will walks quietly across the room and sits on the edge of the couch across from her. He leans forward and clasps his hands in front of him, his elbows resting on his knees.

"I'll explain everything." He says this with a serious, respectful tone to his voice.

"I know you will," she replies evenly.

"Basically, I made a lot of assumptions. I thought she was older. She *seemed* older. Once she told me she was eighteen, I guess I assumed she was in college. It's only September; most students aren't eighteen when they start their senior year."

"Most of them. She's only been eighteen for two weeks."

"Yeah, I . . . I realize that now," he says, shooting a look in my direction.

"She wasn't attending school the first week you guys moved in, so I guess I just assumed. Somehow the topic never came up while we were together."

My mother starts to cough again. Will and I wait, but the coughing intensifies and she stands and takes a few deep breaths. I would think she's having a panic attack if I didn't already know she was coming down with something. Will goes to the kitchen and comes back with a glass of water. She takes a sip and turns toward the living-room window that faces the front yard. Caulder and Kel are outside now; I can hear them laughing. My mother walks to the front door and opens it.

"Kel, Caulder! Don't lie in the street!" She closes the door and turns toward us. "Tell me, when *did* the topic come up?" she asks, looking at both of us now.

I can't answer her. Somehow, in the presence of the two of them, I feel small. Two adults hashing it out in front of the children. That's what this feels like.

"We didn't find out until she showed up for my class," Will replies.

My mother looks at me, and her jaw gapes open. "You're in his *class*?" She looks at Will and repeats what she said. "She's in your *class*?"

God, it sounds really bad coming from her mouth.

She stands up and paces the length of the living room as both Will and I allow her time to process. "You're telling me that both of you deny having *any* knowledge of this prior to the first day of school?"

We both nod in agreement.

"Well, what the hell happens now?" she asks. She has both of her hands on her hips. Will and I are silent, hoping she can magically come up with the solution that we've both been searching for all week.

"Well," Will replies. "Lake and I are doing our best to work through this a day at a time."

She glares at him accusingly. "*Lake?* You call her *Lake?*"

Will looks down at the floor and clears his throat, unable to meet her stare.

My mother sighs and takes a seat next to Will on the sofa. "Both of you need to accept the severity of this situation. I know my daughter, and my daughter likes you, Will. *A lot.* If you share even a fraction of those feelings, you will do whatever you can to distance yourself from her. That includes ditching the nicknames. This will jeopardize your career *and* her reputation." She stands up and walks to the front door, holding it open for me to follow her out. She isn't allowing us the opportunity for any private time.

Kel and Caulder brush past us and run toward Caulder's bedroom. Mom watches as they disappear down the hallway. "Kel and Caulder don't need to be affected by this," she says, bringing her attention back to Will. "I suggest we work something out now so that the contact between you and Lake can be minimized."

"Absolutely. I completely agree," he says.

"I work nights and sleep in the mornings. If you want to take them to school, Lake or I will pick them up after school. Where they go from there can be up to them. They seem to do pretty well going back and forth."

"That sounds good. Thank you."

"He's a good kid, Will."

"Really, Julia. It's all fine with me. I haven't seen Caulder this happy in a . . ." Will's voice trails off, and he doesn't finish his sentence.

"Julia?" he asks. "Will you be talking to the school about this? I mean, I completely understand if that's what you need to do. I would just like to be prepared."

She looks at him, then at me, and holds her stare when she speaks. "There's nothing currently going on that I would *need* to inform them about, is there?"

"Not at all. I swear," I quickly reply. I want Will to look at me so he can see the apology in my eyes, but he doesn't. As soon as he shuts his front door behind us, I can't hold my tongue any longer.

"Why would you *do* that?" I yell. "You didn't even give me the opportunity to explain!" I dart across the street and don't look back. I run into the house and into the solitude of my bedroom, where I will remain until she's left for work.

* * *

"LAYKEN, DO WE have any packets of Kool-Aid?" Kel is standing in the entryway, covered in slush. It's not the oddest thing he's ever asked me for, so I don't question him as I grab a package of grape out of the kitchen cabinet and take it to him.

"Not purple, we need red," he says. I grab the purple package from his hands and return with a red one.

"Thanks!"

I close the door behind him and grab a towel and lay it down on the tile of the entryway. It's not even nine in the morning and already Kel and Caulder have been outside in the snow for over two hours.

I take a seat at the bar and finish my cup of coffee, staring at the pile of junk food that I'm no longer excited about eating. My mother got home around seven thirty this morning and climbed into bed, where she'll stay until around two o'clock. I'm still angry with her and don't feel like confronting the situation at all today, so it looks like I have about five more hours before I'll lock myself in my bedroom again. I grab a movie off the bar and, despite my lack of appetite, a bag of chocolate. If there is any man who can take my mind off of Will, it's definitely Johnny Depp.

Halfway through my movie, Kel comes bounding in the house, still covered in snow and slush as he grabs my hand and starts to pull me outside.

"Kel, stop! I'm not going outside!" I snap.

"Please? Just for a minute. You have to see the snow-man we made."

"Fine. Let me get some shoes on at least."

As soon as I pull the second boot on, Kel grabs my hand again and pulls me out the door. I continue to allow Kel to pull me along as I shield my eyes. It's taking them a moment to adjust to the sun's reflection on the snow.

"It's right over here," I hear Caulder saying, but not to me. I look up to see Caulder handling his brother in the same way that Kel is handling me. We are both led to the rear of the Jeep where they position us inches apart, directly in front of a casualty.

I now know the purpose behind the demand for red Kool-Aid. In front of us, lying flat on the ground beneath the rear of my Jeep, is a dead snowman. His eyes are small pieces of twig, shaped into a grim expression. His arms are two thin branches lying at his side, one of them broken in half under my rear tire. His head and neck are sprinkled with a trail of red Kool-Aid that leads to a pool of bright-red snow about a foot down from the snowman.

"He was in a terrible accident," Kel says seriously be-fore he and Caulder break out into a fit of giggles.

Will and I look at one another, and for the first time in a week, he smiles at me. "Wow, I need my camera," he says.

"I'll grab mine," I say. I smile back at him and head

inside. So this is what it's going to be like from now on? Conversing under false pretenses in front of our brothers? Avoiding each other in public? I *hate* the transition.

When I return with the camera, the boys are still admiring the murder scene, so I snap a couple of pictures.

"Kel, let's kill a snowman with Will's car now," Caulder says before they dart across the street.

The tension is thick as Will and I stare excessively at the snowman in front of us, not knowing what else to look at. He eventually glances toward his house at our brothers.

"They're lucky to have each other you know," he says quietly.

I analyze this sentence and wonder if it has a deeper meaning, or if he was just making an observation.

"Yeah, they are," I agree.

We both stand there watching them gather more snow. Will takes a deep breath and stretches his arms out above his head. "Well, I better get back inside," he says. He turns away.

"Will, wait." He swings back around and puts his hands in his pockets, but doesn't say anything.

"I'm sorry about yesterday. About my mom," I say as I stare at the ground between us. I can't look him in the eye for two reasons. One—the snow is still blinding me. Two—it hurts when I look at him.

"It's fine, Layken."

And we're back to the official first name.

He stares at the ground where the "blood" has tinted the snow, and he kicks at it with his shoe. "She's just doing her job as a mom, you know." He pauses and lowers his voice even more. "Don't be so mad at her. You're lucky to have her."

He spins and walks back to his house. Guilt overcomes me as I think of what it's like for them to just have each other, and here I sit complaining about the only parent left among the four of us. I feel ashamed for bringing it up. I feel more ashamed of having been mad at my mother for what she did. It was my fault for not talking to her about it sooner. Will is right, as usual. I *am* lucky to have her.

THE SHOWER IN my mother's bedroom is running after lunch, so I heat up some leftovers and make her a glass of tea. I place them at her usual seat at the bar and wait for her. When she finally emerges from the hallway and sees the food, she gives me a slight smile and takes her seat.

"Is this a peace offering or did you poison my food?" she asks as she unfolds a napkin into her lap.

"I guess you'll have to eat it first to find out."

She eyes me cautiously and takes a bite of her food. She chews for a minute and takes another bite after she fails to keel over.

"I'm sorry, Mom. I should have talked to you about it sooner. I was just really upset."

She looks at me with pity in her eyes, so I turn away from her and busy my hands with the dishes.

"Lake, I know how much you like him, I do. I like him, too. But like I said yesterday, this can't happen. You have to promise me you won't do anything stupid."

"I swear, Mom. He's made it clear he wants nothing to do with me, so you don't have anything to worry about."

"I hope not," she says as she continues to eat.

I finish up the dishes and return to the living room to continue my affair with Johnny.

6.

Your heart says not again
What kind of mess have you got me in?
But when the feeling's there
It can lift you up and take you anywhere.

—THE AVETT BROTHERS, "LIVING OF LOVE"

THE NEXT FEW WEEKS FLY BY AS MY HOMEWORK GETS more intense, along with the isolation in Will's classroom. We haven't spoken since the day the snowman was murdered. We haven't had eye contact since then, either. He avoids me like the plague.

I haven't been adjusting very well to Michigan. Maybe everything that happened with Will ended up making the move even harder. All I ever feel like doing is sleeping. I guess because it doesn't hurt as bad when you're asleep.

Eddie keeps bringing up possible fillers for the obvious hole in my boyfriend department, but I've rejected them all. She has finally resorted to switching places in Will's class with Nick in the hopes that something will bloom there.

It won't.

"Hey, Layken," Nick smiles as he sits in his new spot nearest me. "Got another one for ya. Wanna hear it?"

In the past week alone, I've had to endure at least three Chuck Norris jokes a day from Nick. He incorrectly assumes that since I'm from Texas, I must be obsessed with *Walker, Texas Ranger*.

"Sure." I don't try to deny him this privilege anymore; it doesn't work.

"Chuck Norris got a Gmail account today. It's gmail@ chucknorris.com."

It takes me a second to process. I'm normally quick with jokes, but my mind has been sluggish lately, and for good reason.

"Funny," I reply flatly in order to appease him.

"Chuck Norris counted to infinity. Twice."

As much as I didn't feel like laughing, I did. Nick did annoy me quite a bit, but his ignorance was endearing.

When Will walks into the classroom, his eyes dart to Nick. Although he still doesn't look at me, I like to imagine a twinge of jealousy building up inside of him. I've been making it a point recently to become more attentive toward Nick once Will comes into the room. I hate this new desire that has overcome me, the desire to make Will jealous. I know I need to stop before Nick starts to get the wrong idea, but I can't. I feel like this is the only aspect of this entire situation that I have any control over.

"Get out your notebooks, we're making poetry today," Will says as he takes a seat at his desk. Half the class groans. I hear Eddie clapping.

"Can we have partners?" Nick asks. He starts inching his desk toward mine.

Will glares at him. "No."

Nick shrugs and scoots his desk back into place.

"Each of you needs to write a short poem, which you will perform in front of the class tomorrow."

I start taking notes on the assignment, not willing to watch him as he speaks. Remaining in his class was a very bad idea. I can't focus on anything he's saying. I'm constantly wondering what's going on inside his head, whether he's thinking about us, what he does inside his house at night. Even at home he's been the only thing I can think about. I find myself stealing glances across the street any chance I get. Honestly, if I had switched classes it probably wouldn't have made a difference. I would just rush to get home first so I could watch from the window when he pulls up to the house. This game I'm playing with myself is so exhausting. I wish I could find a way to break the hold he has on me. He seems to have done a pretty good job of moving on.

"You just need to start out with about ten sentences for tomorrow's presentation. We can expand over the next couple of weeks, giving you something to prepare for the slam," Will says. "And don't think I've forgotten. So far no one in here has shown up at the slam. We made a deal."

The entire class starts to protest.

"That wasn't the deal! You said we just had to observe. Now we have to perform?" says Gavin.

"No. Well, technically not. Everyone in here is required to attend one slam. You aren't required to perform; I just want you to observe. However, there's a chance you could be chosen to be the sacrifice, so it wouldn't hurt to have something prepared."

Several students ask what the sacrifice is in unison. Will explains the term and how it can be anyone chosen at random. Therefore, he wants everyone to have a piece ready before the night they are to attend, just in case.

"What if we want to perform?" Eddie asks.

"I'll tell you what. We'll make one more deal. Whoever willingly slams will be exempt from the final."

"Sweet, I'm in," Eddie says.

"What if we don't go?" Javi asks.

"Then you're missing out on something amazing. *And* you get an F for participation," he replies.

Javi rolls his eyes and groans at Will's response.

"So, what kinds of things can we write about?" Eddie asks.

Will moves to the front of the desk and sits, only inches from me.

"There are no rules, you can write about anything.

You can write about love, food, your hobby, something significant that's happened in your life. You can write about how much you hate your Poetry teacher. Write about anything, as long as it's something you're passionate about. If the audience doesn't feel your passion, they won't feel you—and that's never fun, believe me." He says this as though he speaks from experience.

"What about sex? Can we write about that?" Javi asks. It's obvious he's trying to push Will's buttons. Will remains cool.

"Anything. As long as it doesn't get you in hot water with your parents."

"What if they don't let us go? I mean, it *is* a club," a student asks from the back of the room.

"I understand if they have hesitations. If there are any parents that don't feel comfortable, I'll talk to them about it. I also don't want transportation to be an issue. This club is somewhat of a drive, so if it's an issue, I'll take a school vehicle. Whatever the obstacle, we'll work through it. I'm very passionate about slam poetry and don't feel I'll be doing you justice as your teacher if I don't allow you the opportunity to experience this in person.

"I'll answer questions throughout the week regarding the semester requirement. But for now, let's get back to today's assignment. You have the entire class period to complete the poem. We'll start presenting them tomorrow. Get to it."

I open my notebook and lay it flat on my desk. I stare

at it, not having the first clue as to what to write about. The only thing that's been on my mind lately is Will, and there's no way I'm doing a poem about him.

By the end of the class period, the only thing that's written on my paper is my name. I glance up to Will, who is seated at his desk, biting the corner of his bottom lip. His eyes are focused on my desk, down on the poem that I've yet to write. He glances up and sees me watching him. It's the first eye contact we've had in three weeks. Surprisingly, he doesn't immediately look away. If he had any idea how this lip-biting quirk affects me, he'd stop. The intensity in his eyes causes me to flush, and the room suddenly becomes warm. His stare is unwavering until the class dismissal bell rings. He stands and walks to the door and holds it open for the students exiting. I immediately put away my notebook and throw my bag over my shoulder. I don't make eye contact when I leave the classroom, but I can feel him watching me.

Just when I think he's forgotten about me, he goes and does something like this. The entire rest of the day I'm extremely quiet as I attempt to analyze his actions. I eventually come up with just one conclusion: He's just as confused as I am.

I'M RELIEVED TO feel the warm sun beating down on my face as I walk toward my Jeep. The weather was insanely cold going into October. The predictions are that the next two weeks will be a nice respite from the snow before winter begins. I insert the key into the ignition and turn it.

Nothing happens.

Great, my Jeep is shot. I have no idea what I'm doing, but I pop the hood on the Jeep and take a look. There's a bunch of wires and metal; that's about all I can comprehend from a mechanical standpoint. I do know what the battery looks like, so I grab a crowbar from the trunk and tap it against the battery. After another failed attempt at getting the ignition to turn over, I resort to pounding a little harder until I'm pretty much bludgeoning the battery out of sheer frustration.

"That's not a good idea." Will walks up beside me, satchel across his chest, looking very much like a teacher and less like Will.

"You've made it clear that you don't think a lot of what I do is a very good idea," I say as I return my focus back under the hood.

"What's wrong, it won't crank?" He bends forward under the hood and starts to mess with wires.

I don't understand what he's doing. One minute he tells me he doesn't want to speak to me in public, the next minute he's staring me down in class, and now he's under my hood, trying to help me. I'm not a fan of inconsistency.

"What are you doing, Will?"

He rises out from under the hood and cocks his head at me. "What does it look like I'm doing? I'm trying to figure out what's wrong with your Jeep." He walks around to the driver's side and attempts to turn the ignition.

I follow him to the door. "I mean, *why* are you doing this? You've made it pretty clear you don't want me to speak to you."

"Layken, you're a student stranded in the parking lot. I'm not going to get in my car and just drive away."

I know his reference to me as a student isn't meant as an insult, but it sure feels like one. He realizes his poor choice of words and sighs as he gets out of the car and looks back under the hood. "Look, that's not how I meant it," he says, fidgeting with more wires.

I lean under the hood next to him in an attempt to look natural as I continue my point. "It's just been really hard, Will. It was so easy for you to accept this and move past it. It hasn't been that easy for me. It's all I think about."

Will grips the edge of the hood with his hands and turns his head toward me. "You think this is easy for me?" he whispers.

"Well, that's how you make it seem."

"Lake, nothing about this has been easy. It's a daily struggle for me to come to work, knowing this very job is what's keeping us apart." He turns away from the car and leans against it. "If it weren't for Caulder, I would have quit that first day I saw you in the hallway. I could have taken the year off . . . waited until you graduated to go back." He turns toward me, his voice lower than before.

"Believe me, I've run every possible scenario through my mind. How do you think it makes me feel to know that I'm the reason you're hurting? That I'm the reason you're so sad?"

The sincerity in his voice is surprising. I had no idea. "I . . . I'm sorry. I just thought—"

Will cuts me off midsentence and turns back toward the car. "Your battery is fine; looks like it might be your alternator."

"Car won't start?" Nick asks as he walks up beside us, explaining the reason behind Will's sudden guarded behavior.

"No, Mr. Cooper thinks I need a new alternator."

"That sucks," Nick says as he glances under the hood. "I'll give you a ride home if you need one."

I start to decline when Will interrupts.

"That would be great, Nick," Will says as he closes the hood of the Jeep.

I shoot Will a glance, and he ignores my silent protest. Will walks away and leaves me with Nick and no other option for a ride home.

"I'm parked over here," Nick says, heading to his car.

"Let me grab my stuff first." I reach for my bag and my hand goes up to find the ignition empty. Will must have accidentally taken my keys. I leave the door unlocked just in case he doesn't have them. I don't want to add a locksmith charge on top of our already mounting debt.

"Wow. Nice car," I say when we reach Nick's vehicle. It's a small black sports car. Not sure what kind, but there isn't a speck of dirt on it.

"It's not mine," he says as we climb inside. "It's my dad's. He lets me drive it when he's off work."

"Still, it's nice. Do you mind if we swing by Chapman Elementary? I'm supposed to pick up my little brother."

"No problem," he says, turning left out of the parking lot.

"So, new girl. You miss Texas yet?" Although it's been a month, he still calls me new girl.

"Yep," I reply shortly.

He attempts to make more small talk but I treat his questions as if they were rhetorical, even though they aren't. I can't stop thinking about the things Will said to me before Nick interrupted us. Nick finally grasps the idea that I'm not in a chatty mood, so he turns on the radio.

We pull up to Kel's school, and I get out of the car so Kel can spot me, since I'm not in my Jeep. When Kel notices me, he comes running up to me, followed by Caulder. "Hey, where's your Jeep?"

"Won't start. Hop in, Nick is giving us a ride home."

"Oh. Well, Caulder is supposed to go with us today."

I open the back door as the two climb in the small backseat. They immediately start oohing and aahing. The remainder of the short drive consists of transformer comparisons and Nick's car. When we arrive at the house, Kel and Caulder jump out of the car and run inside. I thank Nick and follow the boys toward the house when I hear Nick open his door.

"Layken, wait," Nick calls after me.

Ugh. Almost in the clear. I turn to see him standing in my driveway, looking nervous.

"Later this week, Eddie and Gavin and I are going to Getty's. You wanna come?"

I definitely should have laid off on the obvious flirtation with Nick. I feel guilty, knowing good and well I've sent him the wrong signals. "I don't know. I'd have to run it by my mom. I'll let you know tomorrow, okay?" I see the hope fill his eyes, and wish I had gone ahead and turned him down. I don't want to give him any more false hope than I already have.

"Yeah. Tomorrow. See ya," Nick says.

When I walk in the house, Kel and Caulder are both at the bar with their homework out. "Caulder, do you live with us now or what?"

He looks at me with his big green Will-looking eyes. "I can go home if you want me to."

"No. I was just kidding. I like you being here; it keeps this little creeper away from me." I squeeze Kel's shoulders, then walk into the kitchen and grab a drink.

"So is that Nick guy your boyfriend? I thought my brother was going to be your boyfriend."

Caulder catches me off guard with his observation, causing juice to spew from my mouth. "No, neither of them is my boyfriend. Your brother and I are just friends, Caulder."

"But Layken," Kel gives Caulder a mischievous grin. "I saw you kissing him that night y'all came home. In the driveway. I was watching from my bedroom window."

My heart jumps to my throat. I walk over to them and place my hands firmly on the bar in front of them. "Kel, don't ever repeat what you just said. Do you hear me?"

His eyes get big, and he and Caulder both lean back in their chairs as I lean forward across the bar.

"I'm serious. You did not see what you thought you saw. Will can get in a lot of trouble if you repeat what you said. I mean it."

They both nod as I back away and turn toward my room. I pull my notebook out of my bag and plop down on the bed next to it to start on my homework, but I can't. The thought of anything getting out about Will and me distracts me. As much as I hate the fact that we can't be together, I hate the thought of him getting fired even more. He needs this job. Will was only one year older than I am now when his parents died, and he essentially became a parent himself. The more I think about it, the guiltier I feel for being so hard on him and the decision he's made. The pain I'm feeling as a result of us not being together pales in comparison to what Will must be going through. I feel less like Will's peer every day and more like his student.

I decide to work on the poem I've yet to start, but

after half an hour I'm still staring at a blank page, when my mother walks in.

"Where's your Jeep?"

"Oh, I forgot to tell you. It won't crank—alternator or something. It's parked at school."

"How can you forget to mention that?" she says, obviously frustrated.

"I'm sorry. You were sleeping when I got home. I know you've been sick this week, so I didn't want to wake you up."

She sighs and sits on my bed. "I don't know when I'll be able to get it fixed. I work the next few days. Do you mind just keeping it at the school for a couple days until I can work it out?"

"I'll ask tomorrow. I doubt they would even notice it's there."

"Okay. Well, I've got to get to work." She stands up to leave.

"Wait. Your shift doesn't start for a few more hours."

"I need to run errands," she quickly replies. She shuts the door, leaving me to question the validity of her response.

I'M DRYING MY hair after my shower when I think I hear the doorbell. I turn the dryer off and listen for a moment, and it eventually rings again. "Kel, get the door!" I yell as I pull on my sweats. I pile my still-wet hair into a band and double it up on top of my head as I throw on a tank top. The doorbell rings again.

I make my way to the front door and check the peephole. Will is standing outside with his arms crossed, staring at the ground. My heart skips a beat at the sight of him, and I turn to check my reflection in the entryway mirror. Sure enough, I look like I just got out of the shower. At least I'm not wearing Kel's house shoes. Ugh! Why do I even care?

I open the door and motion for him to come inside. He steps in far enough for me to shut the door behind him but doesn't come any further inside.

"I just need Caulder. Bath time."

His arms are still crossed, and his speech is curt. I take this as a sign that I'm not getting any more confessions out of him right now, so I tell him to give me a sec as I go fetch Caulder. I check Kel's room, my mother's room, and eventually my room, when I run out of rooms to check.

"They aren't here, Will," I say as I walk back into the living room.

"Well, they have to be. They aren't at my house." He makes his way down the hallway and checks the rooms as he calls for them. I open the patio door, flick on the outdoor light, and make a quick scan of the small backyard.

"They aren't out back," I say when we meet back in the living room.

"I'll check my house again," he says.

Will makes his way across the street and I follow behind him. It's dark outside and the temperature has dropped since earlier in the day. I become increasingly concerned as we make our way to Will's house. I know Kel and Caulder wouldn't be outside this time of night. If they aren't in one of the houses, I don't know where they could be.

Will makes a quick run of his house. I don't feel comfortable walking through it, since I've never really been further than the hallway, so I stand in the doorway and wait.

"They aren't here," he says, unable to hide the uncertainty in his voice. My hands go to my mouth as I gasp, fully realizing the seriousness of the situation. Will can see the fear in my eyes, and he puts his arms around me.

"We'll find them. They're just off playing somewhere." His reassurance is brief as he lets go and heads back out the front door. "Check the backyard; I'll meet you out front," he says.

We're both calling the boys' names when the panic rises up in my chest. It reminds me of the time I was babysitting Kel when he was four, and I thought I had lost him. I searched the entire house for twenty minutes before finally breaking down and calling my mother. She immediately called the police, who arrived within minutes. They were still searching when she finally made it home—the panic in her eyes when she walked through the door cut through me and we both started to cry. After searching for over fifteen minutes, an officer found Kel passed out on the folded towels in the bathroom cabinet. Apparently he had been hiding from me when he fell asleep.

I'm hoping to find the same sense of relief when I look through Will's backyard, but they aren't here. I make my way around the side of his house and see Will standing in the driveway, staring inside his car. When he sees me running toward him, his finger goes up to his mouth, instructing me to be quiet. I peer into the backseat, where Kel and Caulder are both crouched on the floorboard, their fingers and hands clamped together in the shape of guns; they're both passed out.

I breathe a sigh of relief.

"They would make horrible guards," he whispers.

"Yeah, they sure would."

We both stand there, staring at our little brothers. Will's arm goes around me, and he gives my shoulders a quick squeeze. His hug doesn't linger at all though, so I know it's nothing more than a gesture expressing relief that our brothers are safe.

"Hey, before you wake them up, I've got something of yours inside." He walks toward his house, so I follow him inside and into the kitchen.

My heart is still pounding against my chest, although I can't distinguish if it's the aftermath of the search for our brothers, or if it's just being in Will's presence.

He pulls something out of his satchel and hands it to me. "Your keys," he says, dropping them into my hand.

"Oh, thanks," I say, somewhat disappointed. I don't know what I expected him to have, but I was fantasizing that maybe it was his resignation letter.

"It's running fine now. You should be able to drive it home tomorrow." He makes his way to his couch and sits.

"What? You fixed it?" I say.

"Well, *I* didn't fix it. I know a guy who was able to put an alternator on it this afternoon."

His reference in the parking lot comes back to mind. Somehow I doubt he would have an alternator put on any other student's vehicle.

"Will, you didn't have to do that," I say as I sit down beside him on the couch. "Thanks, though. I'll pay you back."

"Don't worry about it. You guys have helped me a lot with Caulder lately; it's the least I can do."

And yet again, I'm at a loss for what to say next. It feels like that first day I was standing in his kitchen, contemplating my next move after he helped me with my bandage. I know I should get up and leave, but I like being here next to him. Even if I am finding myself in his debt again. I somehow find the confidence to speak again.

"So, can we finish our conversation from earlier?" I say.

He adjusts himself on the couch and props his feet on the coffee table in front of us. "That depends," he says. "Did you come up with a solution?"

"Well, no," I reply, just as a possible solution comes

to mind. I lean my head against the back of the couch and meekly suggest my idea. "Suppose these feelings we have just get more . . . complex." I pause for a moment. I'm not sure how he's going to take this new suggestion of mine, so I tread lightly.

"I wouldn't be opposed to the idea of getting a GED."

"That's ridiculous," he says, eyeing me sharply. "Don't even think like that. There's no way you're quitting school, Lake."

I'm *Lake* again.

"It was just an idea," I say.

"Well, it was a dumb one."

We both think silently, neither of us coming up with any other solutions. My head is still resting against the back of the couch as I watch him. His hands are clasped behind his head, and he's staring up at the ceiling. His jaw is clenched tight, and he's absentmindedly popping his knuckles.

He's no longer wearing the clothes he wears as a teacher. Instead, he has a plain white fitted T-shirt on and gray jogging pants that are almost identical to the ones I'm wearing. For the first time tonight, I notice his hair is wet. I haven't been this close to him in weeks; I was beginning to forget what he smells like. I inhale and take in the scent of his aftershave. It smells like the air in Texas right before it starts to rain.

There's a small dab of shaving cream right below his left ear. My hand instinctively moves up to his neck and I wipe it away. He flinches and turns toward me, so I defensively hold up my finger as if to prove my reason for touching him. He pulls my hand toward him and rubs my finger across his shirt, wiping off the excess shaving cream.

Our hands come to rest on his chest and we continue to look at each other in silence. My palm is flat against his heart, and I can feel it rapidly beating against my hand. I know this exchange between us is wrong, but it feels incredibly right.

He allows my hand to remain on his chest as it moves up and down to the rhythm of his breath. The look in his eyes is the exact look he had when he was watching me in class today. But this time my physical response is more intense, and I struggle to control the powerful urge to lean in and kiss him. I've wanted to talk to him like this for over a month now. I still had so much to say before he started pretending I didn't exist. I'm afraid that as soon as I walk out of his house tonight, the isolation will return, so I decide to tell him what I've wanted to say to him for weeks.

"Will?" I whisper. "I'll wait for you—until I graduate."

He exhales and closes his eyes, stroking his thumb across the back of my hand. "That's a long wait, Lake. A lot can happen in a year." His pulse increases against my palm.

I don't know what comes over me, but I lean closer and turn his face toward mine. I just need him to look at me.

He doesn't meet my gaze. Instead, his eyes focus on his hand as he slowly moves it up my arm. All the same sensations that flowed through me the first night we kissed come flooding back. I've missed his touch so much.

He moves his hand to my shoulder and slides his fingers underneath the strap of my shirt, slowly tracing along the edges of it. His movements are slow and methodical as he pulls his legs off of the table in front of him and turns his body toward me. His expression seems full of conflict, but he slowly leans in and presses his lips against my shoulder. I place my hands on the back of his neck and inhale. His breath becomes heavier as his lips slowly move across my shoulder and onto my neck. The room starts to spin, so I close my eyes. His lips make their way to my jaw and closer to my mouth. When I feel him pull away, I open my eyes and he's watching me. There's a slight moment of hesitation in his eyes just before his lips close over mine.

In the past, his kisses have been very delicate and smooth. There's a different hunger behind him now. He slides his hands under my shirt and grasps at my waist. I return his kisses with the same feverish passion. I run my hands through his hair and pull him to me as I lie back on the couch. As soon as he begins to ease his body on top of mine, his lips break away and he sits back up.

"We've got to stop," he says. "We can't do this." He squeezes his eyes shut and rests his head against the couch.

I sit back up and ignore his protest, sliding my hands

up his neck and through his hair. I press my lips to his and pull myself onto his lap. His hands wrap around my waist again and he pulls me into him, returning my kiss with even more intensity than before.

He's right; they do get better every time.

My hands find the bottom edge of his shirt and I slide it up. Our lips separate for a brief moment when his shirt passes between us. I place my hands on his chest and run them over the contours of his muscles as we continue to kiss. He grips my arms and pushes me down onto the couch. I wait for him to find his way back to my mouth, but instead he pushes away from me and stands up.

"Layken, get up!" he demands. He grabs my hand and pulls me up from the couch.

I stand up, still caught up in the moment and unable to catch my breath.

"This—this can't happen!" He's attempting to catch his breath, too. "I'm your teacher now. Everything has changed—we can't do this."

His timing sucks. My knees are weak, so I sit back down on the couch for support. "Will, I won't say anything. I swear." I don't want him to regret what just happened between us. For a moment, it felt like we were back where we belonged. Now, seconds later, I'm confused again.

"I'm sorry, Layken, but it's not right," he says, pacing the floor. "This isn't good for either of us. This isn't good for *you*."

"You don't know what's good for me," I snap. I'm getting defensive again.

He stops pacing and turns toward me. "You won't wait for me. I won't let you give up what should be the best year of your life. I had to grow up way too fast; I'm not taking that away from you, too. It wouldn't be fair. I don't want you to wait for me, Layken."

The shift in his demeanor and the way my entire first name is flowing from his mouth is causing the oxygen to deplete from the room. I'm dizzy. "I won't be giving *anything* up," I reply weakly. I would have screamed it if I could muster enough energy.

He grabs his shirt and pulls it on over his head as he moves further away from me. He walks to the opposite side of the living room and around the back of the couch. He grips the back of it and lets his head fall between his shoulders, avoiding eye contact again. "My life is nothing but responsibilities. I'm raising a *child*, for Christ's sake. I wouldn't be able to put your needs first. Hell, I wouldn't even be able to put them *second*." He slowly raises his head and brings his gaze back to mine. "You deserve better than third."

I go to him and kneel on the couch in front of him, placing my hands on top of his. "Your responsibilities *should* come before me, which is why I want to wait for you, Will. You're a good person. This thing about you that you think is your flaw—it's the reason I'm falling in love with you."

My last few words trickle out as though I've lost what little control over myself I had left. I don't regret saying it, though.

He pulls his hands out from under mine and places them firmly on either side of my face. He looks me directly in the eyes. "You are *not* falling in love with me." He says this as if it's a command. "You *cannot* fall in love with me." His eyes are hard and he clenches his jaw again. I feel the tears begin to well in my eyes as he releases me and walks toward the front door.

"What happened tonight—" He's pointing to the couch as he speaks. "That can't happen again. That *won't* happen again." He says this as though he's trying to convince more than just me.

After he walks outside, he slams the door behind him, and I'm left alone in his living room. My hands clutch at my stomach; my nausea intensifies. I'm afraid if I don't regain my composure soon, I won't be able to stand long enough to make it out of the house. I inhale through my nose and exhale from my mouth, then count backward from ten.

It's a coping technique I learned from my father when I was younger. I used to have what my parents referred to as "emotional overloads." My dad would wrap his arms around me and squeeze me as tight as he could as we counted down. Sometimes I would fake the tantrums just so he would have to squeeze me. What I wouldn't give for my dad's embrace right now.

The front door opens, and Will reenters, carrying a sleeping Caulder in his arms. "Kel woke up; he's walking home now. You should go, too," he says quietly.

I feel completely embarrassed. Embarrassed by what just happened between us and the fact that he's making me feel desperate, *weaker* than him. I snatch my keys off the coffee table and turn toward the door, stopping in front of him.

"You're an *asshole*," I say. I turn and leave, slamming the door behind me.

As soon as I get to my bedroom, I collapse onto the bed and cry. Although it's negative, I finally have inspiration for my poem. I grab a pen and start writing as I wipe smudged tears off of the paper.

7.

You can't be like me
But be happy that you can't
I see pain but I don't feel it
I am like the old Tin Man.

—THE AVETT BROTHERS, "TIN MAN"

ACCORDING TO ELISABETH KÜBLER-ROSS, THERE ARE FIVE stages of grief a person passes through after the death of a loved one: denial, anger, bargaining, depression, and acceptance.

I took a psychology class during the last semester of my junior year when we lived in Texas. We were discussing stage four when the principal walked into the room, pale as a ghost.

"Layken, can I see you in the hallway please?"

Principal Bass was a pleasant man. Plump in the belly, plump in the hands, plump in places you didn't know could be plump. It was an unusually cold spring day in Texas, but you wouldn't know it from the rings of sweat underneath his arms. He was the type of principal who hung out in his office rather than the halls. He never went looking for trouble, just waited for it to come to him. So why was he here?

I had a sinking feeling deep in the pit of my stomach as I stood up and walked as slowly as I could to the classroom door. He wouldn't make eye contact with me. I remember I looked right at him, and his eyes darted to the floor. He felt sorry for me. But why?

When I walked out into the hallway my mother was standing there, mascara streaked down her cheeks. The look in her eyes told me why she was there. Why *she* was there, and my father wasn't.

I shook my head, refusing to believe what I knew to be true. "No," I cried repeatedly. She threw her arms around me and started to collapse to the floor. Rather than hold her up, I simply melted with her. That day I experienced my first stage of grief in the hallway floor of my high school: denial.

GAVIN IS PREPARING to perform his poetry. He's standing in front of the class, his paper shaking between his fingers as he clears his throat and prepares to read from it.

I wonder, as I ignore Gavin's presence and focus on

Will, do the five stages of grief only apply to the death of a loved one? Could it not also apply to the death of an aspect of your life? If it does, then I'm definitely smack-dab in the center of stage two: anger.

"What's it called, Gavin?" Will asks. He's sitting at his desk, writing notes into his pad as students perform. It pisses me off—the way he's being so attentive, focused on everything except me. His ability to make me feel like this huge invisible void pisses me off. The way he pauses to chew on the tip of his pen pisses me off. Just last night, those same lips that are wrapped around the tip of his ugly red pen were making their way up my neck.

I push the thought of his kiss out of my mind as quickly as it crept in. I don't know how long it will take, but I'm determined to break from this hold he has on me.

"Um, I didn't really give it a title," Gavin responds. He's standing at the front of the classroom, second to last person to perform. "I guess you can call it 'Preproposal'?"

"'Preproposal'—go ahead then," Will states in a teacherish voice that also pisses me off.

"Ahem." Gavin clears his throat. His hands start trembling even more as he begins to read.

One million fifty-one thousand and
two hundred minutes.
That's approximately how many minutes

I've loved you,

It's how many minutes I've *thought* about you,

How many minutes I've *worried* about you,

How many minutes I've thanked *God* for you,

How many minutes I've thanked *every deity* in the

Universe for you.

One million

Fifty-one thousand

And

Two

Hundred

Minutes . . .

One million fifty-one thousand and

two hundred times.

It's how many times you've made me *smile*,

How many times you've made me *dream*,

How many times you've made me *believe*,

How many times you've made me *discover*,

How many times you've made me *adore*,

How many times you've made me *cherish*,

My life.

(Gavin walks toward the back of the room, where Eddie is sitting. He bends down on one knee in front of her as he reads the last line of his poem.)

And exactly *one million fifty-one thousand and two*

hundred minutes from now, I'm going to *propose* to you, and ask that you share *all* the rest of the minutes of your *life* with me.

Eddie is beaming as she leans down and hugs him. The classroom is divided as the boys groan and the girls swoon. I simply squirm in my seat, anticipating the last poet of the day: me.

"Thanks, Gavin, you can take your seat. Good job." Will doesn't look up from his notes when he calls me to read my poem. His voice is soft, full of trepidation when he says my name. "Layken, it's your turn."

I'm ready. I feel good about my piece. It's short but to the point. I already have it memorized so I leave the poem on my desk and walk to the front of the classroom.

"I have a question." My heart races when I realize this is the first time I've spoken out loud to Will in his classroom since I entered it a month ago. He hesitates as though he can't decide if he should acknowledge that I even have a question. He gives me a slight nod.

"Is there a time minimum?" I say.

I'm not sure what he thought I was about to ask, but he looks relieved that this was my question.

"No, it's fine as long as you get your point across. Remember, there are no rules." His voice cracks slightly when he replies. I can see on his face that what happened between us last night is fresh on his mind. All the better.

"Good. Okay then," I stammer. "My poem is called 'Mean.'" I face the front of the classroom and proudly recite my poem by heart.

According to the thesaurus . . .
and according to *me* . . .
there are over thirty different meanings and
substitutions for the word
mean.

(I quickly yell the following words; the entire class flinches—including Will.)

Jackass, jerk, cruel, dickhead, unkind, harsh, wicked,
hateful, heartless, vicious, virulent, unrelenting,
tyrannical, malevolent, atrocious, bastard,
barbarous, bitter, brutal, callous, degenerate,
brutish, depraved, evil, fierce, hard, implacable,
rancorous, pernicious, inhumane, monstrous,
merciless, inexorable.
And *my* personal favorite—*asshole.*

I glance at Will as I return to my seat and his face is red, his teeth clenched. Eddie is the first to clap, followed by the rest of the girls in the class. I fold my arms across my chest and focus my eyes solely on my desk.

"Man," Javi says. "Who pissed you off?"

The bell rings and the students begin to file out. Will

never utters a word. I begin to pack my things into my bag, when Eddie runs up to me.

"Have you talked to your mom yet?" she asks.

"My mom? About what?" I have no clue what she's referring to.

"The date. Nick asked you out yesterday? You said you'd have to ask your mom?"

"Oh, that," I respond.

That was yesterday? It seems like a lifetime ago. I shoot a quick glance in Will's direction and see that he's watching me, waiting for my response to Eddie. His expression is stone cold. I wish at this moment he were easier to read. I assume his internal expression is jealousy, so I go with it.

"Yeah, sure. Tell Nick I'd love to," I lie as I keep my eyes locked on Will. He grabs his pen and paper and opens one of the desk drawers and drops them in, slamming it shut. The action startles Eddie and she jumps, spinning around to look at him. He's aware of the attention he brought upon himself, so he stands up and acts oblivious to us as he erases chalk off the board. Eddie turns back toward me.

"Great! Oh, and we decided on Thursday, so after Getty's we can go to the slam. We've only got a few weeks—might as well get it out of the way. You want us to pick you up?"

"Uh, sure."

Eddie claps excitedly and bounces out of the room.

Will continues to erase away nothing as I start toward the exit.

"Layken," he says with a hardness to his voice.

I pause at the door but don't turn toward him.

"Your mom works Thursday nights. I always get a sitter for Thursdays since I go to the slams. Just send Kel over before you leave. You know, before your *date*."

I don't respond. I simply walk out.

Lunch is awkward. Eddie has already informed Nick that I've agreed to go out with them, so everyone is extremely chatty about our new plans. Everyone except me. Other than the occasional nod and mutters of agreement, I don't speak. I have no appetite, so Nick eats the majority of my food. I stir the rice pudding around on my tray with my spoon, dribbling in traces of ketchup here and there. It reminds me of the remnants of the murdered snowman in my driveway. For days, every time I backed out, my tire would glide over his ice-hard body. I wonder if that's how quiet my Jeep would be if I were to run over Will? Just accidentally back up over him, then put my car in drive and continue on.

"Layken, are you just going to ignore him?" Eddie says.

I look up to see Will standing behind Nick, staring down at the mess I've made of my tray.

"What?" I say to Eddie.

"Mr. Cooper needs to see you," she says, nudging her head in Will's direction.

"I bet you're in trouble for saying 'asshole,'" Nick says.

I put my hand against my throat, afraid it's about to explode. What is he *doing*? Why is he asking me to go with him in front of everyone? Has he lost his mind?

I slide my chair back and leave my tray on the table as I eye him cautiously. He walks out of the cafeteria toward his classroom and I follow him. It's a long walk. A long, awkward, tension-filled, quiet walk.

"We need to talk," he says as he shuts his door behind us. "Now."

I don't know if he's being "Will" right now. I don't understand the angle he's coming at me from. I don't know whether to obey him—or punch him. I don't walk very far into his room. I fold my arms across my chest and attempt to look annoyed.

"Then talk!" I say.

"Dammit, Lake! I'm not your enemy. Stop hating me."

He's being Will.

I rush toward him and throw my hands up in the air in frustration. "Stop *hating* you? Make up your freaking mind, Will! Last night you told me to stop loving you, now you're telling me to stop *hating* you? You tell me you don't want me to wait for you, yet you act like an immature little boy when I agree to go out with Nick! You want me to act like I don't know you, but then you pull me out of the lunchroom in front of everyone! We've got this whole facade between us, like we're different people all the time, and it's exhausting! I never know when you're Will or Mr. Cooper and I *really* don't know when I'm supposed to be Layken or Lake."

I'm tired of playing his head games. I'm so tired. I throw myself into the seat I occupy during his class. He's hard to read as he stands motionless. Expressionless. He slowly walks around me and takes a seat in the desk behind me. I continue facing forward when he leans forward over the desk, close enough to whisper. My body tenses and my chest tightens when he speaks.

"I didn't think it would be this hard," he says.

I don't want to give him the gratification of seeing the tears that are making their way down my cheeks.

"I'm sorry I said that to you earlier, about Thursday," he says. "I was being sincere for the most part. I know you'll need someone to watch Kel, and I did make the slam a required assignment. But I shouldn't have reacted like that. That's why I asked you to come here: I just needed to apologize. It won't happen again, I swear."

The door to the classroom swings open, and Will hops up out of the seat. His sudden movement startles Eddie, and she eyes us curiously from the doorway. She's holding the backpack that I left in the cafeteria. I can't conceal the tears that are still flowing from my eyes, so I turn away from her. There's nothing Will or I could do at this point to mask the tension between us.

Eddie holds her palms up and gently lays my backpack on the desk closest to the door. She backs out of the room and whispers, "My bad . . . continue." She closes the door behind her.

Will runs his hands through his hair and paces the floor. "That's just great," he mutters.

"Let it go, Will," I say as I stand up and walk to my backpack. "If she asks me about it, I'll just tell her you were upset because I said 'asshole.' And jackass. And dickhead. And bastar—"

"I get your point!"

My hand is on the doorknob when he calls my name again so I pause.

"I also want to say I'm sorry . . . about last night," he says.

I turn toward him when I speak. "Are you sorry it happened? Or sorry about the way you stopped it?"

He cocks his head and shrugs his shoulders as if he doesn't understand my question. "All of it. It never should have happened."

"Bastard," I finish.

THE ENGINE OF my Jeep purrs its familiar sound when I crank it, and that pisses me off, too. I slam my fist against the steering wheel, wishing so many things. I wish I hadn't met Will the first week I was here. It would have been so much easier if I'd met him in class first. Or better yet, I wish we had never even moved to Ypsilanti. I wish my dad were alive. I wish my mother weren't being so vague about her *errands*. I wish Caulder weren't at our house every day. Seeing him just makes me think of Will. I wish Will had never fixed my Jeep. I hate that he does considerate things like that. It would make it so much easier to hate him if he really *were* all those things I called him. Oh my god, I can't believe I called him all those names. Wait, no regrets.

I PICK THE boys up from school and drive home. I beat Will home today, but I won't be waiting at the window. I'm done waiting at the window.

"We'll be at Caulder's," Kel yells as they slam the Jeep door.

Good.

When I walk down the hallway, I hear my mother talking to someone in her bedroom, so I pause outside her door. It's a one-sided conversation, so she must be on the phone. Normally, I would never eavesdrop on one of her conversations. However, her behavior lately warrants a little nosiness. Or maybe *my* behavior warrants a little rebellion. Either way, I cup my ear to the door.

"I know. I *know*. I'll tell them soon," she says.

"No, I think it will go over better if I tell them alone . . ."

"Of course I will. I love you too, babe."

She's signing off. I quietly tiptoe to my bedroom and

slip inside. I shut the door behind me and slide to the floor.

Seven months. It took her all of seven months to move on. She can't be seeing someone else already, but her words on the phone couldn't have been more clear. I'm in stage one again: denial.

How could she? And whoever he is, he already wants her to introduce us to him? I already don't like him. And her nerve! How could she accost Will like she did, when what she's doing is just as deplorable, if not worse? Stage one is extremely brief. I'm back in stage two again: anger.

I decide not to bring it up right away. I want to find out more before I confront her about it. I want the upper hand in this situation, and it's going to take some thought.

"Lake? Are you back?" She's knocking on my door. I have to roll forward and hop up to get out of the way when she opens it. She sees me jump up and she eyes me curiously.

"What are you doing?" she asks.

"Stretching. My back hurts."

She doesn't buy it, so I clasp my hands behind me and stretch my arms upward, bending forward.

"Take some aspirin," she says.

"Okay."

"I'm off tonight, but I have a lot of sleep to catch up on. I didn't get any at all today so I'm going to lie down. Can you make sure Kel gets a bath before he goes to bed?"

"Sure."

We both start down the hallway. "Wait—Mom?"

She turns back to me, her lids dragging over her blood-shot eyes.

"I'm going out Thursday night. Is that okay?"

She eyes me suspiciously. "With who?"

"Eddie, Gavin, and Nick."

"Three guys? You aren't going anywhere with three guys."

"No. Eddie's a girl. She's my friend. Her boyfriend is Gavin, and we're double-dating. I'm going with Nick."

Her eyes brighten a little. "Oh. Well, good." She smiles and opens the door to her bedroom. "Wait," she says. "I work Thursday. What about Kel?"

"Will has a sitter on Thursdays. He already said Kel could stay there."

She looks pleased, but only for a second. "Will agreed to pay a sitter? To watch Kel? So you could go on a *date*?"

Crap. I didn't realize how this would look. "Mom, it's been weeks. We went on one date; we're over it."

She stares at me for several seconds. "Hmm." She returns to her room, still unappeased.

Her suspicion brings me a small sense of gratification. She thinks I'm lying about something. Now we're even.

"I'm not going to third period," I say to Eddie as we exit history.

"Why not?"

"I just don't feel like it. Headache. I think I'll go sit in the courtyard and get some fresh air."

I turn and start to head to the courtyard when she grabs my arm.

"Layken? Does this have anything to do with what happened at lunch yesterday with Mr. Cooper? Is everything okay?"

I smile at her reassuringly. "No, it's fine. He just wants me to refrain from my colorful choice of words in his class."

She purses her lips together and walks away with the same unappeased look my mother had last night.

The courtyard is empty. I guess none of the other students needs a breather from the teacher they're secretly in love with. I sit at a bench and pull my phone out of my pocket. Nothing. I've only spoken to Kerris once since I moved. She was the friend in Texas I was closest to, but *she* was actually best friends with *another* girl. It's odd when your best friend has an even better best friend. I chalked it up to the fact that I was too busy for best friends, but maybe it was more than that. Maybe I'm not a good listener. Maybe I'm not a good *sharer*.

"Mind if I join you?"

I look up and Eddie is taking a seat on the bench across from me. "Misery loves company," I say.

"Misery? And why are we miserable? You have a date

to look forward to tomorrow night. And your best friend is me," she says.

Best friend. Maybe. Hopefully.

"You don't think Will is going to come looking for us?" I say.

She cocks her head at me. "*Will*? You mean Mr. Cooper?"

Oh god, I just called him Will. She's already suspicious. I smile and come up with the first excuse that pops into my head.

"Yeah, Mr. Cooper. We called teachers by their first names at my last school."

She doesn't respond. She's picking at the paint on the bench with her blue fingernail. Nine of her fingernails are green; just the one is blue. "I'm just going to say something here," she says. Her voice is calm. "Maybe I'm way off base, maybe I'm not. But whatever I say, I don't want you to interject."

I nod.

"I think what was happening at lunch yesterday was more than just a slap on the wrist for inappropriate verbal usage. I don't know how *much* more, and honestly it's none of my business. I just want you to know you can talk to me. If you need to. I'd never repeat anything; I don't have anyone besides Gavin to repeat stuff to."

"No one? Best friends? Siblings?" I hope this changes the subject.

"Nope. He's all I have," she says. "Well, technically,

if you want to know the truth, I've had seventeen sisters, twelve brothers, six moms, and seven dads."

I can't tell if she's making a joke, so I don't laugh in case she isn't.

"Foster care," she says. "I'm on my seventh home in nine years."

"Oh. I'm sorry." I don't know what else to say.

"Don't be. I've been with Joel for four of those nine years. He's my foster dad. It works. I'm content. He gets his check."

"Were any of your twenty-nine siblings blood related?"

She laughs. "Man, you pay attention. And no, I'm an only child. Born to a mother with a yen for cheap crack and pricey babies."

She can see I'm not following.

"She tried to sell me. Don't worry, nobody wanted me. Or she was just asking too much. When I was nine she offered me to a lady in a Walmart parking lot. She gave her a sob story about how she couldn't take care of me, yada yada, offered the lady a deal. A hundred bucks was my going rate. It wasn't the first time she tried this right in front of me. I was getting bored with it, so I looked right at the lady and said, 'You got a husband? I bet he's hot!' My mother backhanded me for ruining the sale. Left me in the parking lot. The lady took me to the police station and dropped me off. That's the last time I ever saw my mom."

"God, Eddie. That's unreal."

"Yeah, it is. But it's my real."

I lie down on the bench and look up at the sky. She does the same.

"You said Eddie was a family name," I say. "Which family?"

"Don't laugh."

"But what if I think it's funny?"

She rolls her eyes. "There was a comedy DVD my first foster family owned. Eddie Izzard. I thought I had his nose. I watched that DVD a million times, pretending he was my dad. I had people refer to me as Eddie after that. I tried Izzard for a while, but it never stuck."

We both laugh. I pull my jacket off and pull it on top of me, sliding my arms through it backward so that it warms the parts of me that have been exposed to the cold for too long. I close my eyes.

"I had amazing parents," I sigh.

"Had?"

"My dad died seven months ago. My mother moved us up here, claimed it was for financial reasons, but now I'm not so sure she was being honest. She's seeing someone else already. So yes, amazing is past tense at the moment."

"Suck."

We both lie there pondering the hands we were dealt. Mine pales in comparison to hers. The things she must have seen. Kel is the same age now that Eddie was when she was put into foster care. I don't know how she walks around so happy, so full of life. We're quiet. Everything is comfortably quiet. I silently wonder if this is what it feels like to have a best friend.

She sits up on her bench after a while, hands stretched out in front of her as she yawns. "Earlier, the thing I said about Joel—and me being a check to him? It's not like that. He's really been a great guy. Sometimes when things get too real, my sarcasm takes over."

I smile at her in understanding. "Thanks for skipping with me, I really needed it."

"Thanks for needing it. Apparently I did, too. And about Nick—he's a good guy, just not for you. I'll drop it. But you still have to go with us tomorrow."

"I know I do. If I don't, Chuck Norris will hunt me down and kick my ass." I flip my jacket around and ease my arms in as we walk through the door and back into the hallway.

"So if Eddie is something you made up, what's your real name?" I ask her before we part ways. She smiles and shrugs her shoulders.

"Right now, it's Eddie."

8.

I wanna have friends
that will let me be
All alone when being alone
is all that I need.

—THE AVETT BROTHERS,
"THE PERFECT SPACE"

"WHERE'S MOM?" I ASK KEL. HE'S SITTING AT THE BAR with his homework out.

"She just dropped me and Caulder off. Said she would be back in a couple of hours. She wants you to order pizza."

If I'd been home a few minutes sooner, I would have followed her. "Did she say where she was going?" I ask him.

"Can you ask them to put the pepperonis under the sauce this time?"

"Where'd she say she was going?"

"No, wait. Tell them to put the pepperonis on first, then the cheese, then the sauce on top."

"Dammit, Kel! Where did she go?"

His eyes grow wide as he climbs off the stool and walks backward toward the front door. He slumps his shoulders and slips his shoes on. I've never cussed at him before.

"Know don't I. Caulder's to going I'm."

"Be back by six, I'll have your pizza."

I decide to knock my homework out first. Mr. Hanson may be half deaf and half blind, but he makes up for that in the sheer volume of homework he assigns. I finish within an hour. It's just four thirty.

I take this opportunity to play detective. Whatever she's up to and whomever she's with, I'm determined to find out. I rummage through kitchen drawers, cabinets, hallway closets. Nothing. I've never snooped in my parents' room before. Ever. This is definitely a year of firsts, though, so I let myself in and close the door behind me.

Everything is the same as it was in their old bedroom. Same furniture, same beige carpet. If it weren't for the lack of space, I would hardly be able to tell the difference between this room and the one she shared with my father. I check the obvious first: the underwear drawer. I don't find anything. I move to the edge of the bed and slide open the drawer to her nightstand. Eye mask, pen, lotion, book, note—

Note.

I slip it out of the drawer and open it. It's written in black ink, centered down the page. It's a poem.

Julia,
I'll paint you a world one day
A world where smiles don't fade
A world where laughter is played
In the background
Like a PSA
I'll paint it when the sun goes down
While you're lying there in your gown
The moment your smile turns around
I'll paint right over your frown
I'll be finished when the sun breaks in
You'll wake with a still-wet grin
You'll see that I finish what I begin
The world I've painted on your chin . . .

It's pathetic. The world I've painted on your chin? Like a PSA? What is that, anyway? Public service announcement? Who rhymes with acronyms? Whoever he is, I don't like him. I hate him. I fold the note up and put it back in its place.

I call Getty's and order two pizzas. Mom is pulling up in the driveway when I hang up the phone. Perfect opportunity for a shower. I lock myself in the bathroom before she makes it inside. I don't want to see the look on her face. That look of "falling in love."

* * *

"WHAT THE HELL?" my mother says when she opens up the box of pizza.

"That's Kel's. It's backward," I tell her. She rolls her eyes as she pulls the second box toward her. It makes me cringe how her eyes scroll over all the slices of pizza like she's trying to find the one that tastes the best. They're all slices from the same pizza!

"Just pick one!" I snap.

She flinches. "Jeez, Lake. Have you eaten today? Quite the crab, are we?" She picks up a slice and thrusts it toward me. I throw it on my plate and plop down at the bar, when Kel comes running in backward.

"Here pizza the is?" he asks, right before he trips over the rug and lands on his butt.

"God, Kel, grow up!" I snap.

My mother shoots me a look. "Lake! What is your problem? Is there something you need to talk about?"

I push my pizza across the table and get up from the bar. I can't pretend anymore.

"No, Mother! There's nothing I need to talk about. *I* don't *keep* secrets!"

She sucks in a small gasp of air. This is it—she knows I know.

I expect her to defend herself, yell at me, put up a fight, send me to my room. *Something.* Isn't that what happens when things come to fruition? The climax?

Instead, she simply looks away and grabs a plate for Kel, filling it with slices of backward pizza.

I march to my room and slam the door. Again. Who knows how many doors I've slammed since we moved here? I'm constantly leaving or entering rooms, pissed off at someone. Will slams poems; I slam doors.

THE ALARM CLOCK is flashing red when I wake up. The power must have gone out overnight. The sun is unusually bright for this early in the morning, so I grab my phone to check the time, and sure enough, we overslept. I jump out of bed and throw on my clothes, brush my teeth, and pull my hair on top of my head. No time for makeup. I wake Kel up and rush him to get dressed while I gather my homework. No time for coffee, either.

"But I ride to school with Caulder in the mornings," Kel whines as we pull our jackets on.

"Not today. We overslept."

It's apparent we aren't the only ones who overslept when I see Will's car still in his driveway. *Great!* I can't just leave and not wake them up.

"Kel, go knock on their door and wake them up."

Kel runs across the street and beats on the door as I climb inside my Jeep and crank it. I turn the heater up full blast and grab the scraper and start wiping the frost away from the windows. I get the final window cleared when Kel returns.

"No one answered the door. I think they're still asleep."

Ugh! I hand the scraper to Kel and tell him to get inside the Jeep; then I walk to Will's house. Kel already tried the front door, so I walk to the side of the house that the bedrooms are on. I don't know which one is Will's, so I knock on all three windows just to be sure I wake someone up.

As I round the front of the house, the front door swings open and Will is standing there, shielding his eyes from the sun, *shirtless*. My hands have touched those abs before. I force myself to look away.

"Power went out. We overslept," I tell him. "We" feels odd. It's like I'm insinuating we're a team.

"What?" he says groggily, rubbing his face. "What time is it?"

"Almost eight."

He immediately perks up.

"Shit!" he says, remembering something. "I've got a conference at eight!"

He turns back inside but leaves the door open. I peek my head further inside but don't dare step over the threshold.

"Do you need me to take Caulder to school?" I yell after him.

He reappears from the hallway.

"Would you? Can you? You don't mind?" He's really

frantic. He's got a tie around his neck, but still no shirt.

"I don't mind. Which one is his room? I'll get him ready."

"Oh. Yeah. That would be great. Thanks. First one on the left. Thank you." He disappears down the hallway again.

I go to Caulder's room and shake him awake. "Caulder, I'm taking you to school. You need to get dressed."

I assist Caulder while he gets ready, catching glimpses of Will running back and forth. The front door eventually shuts, followed by a car door. He's gone. I'm in his house. Awkward.

"Ready, buddy?"

"I'm hungry."

"Oh, yeah. Food. Let me see." I rummage through cabinets in Will's kitchen. The canned goods are stacked according to their labels. There's an abundance of pasta. It's easy enough to cook, I guess. Everything's so clean. Not like most twenty-one-year-old guys' kitchens. I locate some Pop-Tarts above the fridge and grab one for Kel and one for Caulder.

I'M HALF AN hour late for first period, so I decide to sit it out in my Jeep. That's two classes in two days. I'm becoming a real rebel.

I take my seat in history and Eddie swings in behind me.

"You skip Math, and you don't take me with you?" she whispers from behind me.

I turn around, and she draws her neck in and pouts.

"Oh. You overslept."

Makeup. I forgot to bring my makeup. Eddie reaches into her purse and pulls out a cosmetic bag. She can read my mind. Isn't that what best friends do?

"My hero," I say as I take it from her and turn around. I pull lipstick and mascara out, along with a mirror. I apply it quickly and hand her back the bag.

When we walk into third period, Will makes eye contact with me and mouths, "Thank you." I smile and shrug my shoulders, letting him know it wasn't a big deal. Eddie pinches my arm when she walks past me, letting *me* know she saw our exchange.

You wouldn't know by looking at him that Will got ready in less than three minutes. His black pants are wrinkle free, his white shirt tucked in at the waist. His tie . . . oh my god, his tie. I let out a laugh and he glances in my direction. He must not have noticed he put his tie on first this morning; it's barely visible underneath his white shirt. I tug at the collar of my shirt and point to him. He glances down and pats his chest where his tie should be. He laughs as he turns and faces the chalkboard and corrects his wardrobe malfunction. The other students were still taking their seats and chatting, but I know Eddie saw what just happened. I can feel her staring a hole into my back.

* * *

NICK THROWS HIMSELF into the seat next to me at lunch.
Eddie is sitting right across from me. I expect her to give
me the eye but she doesn't. She's just as exuberant as ever.
She already knows too much. I'm afraid she may assume
it's more than it is. I was late for school today; Will obviously got dressed in a hurry. She has every right to bom-
bard me with questions, but she doesn't. I respect her for
that—for respecting me.

"New girl, what time we leavin'?" Nick asks as he
piles his food together.

"I don't know. Who's driving?"

"I'll drive," Gavin says.

Nick looks up at Gavin. "No way, man. We're taking
my dad's car. No way I'm riding in Monte Car-no."

"Monte Car-no?" I look at Gavin.

"My car," Gavin replies.

"What's your address, Layken?" Eddie asks. I'm
shocked she failed to obtain it the first time we met.

"Oh, I know where she lives," Nick says. "I gave her
a ride home. Same street as Mr. Cooper. We'll pick her
up last."

How does Nick know that? I glance down to my tray
and stir my mashed potatoes, attempting to seem oblivious to Eddie's stare.

* * *

NICK AND GAVIN are both sitting in the front seat, so I take the backseat with Eddie. When I climb in she smiles a friendly smile. She's not going to press me. I breathe a sigh of relief.

"Layken, we need your help," Gavin says. "Settle something for us, will ya?"

"I like disputes. Shoot," I say as I put on my seat belt.

"Nick here thinks Texas is nothing but tornadoes. He says they don't have hurricanes because there's no beach. School him."

"Well, he's wrong on both counts," I say.

"I can't be," Nick says.

"There *are* hurricanes," I say. "You forgot about the little area known as the *Gulf of Mexico*. But there aren't any tornadoes."

They both pause.

"There's definitely tornadoes," Gavin says.

"No," I say. "There's no such thing as tornadoes, Gavin. Chuck Norris just hates trailer parks."

There's a moment of silence before they break out in laughter. Eddie scoots closer to me in the backseat and cups her hand to my ear.

"He knows."

I hold my breath, thinking back on conversations that might give me a clue who she's talking about.

"*Who* knows? And what does he know?" I finally ask.

"Nick. He knows you aren't interested. He's fine

with it. There's no pressure. We're just friends tonight, all of us."

I'm relieved. *So* relieved. I was already planning out how I would let him down.

I NEVER DID get to taste the pizza from Getty's that I had delivered the night before. It's heaven. We had to order two, since Nick is eating a whole one by himself. I haven't thought about being mad at my mother so far. I haven't even thought about Will (that much). I'm having fun. It's nice.

"Gavin, what's the stupidest thing you've ever done?" Nick asks.

We all quiet down at this question.

"I can only pick one?" Gavin asks.

"*The* one. The *stupidest* one," Nick replies.

"Hmm. I guess it would have to be the time I was visiting my grandparents on their ranch right outside of Laramie, Wyoming. I had to use the bathroom so bad. It's not a big deal: I'm a guy. We can whip it out anywhere. The big deal was that it was *my* turn."

"For what?" I ask.

"To complete the dare. My brothers used to dare me to do stuff all the time. They would do it first, and then I'd have to do it. The only problem was, I was younger by several years, so they always outsmarted me somehow. This particular day, they told me my rubber boots were too wet to wear so I had to throw on my hiking boots. They, of course, wore their rubber boots. Well, they came up with the dare to see who would pee on the electric fence."

"You didn't," Eddie laughs.

"Oh, just wait, babe. It gets better. They went first, and I realize now that rubber blocks electricity, so they didn't feel anything. I, on the other hand, was not so lucky. It knocked me on my back, and I was crying, trying to get up, when I tripped. I fell forward and met the fence with my mouth. Saliva and electricity don't mix well either. It shocked me so bad my tongue started to swell and my brothers freaked out. Both of them ran home to get my parents while I lay there, unable to move, with my dick hanging out of my pants."

Eddie, Nick, and I are all laughing so hard we get glares from the other customers. Eddie wipes away a tear when Gavin tells her it's her turn.

"I guess when I ran over you with my car," Eddie says.

"Try again," Gavin says.

"What? That's it! That's the stupidest thing I've ever done."

"What about *after* you ran over me? Tell them about that," he laughs.

"We fell in love. The end." She's obviously embarrassed by the aftermath of the swipe.

"You have to tell us now," I say.

"Fine. It was the second day after I got my license. Joel let me drive his car to school so I was being supercareful. I was focused. When Joel was teaching me to drive, he paid careful attention to how I parked. He hates people who double-park. In fact, I knew he was going to have someone drive him through the parking lot just to double-check my parking job, so I really wanted to be perfect. So that's what I was focused on. I didn't like how I parked the first time—"

"Or the second, third, or fourth time," Gavin says.

Eddie smirks at him. "So on the *fifth* time, I was determined to get it right. I backed out extra far to get a better angle, and that's when it happened. The thud. I turned around and didn't see anyone, so I panicked, thinking I had hit the car next to me or something. I continued to back out of the spot and threw the car in drive and was looking for a better spot so that I could inspect the car for damage. I pulled over in the next lot and got out. That's when I saw him."

"You . . . *dragged* him?" I ask. I'm trying to hold back the laughter.

"Over two hundred yards. After I hit him the first time, I kept backing up, and his pant leg got hung up in the bumper. I broke his leg. Joel was so worried they were going to sue, he made me take food to him at the hospital every day for a week. That's when we fell in love."

"You're lucky you didn't kill him," Nick says. "You'd be locked up on a hit-and-run charge *and* involuntary manslaughter. Poor Gavin would be ten feet under."

"*Six* feet under!" I laugh.

"I'd love to hear your stupid story, Layken, but it's gonna have to wait. We're gonna be late," Eddie says as she scoots out of the booth.

ON OUR DRIVE to the slam, Eddie pulls a folded up sheet of paper out of her back pocket.

"What's that?" I ask her.

"It's my poem. I'm going to slam tonight."

"Seriously? God, you're brave."

"I'm not, really. The first time Gavin and I went, I promised myself I would do one before I turned eighteen. My birthday is next week. When Mr. Cooper told us we could skip the final if we performed, I took it as a sign."

"I would just say I did one. Mr. Cooper won't know. I doubt he'll be there," Nick says.

"No," Gavin says. "He'll be there. He's always there."

The empty feeling in my stomach returns, despite its being full from supper. I slide my hands across my pants and fix my eyes on a star outside the window. I'll wait to join back in the conversation until the subject changes.

"Man, Vaughn really did a number on him," Nick says.

I cock my head in Nick's direction. Eddie sees the interest perk in me, and she folds up her paper and puts it back in her pocket.

"His ex," she says. "They dated their last two years of

high school. They were *the* couple. Homecoming queen, football star . . ."

"Football? He played football?" I'm shocked. This doesn't sound like Will.

"Oh yeah, star quarterback three years running," Nick says. "We were freshmen when he was a senior. He was a nice guy, I guess."

"Can't say the same about Vaughn," Gavin says.

"Why? Was she a bitch?" I ask.

"Honestly, she wasn't that bad in high school. It's what she did to him after they graduated. After his parents . . ." Eddie's voice trails off.

"What'd she do?" I sound too interested, I know.

"She dumped him. Two weeks after his parents were killed in a car wreck. He had a football scholarship but lost it when he had to move back home to take care of his little brother. Vaughn told everyone she wasn't marrying a college dropout with a kid. So that's it. He lost his parents, his girlfriend, and his scholarship *and* became a guardian all in the same two-week time frame."

I return my gaze out the window. I don't want Eddie to see the tears welling up in my eyes. This explains so much. It explains why he's scared to take everything away from me, like it was taken from him. I fade out of the conversation as we drive toward Detroit.

"Here," Eddie whispers, laying something in my lap. A tissue. I squeeze her hand to thank her, then wipe the tears from my eyes.

9.

A slight figure of speech
I cut my chest wide open
They come and watch us bleed
Is it art like I was hoping now?

—THE AVETT BROTHERS,
"SLIGHT FIGURE OF SPEECH"

WHEN WE ENTER THE BUILDING, I IMMEDIATELY SEARCH
for Will. Nick and Gavin lead us to a table on the floor, so
much more exposed than the booth Will and I sat in. The
sac has already performed and they are well into round
one. Eddie goes to the judges' table and pays her money
and comes back.

"Layken, come to the bathroom with me," she says as
she pulls me out of my chair.

When we get in the bathroom, she backs me up to

the sink and stands in front of me with her hands on my shoulders.

"Snap out of it, girl! We're here to have fun." She reaches into her purse and pulls out her makeup bag. She wets her thumbs under the faucet and wipes mascara from underneath my eyes. She meticulously applies my makeup, extremely focused on the task. No one's ever done my makeup before besides me. She pulls a brush out of her purse and pushes me forward, brushing my hair upside down over my head. I feel like a rag doll. She pulls me back up and does some fancy handiwork as her fingers twist and pull at my hair. She steps back and smiles as though she's admiring her accomplishment.

"There."

She turns me to the mirror and my jaw drops to the floor. I can't believe it. I look . . . *pretty*. My bangs are pulled into a French braid that hangs loose down my shoulder. The soft amber hue of eye shadow brings out my eyes. My lips are defined but not too colorful. I look just like my mother.

"Wow. You have a gift, Eddie."

"I know. Twenty-nine brothers and sisters in nine years, you're bound to learn a few tricks."

She pulls me out of the bathroom, and we head back. As we approach our seats, I stop. Eddie stops, too, since she has hold of my hand and is suddenly being jerked back. She follows my gaze to our table and sees Javi . . . and Will.

"Looks like we have company," she says. She winks at

me and pulls me forward, but I pull her hand back. My feet are weighted to the floor beneath me.

"Eddie, it's not like that. I don't want you thinking it's like that."

She faces me and takes my hands in hers. "I don't think *anything*, Layken. But if it really *is* like that, it would explain the obvious tension between you two," she says.

"It's only obvious to you."

"And that's how it shall remain," she says, pulling me forward.

When we reach the table, all eight eyes are focused on me. I want to run.

"Damn, girl, you look good," Javi says.

Gavin glares at Javi and then smiles back at me. "Eddie got hold of you, did she?" He wraps his arm around Eddie's waist and pulls her to him, leaving me to fend for myself. Nick pulls a chair out for me and I take it. I glance up at Will, and he gives me a half smile. I know what it means. He thinks I look pretty.

"All right, we've got four more performers for round one. Next one goes by the name of Eddie. Where is he?"

Eddie rolls her eyes and stands. "I'm a *she*!"

"Oh, my bad. There she is. Come on up, Ms. Eddie."

Eddie gives Gavin a quick peck on the lips and bounces to the stage, her confidence pouring from her smile. Everyone but Will takes a seat. Javi takes the seat to my left, and the only available seat at the table is to my right. Will hesitates before he takes a step and finally sits.

"What are you performing Eddie?" the emcee asks her.

She leans into the microphone and says, " 'Pink Balloon.' "

As soon as the emcee is off the stage, Eddie loses her smile and goes into her zone.

My name is Olivia King

I am five years old.

My mother bought me a *balloon*. I remember the day

she walked through the front door with it. The curly

hot-pink ribbon *trickling* down her arm, *wrapped*

around her *wrist*. She was *smiling* at me as she *untied*

the ribbon and wrapped it around my hand.

"Here, Livie, I bought this for you."

She called me *Livie*.

I was so *happy*. I'd *never* had a *balloon* before. I mean,

I always saw balloons wrapped around *other* kids'

wrists in the parking lot of *Walmart*, but I never

dreamed I would have my very *own*.

My *very own* pink balloon.

I was so *excited*! So *ecstatic*! So *thrilled*! I couldn't

believe my mother bought me something! She'd *never*

bought me *anything* before! I played with it for *hours*.

It was full of *helium*, and it *danced* and *swayed* and

floated as I *pulled* it around from *room* to *room* with

me, thinking of places to take it. Thinking of places

the balloon had *never* been before. I took it into the

bathroom, the *closet*, the *laundry room*, the *kitchen*, the *living room*. I wanted my new best friend to see *everything* I saw! I took it to my mother's **bedroom**!

My mother's

Bedroom?

Where I wasn't supposed to *be?*

With my pink

balloon . . .

I *covered* my *ears* as she *screamed* at me, *wiping* the *evidence* off of her *nose*. She *slapped* me across the face and reminded me of how **bad** I was! How much I **misbehaved**! How I never **listened**! She *shoved* me into the hallway and *slammed* the door, locking my pink balloon inside with her. I wanted him **back**! He was **my** best friend! **Not hers**! The pink ribbon was **still** tied around my **wrist** so I **pulled** and **pulled**, trying to get my new best friend *away* from her.

And

it

popped.

My name is Eddie.

I'm seventeen years old.

My *birthday* is next week. I'll be the big *One-Eight*. My foster dad is buying me these boots I've been wanting.

I'm sure my friends will take me out to eat. My boyfriend will buy me a *gift*, maybe even take me to a *movie*. I'll even get a nice little card from my foster-care worker, wishing me a happy eighteenth birthday, informing me I've aged out of the *system*.

I'll have a good time. I know I will.

But there's *one* thing I know

for *sure*.

I better not get any

shitty-ass pink balloons!

When the crowd cheers for her, Eddie eats it up. She's bouncing up and down on the stage and clapping along with the crowd, forgetting all about the somber poem she just performed. She's a natural. We give her a standing ovation when she comes back to the table.

"That felt so awesome," she squeals. Gavin throws his arms around her and picks her up off the ground and kisses her cheek.

"That's my girl," he says as they sit back down in their seats.

"That was great, Eddie—guess you're exempt," Will says.

"That was so easy! Layken, you really need to do one next week. You've never had one of Mr. Cooper's finals before. They aren't fun, believe me."

"I'll think about it," I say. She did make it look easy.

Will laughs and leans forward. "Eddie, you haven't had one of my finals *either*. I've only been teaching two months."

"Well, I'm sure they suck," she laughs.

They call another performer to the stage and the table grows quiet. Javi's leg keeps brushing against mine.

Something about him gives me the creeps. Maybe it's the obvious creep factor. Throughout the performance, I keep drawing myself in more and more until I have nowhere else to go, but he somehow keeps getting closer. Just when I'm on the verge of punching him, Will moves in and whispers in my ear.

"Trade me seats."

I hop up, and he slides over as I take his seat. I silently thank him with a look. Javi straightens back up and glares at Will. It's obvious there is no love lost between the two of them.

By the start of the second round, everyone at our table is dispersing among the crowd. I spot Nick at the bar chatting up a girl. Javi eventually sulks off, leaving just Will and me at the table with Gavin and Eddie.

"Mr. Cooper, did you see—"

"Gavin," Will interrupts. "You don't have to call me Mr. Cooper here. We went to high school together."

A mischievous grin crosses Gavin's face. He nudges Eddie, and they both smile at Will. "Can we call you—"

"No! You can't!" Will interrupts again. He's blushing.

"I'm missing something here," I say, looking from Will to Gavin.

Gavin leans forward in his chair and puts his elbows on his knees. "You see, Layken, about three years ago—"

"Gavin, I'll fail you. I'll fail your little girlfriend, too," Will says.

Everyone's laughing now, but I'm still lost.

"Three years ago, Duckie here decided to start a prank war with the freshmen."

"Duckie?" I say. I look at Will and his face is buried in his hands.

"It became apparent that Will—I mean Duckie—was the one behind all the pranks. We suffered at the hands of this man." Gavin laughs as he gestures toward Will.

"So, we decided we'd had enough. We came up with a little plan of our own, now known as Revenge on Duckie."

"Dammit, Gavin. I knew it was you! I *knew* it," Will says.

Gavin laughs. "Will was known for his daily naps in his car. Particularly during Mr. Hanson's History class. So, we followed him to the parking lot one day and waited until he was off in la-la land. We got about twenty-five rolls of duct tape and wrapped him inside the car. There had to be six layers of duct tape around his car already before he finally woke up. We could hear him screaming and kicking at the door all the way back to the school."

"Oh my god. How long were you in there?" I ask Will. I don't even hesitate when I speak to him. I like that we're interacting again, even if it is just as friends. This is good.

He cocks an eyebrow at me when he responds. "Now that's the kicker. Mr. Hanson's History class was second period. I wasn't cut out of the car until my dad called the school trying to find me. I don't remember what time it was, but it was dark."

"You were in there almost twelve hours?"

He nods.

"How'd you use the bathroom?" Eddie asks.

"I'll never tell," he laughs.

We can do this. I watch Will as he interacts with Eddie and Gavin; they're all laughing. I didn't think it would be possible before—a friendship between us. But here, right now, I do.

Nick walks back up to the table with a sour look on his face. "I don't feel so hot. Can we go?"

"How much did you eat, Nick?" Gavin says, standing.

Eddie looks at me and tilts her head to the front door, insinuating it's time to go. "See you tomorrow, Mr. Cooper," she says.

"Are you sure about that, Eddie?" Will asks her. "You and your friend here aren't taking another courtyard nap tomorrow?"

Eddie looks back at me and clasps her hand to her mouth, exaggerating a gasp. Will and I stand up as they all file out.

"Just leave Kel at my house tonight," he says after everyone is out of earshot. "I'll get him to school tomorrow. They're probably asleep by now anyway."

"You sure?"

"Yeah, it's fine."

"Okay, thanks."

We both stand there, not certain how to part. He steps out of my way. "See ya tomorrow," he says. I smile and shuffle my way past him, then catch up to Eddie.

"PLEASE, MOM? PLEASE?" Kel says.

"Kel, y'all spent the night with each other *last* night. I'm sure his brother wants some time with him."

"No, he doesn't," Caulder says.

"See? We'll stay in our room. I swear," Kel says.

"Fine. But Caulder, I'll need you to be at your house tomorrow night. I'm taking Lake and Kel to dinner."

"Yes, ma'am. I'll go tell my brother and get my clothes."

Kel and Caulder run out the front door. I squirm in my seat on the couch as I unzip my boots. This dinner she's referring to must be it; the big *introduction*. I decide to press her a little further.

"Where are we going to dinner?" I ask.

She comes to the couch and sits, grabbing the remote to flip on the TV.

"Wherever. Maybe we'll just eat here. I don't know. I just want some alone time, just the three of us."

I pull my boots off and snatch them up. "The three of us," I mumble as I walk to my room. I think about that as I throw my boots in my closet and lie on the bed. It used to be "the four of us." Then it became "the three of us." Now, in less than seven months, she's making it "the four of us" again.

Whoever he is, he will never be included in a count with Kel and me. She doesn't know I know about him. She doesn't even know I've already labeled him and her as "the two of them," and Kel and me as "the two of us." Divide and conquer. That's my new family motto.

We've been living in Ypsilanti for a month now, and I've spent every single Friday night in my room. I grab my phone and text Eddie, hoping she and Gavin won't mind a third wheel tonight on their movie date. She texts me back in a matter of seconds, giving me thirty minutes to get ready. It isn't enough time to thoroughly enjoy a shower, so I go to the bathroom and touch up my makeup. The mail is in a pile on the bathroom counter next to the sink, so I pick it up and look at it. All three envelopes have a big red post office stamp across them. Forward to New Address is stamped over our old Texas address.

Eight more months. Eight more months and I'm moving back home. I contemplate hanging a calendar on my wall so I can start marking down the days. I toss the envelopes back on the counter, when the contents of one of them fall to the floor. When I pick it up, I notice the numbers printed in the top right-hand corner.

$178,343.00.

It's a bank statement. It's an account balance. I snatch up the rest of the mail and run to my room and shut the door.

I look at the dates on the bank statement and then sort through the other envelopes. One of them is from a mortgage company so I tear it open. It's an insurance invoice. An invoice for our house back in Texas that I was told we sold. Oh my god, I want to *kill* her. We aren't broke! We didn't even sell our house! She tore my brother and me from the only home we've ever known for some guy? I hate her. I have to get out of this house before I explode. I grab my phone and throw the envelopes in my purse.

"I'm going out," I say when I walk through the living room toward the front door.

"With who?" she asks.

"Eddie. Going to a movie." I keep my replies short and sweet so she won't hear the fury behind my voice. My whole body is shaking I'm so angry. I just want to get out of the house and process things before I confront her.

She walks over to me and grabs my cell phone out of my hand and starts pressing buttons.

"What the hell are you doing?" I yell as I grab it back out of her grasp.

"I know what you're up to, Lake! Don't pretend with me."

"What am I up to? I'd really like to know!"

"Last night you and Will were *both* gone. He conveniently had a babysitter. Tonight, his brother says he's spending the night, and half an hour later you're *going out?* You aren't going anywhere!"

I throw my phone in my purse and wrap my purse across my shoulder as I head to the front door.

"As a matter of fact, I am going out. With *Eddie*. You can watch me leave with *Eddie*. You can watch me *return* with Eddie." I walk out the front door and she follows me. Luckily, Eddie is pulling up in the driveway.

"Lake? Get back here! We need to talk," she yells from the doorway.

I open the door to Eddie's car and I turn to face her. "You're right, Mom, but I think you're the one that needs to do the talking. I know why we're having dinner tomorrow! I know why we moved to Michigan! I know about everything! So don't you dare talk to *me* about hiding stuff!"

I don't wait for her to respond as I get in the backseat and slam the door.

"Get me out of here. Hurry," I say to Eddie.

I start crying as we drive away. I never want to go back.

"HERE, DRINK THIS." Eddie shoves another soda across the table as she and Gavin watch me drink—and cry. We stopped at Getty's because Eddie said their pizza was the only thing that could help me right now. I couldn't eat.

"I'm sorry I ruined your date," I say to both of them.

"You didn't ruin it. Did she, babe?" Eddie says as she turns to Gavin.

"Not at all. It's a nice change of routine," he says, shoving his pizza into a takeout box.

My phone is vibrating again. It's the sixth time my mother has called, so I hold down the power button and throw it back into my purse.

"Can we still make it to the movie?" I ask.

Gavin looks at his watch and nods. "Sure, if you really feel like going."

"I do. I need to stop thinking about this for a little while."

We pay our bill and head to the theater. It's not Johnny Depp, but any actor will do right now.

10.

She puts her hands against
the life she had.
Living with ignorance,
Blissful and sad.
But nobody knows what lies behind
The days before the day we die.

—THE AVETT BROTHERS, "DIE DIE DIE"

WE PULL UP TO MY HOUSE A FEW HOURS LATER. I DON'T immediately get out of the car as I take a few deep breaths, preparing for the fight that's about to go down.

"Layken, call me later. I wanna know everything. Good luck," Eddie says.

"Thanks, I will." I get out of the car and walk up to the door as they drive away. When I enter, my mother is lying on the couch. She hears the door close and jumps up.

I expect her to continue yelling, but she runs to me and throws her arms around my neck. I stand stiff.

"Lake, I'm so sorry, I should have told you. I'm so sorry." She's crying.

I back away from her and go sit on the couch. There are tissues all over both end tables. She's been crying a lot. Good, she should feel bad. *Awful*, even.

"Dad and I were going to tell you before he—"

"Dad? You were seeing him before Dad even *died*?" I stand up and pace the floor. "Mom! How long has this been going on?" I'm yelling now. And crying again.

I look at her, waiting for her to defend her repulsive behavior, but she's just staring at the table in front of her.

She leans forward and cocks her head at me. "Seeing *who*? What do you think's going on?"

"I don't *know* who! Whoever wrote you that poem in your nightstand! Whoever you've been going to see every time you run errands. Whoever you've been saying 'I love you' to on the phone. I don't know *who* and I really don't care *who*."

She stands up and places her hands on my shoulders. "Lake, I'm not seeing *anyone*. You've misunderstood everything. All of it."

I can tell she's being honest, but I still don't have any answers.

"What about the note? And the bank statements? We aren't broke, Mom. And you never even sold the house!

You lied to us to drag us up here. If it wasn't for some guy, then why? Why are we here?"

She removes her hands from my shoulders and looks down at the floor, shaking her head. "Oh god, Lake. I thought you knew. I thought you figured it out." She takes a seat on the couch again and looks down at her hands.

"Apparently not," I say. This is so frustrating. I don't understand what could possibly be so important about Michigan that she would drag us away from our entire lives. "So tell me."

She looks up at me and places her hand on the couch cushion beside her. "Sit down. Please, sit down."

I sit back down on the couch and wait for her to explain everything. She pauses for a long time as she gathers her thoughts.

"The note, it's just something your dad wrote. He was being silly. He drew on my face one night and left the note on my pillow. I kept it. I loved your dad, Lake. I miss him *so* much. I would never do anything like that to him. There's no one else."

She's being sincere.

"Then why did we move here, Mom? Why did you make us move here?"

She takes a deep breath and turns to face me, placing her hands on top of mine. The look in her eyes makes my heart sink. It's the same look she had in the hallway earlier this year when she came to tell me the news about my dad. She takes another deep breath and squeezes my hands.

"Lake, I have cancer."

DENITAL. I'M DEFINITELY in denial. And anger. Bargaining? Yes, that too. I'm in all three. All five, maybe. I can't breathe.

"Your father and I were going to tell you. After he died, y'all were so devastated. I couldn't bring myself to talk to you about it. When I started getting worse, I wanted to move back here. Brenda begged me to, said she'd help take care of me. She's the one I've been talking to on the phone. There's a doctor in Detroit that specializes in lung cancer. That's where I've been going."

Lung cancer. It has a name. That makes it even more real.

"I was planning to tell you and Kel tomorrow. It's time you guys know, so we can all prepare."

I pull my hands away from her. "Prepare . . . for *what*, Mom?"

She wraps her arms around me and starts crying again. I push her back.

"Prepare for *what*, Mom?"

Just like plump Principal Bass, she can't look me in the eyes. She feels *sorry* for me.

I don't remember walking out of the house, and I don't remember going across the street. The only thing I know is that it's midnight and I'm beating on Will's door.

When he opens it, he doesn't ask any questions. He can see on my face that I just need him to be Will. Just for a little while. He puts his arm around my shoulders and ushers me inside as he shuts the door behind him.

"Lake, what's wrong?"

I can't respond. I can't breathe. He wraps his arms around me just as I start to collapse to the floor and cry. And just like in the school hallway with my mother, he melts to the floor with me. He puts my head under his chin and rubs my hair and just lets me cry.

"Tell me what happened," he finally whispers.

I don't want to say it. If I say it out loud, that means it's real. It *is* real.

"She's dying, Will," I say between sobs. "She has cancer."

He squeezes me tighter, then picks me up and carries me to his bedroom. He lays me on the bed and pulls the covers over me when the doorbell rings. He kisses me on the forehead, then leaves the room.

I can hear her speak when he answers the door, but I can't hear what she says. Will's voice is low, but I'm able to make out what he says.

"Let her stay, Julia. She needs me right now."

A few more things are spoken that I can't make out. I hear him eventually shut the door, and he comes back to the bedroom. He crawls into the bed, puts his arms around me, and holds me while I cry.

part
two

11.

Who cares about tomorrow?
What more is tomorrow,
Than another Day?

—THE AVETT BROTHERS, "SWEPT AWAY"

THE WINDOW IS ON THE WRONG SIDE OF THE ROOM. WHAT time is it? I throw my arm across the bed and reach for the phone on my nightstand. My phone's not there. Neither is the nightstand. I sit up in the bed and rub my eyes. This isn't my room. When it all comes flooding back to me, I lie back down and pull the blanket over my head, wishing it all away.

"LAKE."

I wake up again. The sun isn't as bright, but it's still not my room. I pull the covers tighter over my head.

"Lake, wake up."

Someone is pulling the covers back off my head. I groan and grip them even tighter. I try to wish it all away again, but my bladder is screaming at me. I throw the covers off and see Will sitting on the edge of the bed.

"You really *aren't* a morning person," he says.

"Bathroom. Where's your bathroom?"

He points across the hall. I jump out of the bed and hope I can make it. I run to the toilet and sit, but nearly fall in. The seat's up.

"Boys," I mutter as I let the seat down.

When I emerge from the bathroom, Will is at the bar in the kitchen. He smiles and scoots a cup of coffee to the empty seat next to him. I take the seat and the coffee.

"What time is it?" I say.

"One thirty."

"Oh. Well, your bed's really comfortable."

He smiles and nudges my shoulder. "Apparently," he says.

We drink our coffee in silence. *Comfortable* silence.

Will takes my empty cup to the sink and rinses it out before putting it in the dishwasher. "I'm taking Kel and Caulder to a matinee," he says. He turns on the dishwasher and wipes his hands on a rag. "We're leaving in a few minutes. I'll probably take them to dinner afterward, so we'll be back around six. Should give you and your mom time to talk."

I don't like how he throws that last sentence in there,

like I'm susceptible to his manipulation. "What if I don't want to talk? What if I want to go to a matinee?"

He lays his elbows on the bar and leans toward me. "You don't need to watch a movie. You need to talk to your mom. Let's go." He grabs his keys and jacket and starts walking toward the door.

I lean back in my chair and fold my arms across my chest. "I just woke up. The caffeine hasn't even kicked in yet. Can I stay here for a while?"

I'm lying. I just want him to leave so I can crawl back into his comfortable bed.

"Fine." He walks toward me and kisses me on top of my head. "But not all day. You need to talk to her."

He puts his jacket on and walks out, shutting the door behind him. I walk to the window and watch as Kel and Caulder climb into the car, and they all drive away. I look across the street at my house. My house that's not a home. I know my mom is inside, just yards away. I have no idea what I would begin to say to her if I walked over there right now. I decide not to go right away. I don't like that I'm so mad at her. I know this isn't her fault, but I don't know whom else to blame.

My gaze falls on the gnome with the broken red hat, perched upright in the driveway. He's staring right at me, grinning. It's like he knows. He knows I'm over here, too scared to go over there. He's taunting me. Just as I'm about to shut the curtain and let him win, Eddie pulls up in our driveway.

I open the front door to Will's house and wave when she gets out of her car. "Eddie, I'm over here!" She looks at me, back toward my house, then back at me with a confused look on her face before she crosses the street.

Great. Why did I just do that? How am I going to explain this?

I step aside and hold the door open for her when she enters, eyeing the living room curiously. "Are you okay? I've called you a hundred times!" she says. She plops down on the sofa and puts her foot on the coffee table and starts removing her boots. "Whose house is this?"

I don't have to answer her. The family portrait hanging on the wall in front of her answers for me.

"Oh," she says. That's *all* she says about it, though. "Well? What happened? Did she tell you who he is? Do you know him?"

I walk to the couch, step over her legs and take the seat next to her. "Eddie? Are you ready to hear my version of the stupidest thing I've ever done?"

She raises her eyebrows and waits for me to spill it.

"I was wrong. She's not seeing anyone, she's sick. She has cancer."

Eddie places her boots beside her and brings her feet back up to the coffee table as she leans back against the couch. Her socks are mismatched.

"Man, that's unreal," she says.

"Yeah, it is. But it's my real."

She sits there for a moment, picking at her black fingernails. I can tell she doesn't really know what to say. Instead of saying anything, she just leans across the couch and hugs me right before she bounces up.

"So, what's Mr. Cooper got to drink around here?" She walks to the kitchen and opens the refrigerator and removes a soda. She grabs two glasses and fills them with ice and brings them back to the living room, where she fills them with the soda.

"Couldn't find any wine. He's such a bore," she says. She hands me my drink and pulls her legs up onto the couch. "So, what's her prognosis?"

I shrug. "I don't know. It doesn't sound good, though. I left right after she told me last night. I haven't been able to face her." I turn my head toward the window and look at our house again. I know it's inevitable. I know I'll have to face her; I just want one more day of normalcy.

"Layken, you need to go talk to her."

I roll my eyes. "God, you sound just like Will."

She takes a sip of her drink and returns it to the coffee table. "Speaking of *Will*."

Here we go.

"Layken, I'm trying so hard to mind my business. I really am. But you're in his house! You're wearing the same clothes I dropped you off in last night. If you don't at least *deny* there's something going on, then I'll have to assume you're *admitting* it."

I sigh. She's right. From her standpoint, it seems like more is going on than there really is. I don't have a choice but to be honest with her, or she'll assume the worst of him.

"Fine. But Eddie, you have to—"

"I swear. Not even to Gavin."

"Okay. Well, I met him the first day we moved here. There was something there, between both of us. He asked me out, we went out. We had a great time. We kissed. It was probably the best night of my life. It *was* the best night of my life."

She's smiling now. I hesitate before I continue. She can tell by my body language that it's not a happy ending, and her smile fades.

"We didn't know. Until my first day of school, I didn't know he was a teacher. He didn't know I was in high school."

She stands up. "The hallway! That's what was going on in the hallway!"

I nod.

"Oh my god. So he ended it?"

I nod again. She falls back onto the couch.

"Shit. That sucks."

I nod again.

"But you're here. You spent the night," she grins. "He couldn't hold back, could he?"

I shake my head. "It's not like that. I was upset so he let me stay here. Nothing happened. He's just being a friend."

She slumps her shoulders and pouts, making it obvious she was hoping we caved.

"Just one more question. Your poem. It was about him, wasn't it?"

I nod.

"Nice," she laughs. She's quiet again, but not for long. "Last question. I swear. For real."

I look at her, letting her know it's okay to continue.

"Is he a good kisser?"

I smile. I can't help but smile. "Oh my god, he's so freakin' hot!"

"I know!" She claps her hands and bounces on the couch.

Our laughter fades as the reality of the moment returns. I turn and look out the window again and gaze at our house across the street while she takes our glasses to the sink. When she walks back through the living room, she grabs my hand and pulls me off the couch.

"Come on, we're going to talk to your mom."

We? I don't object. There's something about Eddie that you just don't object to.

12.

With paranoia on my heels
Will you love me still
When we awake and you see that
The sanity has gone from my eyes?

—THE AVETT BROTHERS,
"PARANOIA IN B-FLAT MAJOR"

EDDIE HAS NEVER BEEN INSIDE MY HOUSE BEFORE. YOU wouldn't know that by watching her bounce through the front door. She's still pulling me along behind her when we walk inside. My mother is sitting on the sofa, watching this stranger scamper toward her with a smile on her face, dragging her angry daughter behind her. I have to admit, the surprise on my mom's face is gratifying.

Eddie pulls me to the couch and pushes my shoulders down until I'm seated next to my mother. Eddie proceeds to take a seat on the coffee table directly in front of us, posture straight, head held high. She is in charge.

"I'm Eddie, your daughter's best friend," she says to my mother. "There. Now that we all know each other, let's get down to the nitty-gritty."

My mother looks at me, then back at Eddie, and doesn't respond. I actually have nothing to say either. I don't know where Eddie is taking this, so all I can do is allow her to continue.

"Julia, right? That's your name?"

My mother nods.

"Julia, Layken has questions. Lots of questions. You have answers." Eddie looks at me. "Layken, you ask questions, and your mother will answer them." She looks at both of us simultaneously. "That's how you do it. Any questions? For me, I mean?"

My mother and I both shake our heads. Eddie stands up. "All right, then. My work here is done. Call me later."

Eddie steps over the coffee table and heads for the front door, but spins on her feet and comes back to us. She wraps her arms around my mother's neck. My mother looks at me wide-eyed before she returns the hug. Eddie continues to squeeze my mother's neck for an unusually long time before she finally lets go. She smiles at us, hops over the coffee table, and walks out the front door. And she's gone. Just like that.

We both sit in silence, staring at the front door. I'm

confused as to where exactly things went wrong with Eddie. Or where exactly they went *right*. It's hard to tell. I glance back at my mother and we both laugh.

"Wow, Lake. You sure know how to pick 'em."

"I know. She's great, huh?"

We both settle into the couch, and my mother reaches over and pats the top of my hand. "We better do what she says. Ask me a question; I'll answer it best I can."

I cut right to the chase. "Are you dying?"

"Aren't we all?" she replies.

"That's a *question*. You're supposed to just *answer*."

She sighs like she's hesitating, not really wanting to answer.

"Possibly. Probably," she admits.

"How long? How bad is it?"

"Lake, maybe I should explain it first. It'll give you a better idea of what we're dealing with." She stands and moves to the kitchen and takes a seat at the bar. She motions for me to sit with her as she grabs a pen and a sheet of paper and starts to write something down. "There are two types of lung cancer. Non–small cell and small cell. Unfortunately, I have small cell, which spreads faster."

She's drawing a diagram. "Small cell can either be limited or extensive." She points to an area on a sketched pair of lungs. "Mine was limited. Which means it was contained into this area." She circles an area of the lungs and makes a pinpoint. "This is where they found a tumor.

I was having some symptoms a few months before your father died. He had me go in for a biopsy, and that's when we found out it was malignant. We researched doctors for a few days and finally decided our best course of action would be a doctor we found here in Michigan—in Detroit. He specializes in SCLC. We decided on the move before your father even died. We—"

"Mom, slow down."

She lays down the pen.

"I need a minute," I say. "God, it feels like I'm in science class." I rest my head in my hands. She's had months to think about this. She talks about it like she's teaching me how to bake a cake!

She patiently waits as I get up and go to the bathroom. I splash water on my face and stare at my reflection in the mirror. I look like complete crap. I haven't even glanced in a mirror since before I went out with Gavin and Eddie last night. My mascara is smudged under my eyes. My eyes are puffy. My hair is wild. I wipe the makeup off and brush out my hair before I go back to the kitchen and listen to her tell me how she's going to die.

She looks up at me when I walk back into the kitchen, and I nod, giving her the go-ahead. I take a seat across from her.

"A week after we decided we were moving to Michigan to be closer to the doctor, your father died. I was so consumed with it, with his death and the arrangements and everything. I just tried to push what was going on with me out of my mind. I didn't go back to the doctor for three months." Her voice grows softer. "By that time, it had spread. It was no longer limited small cell; it was extensive."

She looks away, wiping a tear from her eye. "I blamed myself—for your dad's heart attack. I knew it was the stress of the diagnosis that caused it." She stands and walks back into the living room. She leans against the window frame and stares outside.

"Why didn't you tell me? I could have helped you, Mom. You didn't need to deal with all of it on your own."

She rolls her back against the wall and faces me. "I know that now. I was in denial. I was angry. I was hoping for a miracle, I guess. I don't know. The days turned into weeks, then months. Now we're here. I started chemotherapy again three weeks ago."

I scoot my chair back and stand up. "That's good, right? If they're giving you chemo then there's a chance it'll go away."

She shakes her head. "It's not to fight it, Lake. It's to manage my pain. It's all they can do now."

Her words cause me to lose whatever strength I had left in my legs. I fall onto the couch and drop my head in my hands and cry. It's amazing how many tears one person can have. One night after my father died, I had cried so much I started to become paranoid I was doing damage to my eyes, so I googled it. I googled "Can a person cry too much?" Apparently, everyone eventually falls asleep and stops crying in order for their bodies to process normal periods of rest. So no, you can't cry too much.

I grab a tissue and take a few deep breaths in an attempt to hold back the rest of my tears. I'm really sick of crying.

My mother sits next to me and I feel her arms encircle me, so I turn into her and hug her. My heart aches for her. For *us*. I tighten my grip on her, afraid to let her go. I can't let her go.

She eventually starts coughing and has to turn away. I watch her as she stands and continues to cough, gasping for breath. She's so sick. How did I not notice? Her cheeks are even hollower than before. Her hair is thinner. I hardly recognize her. I've been so focused on my own misery that I haven't even noticed my own mother being swept away right before my eyes.

The coughing spell passes and my mother returns to her seat at the bar. "We'll tell Kel tonight. Brenda will be here at seven. She wants to be here, since she'll be his guardian."

I laugh. Because she's joking. *Right?* "What do you mean his *guardian*?"

She looks me in the eyes like *I'm* the one being unreasonable. "Lake. You're still in high school; soon you'll be in college. I don't expect you to give everything up. I don't *want* you to. Brenda has raised children before. She *wants* to do it. Kel likes her."

Of all the things I have been through this year.

This moment, these words that have just come out of her mouth—I have never been more enraged.

I stand up and grip the back of the chair and throw it to the floor with such force that the seat comes loose from the base. She flinches as I sprint toward her, pointing my finger into her chest.

"She is *not* getting Kel! You are not giving her *my* brother!" I scream so loud my throat burns.

She attempts to subdue me by putting her hands on my shoulders, but I spin away from her. "Lake, stop it! Stop this! You're still in high school! You haven't even started college yet. What do you expect me to do? We've got no one else." She walks after me as I head for the front door. "I've got no one else, Lake," she cries.

I open the door and swing around to her, ignoring her tears as I continue to scream. "You aren't telling him tonight! He doesn't need to know yet. You better not tell him!"

"We have to tell him. He needs to know," she says.

She's following me down the driveway now. I keep walking. "Go home, Mother! Just go home! I'm done talking about it! And if you ever want to see me again, you will *not* tell him!"

Her sobs fade as I slam the door to Will's house behind me. I run to his bedroom and throw myself on the bed. I don't just cry; I sob, I wail, I scream.

* * *

I'VE NEVER USED drugs before. If you don't count the sip of my mother's wine when I was fourteen, I've never even willingly had alcohol. It's not that I was too afraid, or too straitlaced. Honestly, I'd just never been offered anything. I never went to parties in Texas. I never spent the night with anyone who ever tried to coerce me into doing something illegal. I have frankly just never been in a situation where I could succumb to peer pressure. I spent my Friday nights at football games. Saturday nights, my dad usually took us out to a movie and to dinner. Sunday, I did homework. That was my life.

There was one exception, when Kerris's cousin had a wedding, and she invited me to go. I was sixteen, she had just gotten her license, and the reception had just ended. We stayed late to help clean up. We were having the best time. We drank punch, ate leftover cake, danced, drank more punch. We realized that someone had laced the punch when we both noticed how much fun we were having. I don't know how much of it we drank. So much that we were already too drunk to stop when we noticed we were drunk. We never even thought twice when we got into the car to go home. We got a mile down the road before she swerved and hit a tree. I got a laceration above my eye, and she broke her arm. We both ended up being okay. In fact, the car was still drivable. Rather than do the smart thing and wait for help, we turned the car around and drove back to the reception to call my dad. The trouble we got into the next day is a different story.

But there was a moment, right before she hit the tree. We were laughing at the way she said "bubble." We just kept saying it over and over until the car started to glide off the road. I saw the tree, and I knew we were about to hit it. But it was as if time slowed down. The tree could have been five million feet away. That's how long it took for the car to hit the tree. The only thing I thought about in that moment was Kel. The *only* thing. I didn't think about school, the boys, the college I would miss out on if I died. I thought about Kel, and how he was the only thing that was important to me. The only thing that mattered in the seconds when I thought I was about to die.

I SOMEHOW FELL asleep in Will's bed again. I know this because when I open my eyes, I'm no longer crying. See? People can't cry forever. Everyone eventually falls asleep.

I expect the tears to return once the fog clears from my mind, but instead I feel motivated, renewed. Like I'm on some sort of mission. I get out of bed and have an odd urge to clean. And sing. I need music. I head to the living room and immediately find what I'm looking for. The stereo. I don't even have to search for music when I turn it on: there's already an Avett Brothers CD inside. I crank up the volume on one of my favorites and get busy.

Unfortunately, Will's house is surprisingly clean for one with two male inhabitants, so I have to search hard for something to keep me busy. I hit the bathroom first, which is good. I know nine-year-olds don't have very good aim, so I start scrubbing. I scrub the toilet, the floor, the shower, the sink. It's clean.

I move on to the bedrooms where I organize, make beds, remake beds. Next I hit the living room, where I dust and vacuum. I mop the bathroom floors and wipe down every surface I can find. I end up at the kitchen sink, where I wash the only two dirty dishes in the house: Eddie's and my glasses.

It's almost seven when I hear Will's car pull up. He and the two boys walk into the house and come to a halt when they see me sitting on his living room floor.

"What are you doing?" Caulder asks.

"Alphabetizing," I reply.

"Alphabetizing what?" Will says.

"Everything. First I did the movies, then I did the CDs. Caulder, I did the books in your room. I did a few of your games, but some of those started with numbers so I put the numbers first, then the titles." I point to the piles in front of me. "These are recipes. I found them on top of the fridge. I'm alphabetizing them by category first; like beef, lamb, pork, poultry. Then behind the categories I'm alphabetizing them by—"

"Guys, go to Kel's. Let Julia know you're back," Will says as he continues to watch me.

The boys don't move. They just stare at the recipe cards in front of me.

"Now!" Will yells. They both jerk their eyes away and start back toward the door.

"Your sister's weird," I hear Caulder say as they leave.

Will sits down on the couch in front of me and watches as I continue to alphabetize the recipes.

"You're the teacher," I say. "Should I put 'Baked Potato Soup' behind potato or soup?"

"Stop," he says. He seems moody.

"I can't stop, silly. I'm halfway finished. If I stop now you won't know where to find . . ." I grab a random card off the floor. "Jerk Chicken?" It *would* be that one. I throw the card back in the pile and continue sorting.

Will eyes the living room, then stands and walks into the kitchen. I see him run his finger along the baseboards. Good thing I thought about those. He walks down the hallway and returns a couple of minutes later.

"You color coded my closet?" He's not smiling. I thought he would be happy.

"Will, it wasn't that hard. You wear like, three different color shirts."

He glides across the living room and bends down, snatching up the recipe cards I've organized into piles.

"Will! Stop! That took me a long time!" I snatch them back out of his hands as fast as he's picking them up.

He finally throws them back on the floor and grabs my wrists and tries to pull me up, but I start kicking at his legs. "Let me go! I'm . . . not . . . done!"

He lets go of my hands and I fall back to the floor. I pick up the recipe cards and start reorganizing them back into piles. He completely took me back to square one! I can't even find the Beef card. I flip over two cards that are upside down but—

"What the hell!" I scream. I'm suddenly drenched in water.

I look up and Will is standing over me with an empty pitcher in his hand and an angry look on his face. I lunge forward and start punching at his legs. He backs away when I start hitting at him, trying to get off the floor.

Why the hell did he just do that? I'm gonna punch him in the face! I stand up and try to hit him, but he steps aside and grabs my arm and twists it behind my back. I flail my other arm at him, and he pushes me toward the hallway and into the bathroom. Before I know it, his arms are around me and he lifts me up. He pulls the shower curtain back and shoves me in. I try to punch him, but his arms are longer than mine. He holds me against the wall with one arm and turns the faucet on with the other. A stream of ice-cold water splashes across my face. I gasp.

"Jerk! Jackass! Asshole!"

He continues to hold me back as he turns the other faucet on and the water gets warmer.

"Take a shower, Layken! Take a damn shower!" He lets go of me and walks out of the bathroom, slamming the door behind him.

I jump out of the shower; my clothes are drenched.

I try to open the bathroom door, but I can't, because he's holding the doorknob from the other side.

"Let me out, Will! Now!" I beat on the door and try to turn the knob, but it doesn't budge.

"Layken," he calmly responds from the other side of the door. "I'm not letting you out of the bathroom until you take off your clothes, get in the shower, wash your hair, and calm down."

I flip him off. He can't see me of course, but it still feels good. I take off my wet clothes and throw them on the floor, hoping I get something dirty. I climb into the shower. The warm water feels good against my skin. I close my eyes and let the water trickle through my hair and down my face.

Dammit. Will is right *again*.

"I NEED A towel!" I yell. I've been in the shower well over half an hour. Will has a showerhead with a jet setting. I turned it on and focused it on the back of my neck for most of the time. It really does relieve tension.

"It's on the sink. So are your clothes," he says from outside the bathroom.

I pull the curtain back and there is definitely a towel there. And clothes. *My* clothes. Clothes he obviously just got out of my house and somehow put in the bathroom. *While* I was in the shower.

I turn the water off and step out of the shower and

dry off. I twist the towel around my head and put on my clothes. He brought me pajamas. Maybe that means I'm sleeping in his comfortable bed again. I hesitate as I turn the doorknob, assuming I still won't be able to open it, but it swings open.

When he hears me open the bathroom door, he jumps over the back of the couch and runs toward me. I back up to the wall, afraid he's about to shove me back in the bathroom, when his arms go around me, and he hugs me.

"I'm sorry, Lake. I'm sorry I did that. You were just *losing* it."

I hug him back. *Of course* I hug him back. "It's okay. I kinda sorta had a bad day," I say.

He pulls away from me and places his hands on my shoulders. "So we're friends? You aren't gonna try to punch me again?"

"Friends," I say reluctantly. That's the last thing I want to be to him right now. His *friend*.

"How was the matinee?" I ask as we walk down the hallway.

"Did you talk to your mom?" He ignores my question.

"Jeez. Deflect much?"

"Did you talk to her? Please don't tell me you spent the entire day cleaning." He walks into the kitchen and takes two glasses out of the cabinet.

"No. Not the *entire* day. We talked."

"And?"

"And . . . she has cancer," I reply frankly.

He looks at me and scowls. I roll my eyes at him and put my elbows on the table, gripping my forehead with my hands. My fingers brush against the towel that's on my head. I bend away from the bar and pull the towel off and flip my head forward, brushing the tangled strands with my fingers to smooth them out.

After I remove all the tangles, I raise my head back up just as Will darts his eyes away from me and to the cup in his hand that's now overflowing with milk. I pretend not to notice the spill and continue to mess with my hair as he wipes up the milk with a rag.

He pulls something out of the cabinet and gets a spoon out of the drawer. He's making me *chocolate* milk.

"Will she be okay?" he asks.

I sigh. He's relentless.

"No. Probably not."

"But she's getting treatment?"

I've been able to go the entire day without thinking about it. I've been comfortably numb since I woke up from my nap. I know this is his house, but I'm beginning to wish he would leave again.

"She's dying, Will. *Dying*. She'll probably be dead within the year, maybe less than that. They're just doing chemo to keep her comfortable. While she *dies*. 'Cause she'll be *dead*. Because she's *dying*. There. Is that what you wanted to hear?"

His expression softens when he sets the milk in front

of me. He grabs a handful of ice out of the refrigerator and drops it into my cup. "On the rocks," he says.

He's good at deflecting and even better at ignoring my snide remarks. "Thanks," I say. I drink my chocolate milk and shut up. It feels like he somehow just won our fight.

THE AVETT BROTHERS are still strumming away in the background when I finish my chocolate milk. I walk to the living room and put the song on repeat. I lie on the floor and stare up at the ceiling with my hands stretched out above my head. It's relaxing.

"Turn the lights off," I tell him. "I just want to listen for a while."

He turns the lights off and I sense him lie down beside me on the floor. A dancing green glow from the stereo illuminates the walls as the Avett Brothers put on a color show. My thoughts drift with the music as we lie there motionless. After the song ends and loops around again, I tell him what's really on my mind.

"She doesn't want me to raise Kel. She wants to give him to Brenda."

He finds my hand in the dark and holds it. He holds it, and I let him just be my friend.

THE LIGHTS FLICK on and I immediately cover my eyes. I sit up and see Will next to me, sound asleep.

"Hey," Eddie whispers. "I knocked, nobody answered." She walks through the front door and sits on the couch. She watches Will as he snores, sprawled out on the living room floor.

"It's Saturday night," she says, rolling her eyes. "Told you he was a bore."

I laugh. "What are you doing here?"

"Checking on you. You haven't answered your phone or texted me back at all today. Your mom has cancer so you decide to swear off technology? Doesn't make sense."

"I don't know where my phone is."

We both stare at Will for a moment. He's snoring really loud. The boys must have worn him out today.

"So, I assume things didn't go well with your mom? Since you're here, sleeping on the damn floor." She looks annoyed that we weren't doing anything more than just sleeping.

"No, we talked."

"And?"

I get up and stretch before I sit on the sofa beside her. She's already got her boots off. I guess going so long without a permanent home makes you feel like you're at home anywhere you go. I pull my feet up and lay back on the arm of the couch, facing her.

"Last week in the courtyard when you were telling me about your mom and what happened when you were nine?"

"What about it?" she says, still watching Will snore.

"Well, I was grateful. I was so grateful that nothing like that would ever happen to Kel. I was grateful that he was able to live a normal nine-year-old life. But now—it's like God has it out for us. Why both of them? Wasn't my dad enough? It's like death came and punched us square in the face."

Eddie turns her gaze away from Will and looks at me.

"It wasn't death that punched you, Layken. It was *life*. Life happens. Shit happens. And it happens *a lot*. To *a lot* of people."

I don't even bother with the worst of the details. I'm too embarrassed to admit to her that my own mother doesn't even want me raising her child.

Will rustles on the floor. Eddie leans over and gives me a squeeze and grabs her boots. "Teacher's waking up, I better get outta here. I just wanted to check on you. Oh, and go find your phone," she says as she walks toward the door.

I watch her as she walks out the front door. She's in a room for three minutes, and her energy is infectious. When I turn back around, Will is sitting up on the floor. He's looking at me like he's about to give me detention. I smile at him as innocently as I can.

"What the hell was she doing here?" he says. He can be really intimidating when he wants to be.

"Visiting," I mutter. "Checking on me." If I don't make it sound like a big deal, maybe he won't either.

"Dammit, Layken!"

Nope. He thinks it's a big deal.

He pushes himself up off the floor and throws his hands up in the air. "Are you *trying* to get me fired? Are you that *selfish* that you don't give a crap about anyone *else's* problems? Do you know what would happen if she let it get out that you spent the night here?" A light bulb goes off in his head, and he takes a step toward me. "Does she know you spent the night here?"

I press my lips into a tight, thin line and look down at my lap, avoiding his eyes.

"Layken, what does she know?" he says, his voice lower. He can see by my body language that I've told her everything.

"Christ, Layken. Go home."

MY MOTHER IS already in bed. Kel and Caulder are sitting on the couch, watching TV. "Caulder, your brother wants you to go home. Kel and I have plans tomorrow, so we won't be home all day."

Caulder grabs his jacket and heads toward the front door. "See ya, Kel." He slips his shoes on and leaves.

I walk to the living room and throw myself into the seat beside Kel. I grab the remote and start flipping through channels, attempting to put the fact that I just pissed Will off out of my mind.

"Where were you?" Kel asks.

"With Eddie."

"What were y'all doing?"

"Driving around."

"Why were you at Caulder's house when we got home from the movies?"

"Will paid me to clean his house."

"Why is Mom sad?"

"Because. She doesn't have enough money to pay me to clean *her* house."

"Why? Our house isn't dirty."

"Do you want to go ice-skating tomorrow?"

"Yes!"

"Then stop asking so many questions."

I press the power button on the remote and send Kel to bed. When I climb into my own bed, I set the alarm for six o'clock. I want to be out of this house before my mother wakes up.

KEL AND I spend the entire day Sunday blowing every cent of my savings account. I take him to breakfast, where we order two meals each off of the menu. We go ice-skating, and we both suck at it, so we don't stay long. I take him to lunch at a concession stand inside an arcade, where we stay for four hours. After the arcade, I take him to an afternoon movie, where we have dinner that consists of even more concession-stand food. I would take him for dessert, but he's now complaining that his stomach hurts.

My mother is at work by the time we get home. My timing isn't accidental by any means. I take a shower, pick out our clothes for school, and put away a load of laundry. I'm so tired that I'm able to fall asleep without confronting anything at all.

13.

Shooting off vicious
collections of words
The losers make facts
by the things they have heard
And I find myself
trying hard to defend them.

—THE AVETT BROTHERS, "ALL MY MISTAKES"

"GOT ANOTHER ONE FOR YA," NICK SAYS AS HE TAKES HIS seat Monday morning.

If I have to hear another Chuck Norris joke, I'm going to explode. "Not today; my head hurts," I reply.

"You know what Chuck Norris does to a headache?"

"Nick, I'm serious. Shut up!"

Nick withdraws and turns to the unfortunate student to his right.

Will's not here. The class waits a few minutes, not

really knowing what to do. Apparently this is uncharacteristic of him.

Javi stands up and gets his books. "Five-minute rule," he says. He walks out the door but walks right back in, followed by Will.

Will shuts the door behind him and goes to his desk and sets a stack of papers down. He's on edge today, and it's obvious to everyone. He hands the first student of each row a smaller stack of the papers to pass back, including me. I look down at my paper and there are about ten sheets stapled together. I start flipping through them and recognize one page as Eddie's poem about the pink balloon. They must all be poems written by students. I don't recognize any of the others.

"Some of you in here have performed at the slam this semester. I appreciate it. I know it takes a lot of courage." He holds up his own copy of the collection of poems.

"These are your poems. Some were written by students in my other classes, some by students in here. I want you to read them. Once you've read them, I want you to score them. Write a number between zero and ten, ten being the best. Be honest. If you don't like it, give it a low score. We're trying to find the best and worst. Write the score in the bottom right of each page. Go ahead." He sits at his desk and watches the class.

I don't like this assignment. It doesn't seem fair. I'm raising my hand. Why am I raising my hand? He looks at me and nods.

"What's the point of this assignment?" I ask.

His eyes slowly make their way around the classroom. "Layken, ask that question again after everyone's finished."

He's acting strange.

I start reading the first poem, when Will grabs two slips of paper off of his desk and walks past me. I glance back just as he lays a slip on Eddie's desk. She picks it up and frowns. He walks back to the front, dropping the other slip on my desk. I pick it up and look it over. It's a detention slip.

I glance back at Eddie, and she just shrugs her shoulders. I wad my slip into a ball and throw it across the room to the trashcan by the door. I make it.

Over the next half hour, students begin to finish their scoring. Will is taking the stacks as they are finished and he's adding up the totals with his calculator. Once the last of the points have been added up, Will writes the totals on a sheet of paper and walks to the front of his desk and sits.

He holds the paper up in the air and shakes it. "Is everyone ready to hear which poems sucked? Which ones got the most points?" He's smiling as he waits on a response.

No one says anything. Except Eddie.

"Some of us who wrote those poems may not *want* to know how many points we got. I know I don't."

Will takes a few steps toward Eddie. "If you don't care how many points it's worth, then why did you write it?"

Eddie is quiet for a moment as she thinks about Will's question.

"Aside from wanting to be exempt from your final?" she asks.

Will nods.

"I guess because I had something to say."

Will looks at me. "Layken, ask your question again."

My question. I try to remember what my question was. Oh yeah, what's his point?

"What's the point of this assignment?" I ask cautiously.

Will holds the paper up in front of him that contains the tallied scores, and he rips it right down the middle. He reaches behind him and picks the stack of poems up that everyone scored and he throws them in the trash. He walks to the chalkboard and begins to write something on the board. When he's finished, he steps aside.

"The *points* are not the *point*; the *point* is *poetry*."
—Allan Wolf

The class is quiet as we take in the words sprawled across the board. Will allows a moment of silence before he continues.

"It shouldn't matter what anyone else thinks about your words. When you're on that stage—you share a piece of your soul. You can't assign points to that."

The bell rings. On any other day, students would be filing out the door. No one has moved; we're all just staring at the writing on the board.

"Tomorrow, be prepared to learn *why* it's important for you to write poetry," he says.

There was a moment, in the midst of all the distraction in my head, when I forgot he was *Will*. I listened to him like he was my *teacher*.

Javi is the first to get up, soon followed by the rest of the students. Will is facing the desk with his back to me when Eddie walks up, detention slip in hand. I had already forgotten he gave us detention. She gives me a wink as she passes me and stops at his desk.

"Mr. Cooper?" She's being respectful, but dramatically so. "It is my understanding that detention commences upon the conclusion of the final class period at approximately three thirty. It is my desire, as I'm sure it is Layken's desire as well, to be punctual, so that we may serve our fairly deserved sentences with due diligence. Would you be so kind as to share with us the location in which this sentence shall be carried out?"

Will never looks at her as he walks toward the door. "Here. Just you two. Three thirty."

And he's gone. Just like that.

Eddie bursts out laughing. "What did you do to him?"

I stand up and walk to the door with her. "Oh, it wasn't just me, Eddie. It was both of us."

She spins around wide-eyed. "Oh my god, he knows I know? What's he going to say about it?"

I shrug my shoulders. "I guess we'll find out at three thirty."

"DETENTION? DUCKIE GAVE you detention?" Gavin laughs.

"Man, he really needs to get laid," Nick says.

Nick's comment causes Eddie to laugh and spew milk out of her mouth. I shoot her a cease-and-desist look.

"I can't believe he gave you detention," Gavin says. "But you aren't positive that's what it's for, right? For skipping? I mean, he already mentioned that at the slam last week, and he didn't seem too mad."

I know what the detention is for. Will wants to make sure he can trust Eddie, but I'm not telling this to Gavin. "He said it's for not turning in the assignment we were supposed to do the day we skipped."

Gavin turns to Eddie. "But you did that one—I remember."

Eddie looks at me and replies to Gavin. "I guess I lost it," she says with a shrug.

EDDIE AND I meet outside the door to Will's classroom at approximately three thirty.

"You know, the more I think about it, this really sucks," Eddie says. "Why couldn't he just call me or something if he wanted to talk about what I know? I had plans today."

"Maybe we won't have to stay long," I say.

"I hate detention. It's boring. I'd rather lay on Will's floor with you than sit in detention," she says.

"Maybe we can try and make it fun."

She turns to open the door but hesitates, then spins around and faces me. "You know, you're right. Let's make it fun. I'm pretty sure detention is an hour long. Do you realize how many Chuck Norris jokes we can make in a whole hour?"

I smile at her. "Not as many as Chuck Norris could."

She opens the door to detention.

"Afternoon, Mr. Cooper," Eddie says as she flurries inside.

"Take a seat," he says, wiping the point of poetry off the board.

"Mr. Cooper, did you know that seats actually *stand up* when Chuck Norris walks into a room?" she says.

I laugh and follow Eddie to our seats. Rather than taking the two front seats, she keeps walking until she's in the very back of the room, where she scoots two desks together. We sit as far from the teacher as possible.

Will doesn't laugh. He doesn't even smile. He sits in his chair and glares at us while we giggle—like high school girls.

"Listen," he says. He stands back up and walks toward us, then leans against the window and folds his arms across his chest. He stares at the floor like he's trying to think of a delicate way to broach the subject. "Eddie, I need to know where your head's at. I know you were at my house. I know you know Layken spent the night. I know she told you about our date. I just need to know what you plan to do about it, if you plan to do *anything* about it."

"Will," I say. "She's not saying anything. There's nothing to say."

He doesn't look at me. He continues to look at Eddie, waiting for her response. I guess mine wasn't good enough. I don't know if it's nerves or the fact that I've had the strangest last three days of my life, but I start laughing. Eddie shoots me a questioning glance, but she can't hold it in. She starts laughing, too.

Will throws his hands up in the air, exasperated. "What? What the *hell* is so *funny*?" he says.

"Nothing," I say. "It's just weird. You gave us *detention*, Will." I inhale as I try to control my laughter. "Couldn't you just, like, come over tonight or something? Talk to us about it then? Why'd you give us detention?"

He waits until our laughter subsides before he continues. When we're finally silent, he straightens up and walks closer to us. "This is the first chance I've had to talk to either of you. I didn't sleep all night. I wasn't sure if I even had a job to come back to today." He looks at Eddie. "If anything gets out . . . if anyone finds out that a student slept in my bed with me, I'd get fired. I'd get kicked out of college."

Eddie stiffens in her seat and turns to me, smiling. "You slept in his *bed* with him? You're holding back vital information. You didn't tell me *that*," she laughs.

Will shakes his head and walks back to the front of the room and throws himself into his chair. He leans onto his desk and sets his face in his hands. It's apparent this isn't going how he had planned.

"You slept in his *bed*?" Eddie whispers, low enough so Will doesn't hear her.

"Nothing happened," I say. "Like you said, he's such a *bore*."

Eddie laughs again, causing me to lose my composure.

"Is this funny?" Will says from his desk. "Is this a joke to you two?"

I can see in his eyes that we're enjoying detention way more than we're supposed to. Eddie isn't fazed, however.

"Did you know Chuck Norris doesn't have a funny bone? It tried to make him laugh once, so he ripped it out," she says.

Will lays his head on his desk in defeat. Eddie and I look at each other and our laughter ceases as we respect that he's attempting to have a serious conversation with us. Eddie sighs and straightens up in her desk. "Mr. Cooper?" she says. "I won't say anything. Swear. It's not that big of a deal anyway."

He looks up at her. "It *is* a big deal, Eddie. That's what I'm trying to *tell* both of you. If you don't treat this as a big deal, you'll get careless. Something might slip. I've got too much at stake."

We both sigh. The energy in the room is nonexistent now. It's like a black hole just sucked all the fun out of detention. Eddie feels it too, so she attempts to rectify it.

"Did you know Chuck Norris likes his steaks med—" Eddie doesn't finish her sentence as Will reaches his limit. He slams his fist against the desk and stands up. Neither Eddie nor I are laughing at this point. I look at her wide-eyed and shake my head, letting her know that Chuck Norris needs to retreat.

"This isn't a *joke*," he says. "This is a *big deal*." He reaches over and takes something out of his drawer and swiftly walks to where we're sitting in the back of the room. He smacks a picture down on the crack where the edges of our desks meet and flips it over. It's a picture of Caulder.

He places his finger on the picture and says, "This boy. This boy is a *big* deal." He backs up a step and grabs a desk and turns it around to face us, then sits down.

"I don't think we're following you, Will," I say. I look at Eddie and she shakes her head in agreement. "What's Caulder got to do with what Eddie knows?"

He takes a deep breath as he leans across his desk and picks the picture back up. I can tell by the look in his eyes that his recollection is unpleasant. He stares at the picture for a while, then lays it down on the desk and leans back in the chair, folding his arms across his chest. He continues to stare at the picture, avoiding our eyes. "He was with them . . . when it happened. He watched them die."

I suck in a breath. Eddie and I give him respectful silence and wait for him to continue. I'm beginning to feel very small.

"They said it was a miracle he survived. The car was totaled. When the first person came on the scene, Caulder was still buckled up in what was left of the backseat. He was screaming for my mom, trying to get her to turn around. For five minutes he had to sit there alone and watch as they died."

Will clears his throat. Eddie reaches under the table and grabs my hand and squeezes it. Neither of us says a word.

"I sat in the hospital with him for six days while he recovered. Never left his side—not even for their funeral. When my grandparents came to pick him up and take him home with them, he cried. He didn't want to go. He wanted to stay with me. He begged me to take him back to campus with me. I didn't have a job. I didn't have insurance. I was nineteen. I didn't know the first thing about raising a kid . . . so I let them take him."

Will stands up and walks to the window. He doesn't say anything for a while as he watches the parking lot slowly empty. His hand goes to his face and it looks like he's wiping at his eyes. If Eddie weren't in here right now, I would hug him.

He eventually turns to face us again. "Caulder hated

me. He was so mad at me he wouldn't return my calls for days. It was in the middle of a football game when I started to question the choice I made. I was studying the football in my hands, running my fingers over the pigskin, across the letters of the brand name printed on the side. This elongated spheroid that didn't even weigh a whole pound. I was choosing this ridiculous ball of leather in my hands over my own flesh and blood. I was putting myself, my girlfriend, my scholarship—I was putting everything before this little boy that I loved more than anything in the world.

"I dropped the football and walked right off the field. I got to my grandparents' house at two in the morning and grabbed Caulder right out of bed. I brought him home that night. They begged me not to do it. Said it would be too hard on me and that I wouldn't be able to give him what he needed. I knew they were wrong. I knew all Caulder really needed—was *me*."

He slowly walks back to the desk in front of us and places his hands on the back of it. He looks at both of us, tears streaming down our faces.

"I've spent the last two years of my life trying to convince myself that I made the right decision for him. So my *job*? My *career*? This life I'm trying to build for this little boy? I take it very seriously. It *is* a big deal. It's a *very* big deal to me."

He calmly returns the desk to its place in the aisle and walks back to the front of the room, grabs his things, and leaves.

Eddie gets up and walks to Will's desk and grabs a box of tissues. She brings the box and slumps back down in her seat. I pull out a tissue and we both wipe at our eyes.

"God, Layken. How do you do it?" she says. She blows her nose and grabs another tissue out of the box.

"How do I do what?" I sniff as I continue to wipe the tears from my eyes.

"How do you not fall in *love* with him?"

The tears begin flowing just as quickly as they had ceased. I grab yet another tissue. "I *don't* not fall in love with him. I don't not fall in love with him *a lot!*"

She laughs and squeezes my hand. We spend the next hour alone, willingly sitting out our much-deserved detentions.

14.

And I know you need me in the next room over
But I am stuck in here all paralyzed.

—THE AVETT BROTHERS, "TEN THOUSAND WORDS"

I'VE NEVER HAD SEX. I CAME REALLY CLOSE ONCE BUT chickened out at the last minute. My longest relationship was with a boy I met through Kerris right before I turned seventeen.

Kerris had a brother who was in college, and he brought a friend home with him during spring break two summers ago. His name was Seth, and he was eighteen. I thought I loved him. I think I really just loved having a boyfriend.

He attended the University of Texas, which was a good four-hour drive away. We talked on the phone and online a lot. By the time we had been together for about six months, we had discussed it plenty, so I decided I was ready to have sex with him. I had a midnight curfew that night, so he rented a hotel room, and we told my mother we were going to the movie theater.

When we got to the hotel, my hands were shaking. I knew I had changed my mind, but was too scared to tell him. He had put so much effort into everything. He even brought his own sheets and blankets from home so it would feel more intimate. We had been kissing for a while on the bed when he took off my shirt. His hands were making their way to my pants when I started crying. He immediately stopped. Never pressured me, never made me feel guilty for changing my mind. He just kissed me and told me it was okay. We stayed in bed and rented a movie instead.

It was seven hours later and daytime when we finally woke up. We were both frantic. No one knew where we were; both of our phones had been turned off all night. I knew my parents were worried sick. He was too scared to face them with me, so he dropped me off at my driveway and left. I remember staring at my house, wanting to be anywhere else but there. I knew they were going to make me talk to them, tell them about where I had been. I hated confrontation.

I'M STANDING IN front of my Jeep now, staring at the gnome-filled yard of our house that's not our home. That same feeling of trepidation deep within the pit of my stomach is back. I know my mother is going to want to talk about it all. The cancer. Kel. She'll want to confront it, and I'll want to hide.

I slowly make my way to the front door and turn the knob, wishing someone were holding it shut from the other side. She, Kel, and Caulder are all seated at the bar.

They're carving pumpkins. She can't talk now. This is good.

"Hey," I say to no one in particular when I walk through the front door. She doesn't acknowledge me.

"Hey, Layken. Check out my pumpkin!" Kel says. He swings it around to face me. Its eyes and mouth are three big Xs, and he's taped a bag of candy to the side of the pumpkin's face.

"He's making a sour face. 'Cause he ate some Sour Skittles," he says.

"Creative," I say.

"Look at mine," Caulder says as he turns his around. There's just a bunch of huge holes where the pumpkin's face should be.

"Oh . . . what is it?" I ask him.

"It's God."

I cock my head at him, confused. "God?"

Caulder laughs. "Yeah, God." He looks at Kel, and in unison they both say, "Because he's *holy*."

I roll my eyes and laugh. "I don't know how you two found each other."

I look at my mom and she's watching me, trying to gauge my mood.

"Hey," I say, specifically to her this time.

"Hey," she smiles.

"So," I say, hoping she'll grasp the double meaning behind what I'm about to say. "Do you mind if we *just* carve pumpkins tonight? Is it okay if that's *all* we do? Just carve pumpkins?"

She smiles and turns her attention back to the pumpkin in front of her.

"Sure. But we can't carve pumpkins every night, Lake. One of these nights we'll eventually have to stop carving pumpkins."

I grab one of the available pumpkins off the floor and set it on the bar and take a seat, when someone knocks at the door.

"I'll get it," Caulder yells as he jumps down.

My mother and I both turn to the front door when he opens it. It's Will.

"Hey, Buddy. You answering doors here now?" Will says to him.

Caulder grabs his hand and pulls him inside. "We're carving pumpkins for Halloween. Come on, Julia bought one for you, too." He's pulling Will through the living room and toward the kitchen.

"No, it's fine. I'll carve mine another time. I just wanted to bring you home so they can have some family time."

My mother pulls out the available chair on the other side of her. "Sit down, Will. We're just carving pumpkins tonight. That's *all* we're doing. Just carving pumpkins."

Caulder already has a pumpkin and is placing it at the table in front of Will's chair.

"Okay, then. I guess we're carving pumpkins," Will says.

Caulder hands him a knife and we all sit at the bar—and just carve pumpkins.

Kel creates the first awkward moment when he asks why I'm so late getting home from school. Mom eyes me, waiting for my response, while Will just cuts away at his pumpkin and doesn't look up.

"Eddie and I had detention," I say.

"Detention? What were you in detention for?" my mom asks.

"We skipped class last week, took a nap in the courtyard."

She brings her scooper down to the table and looks at me, obviously disappointed.

"Lake, why would you do something like that? What class did you skip?"

I don't reply. I purse my lips together and nudge my head toward Will. My mother looks at Will just as he looks up from his pumpkin.

He shrugs his shoulders and laughs. "She skipped my class! What was I supposed to do?"

My mother stands up and pats him on the back as she picks up the phone book. "I'm buying you supper for that."

* * *

THE WHOLE EVENING is surreal. Everyone's eating pizza, talking, laughing, including my mother. It's good to hear her laugh. I can see a difference in her tonight. I think simply being able to tell me she was sick has helped relieve some of her stress. I can see it in her eyes, she's more at ease.

We listen as Kel and Caulder talk about what they want to be for Halloween. Caulder keeps switching back and forth between a Transformer and an Angry Bird. Kel still hasn't come up with anything.

I wipe up pumpkin remnants off the floor and take the rag to the sink and rinse it out. I put my elbows on the counter and rest my chin in my hands as I watch them. This is more than likely my mother's last time to carve pumpkins. Next month will be the last time she sees Thanksgiving. After that, she'll have her last Christmas. But she's just sitting here, talking to Will about Halloween plans, laughing. I wish I could freeze this moment. I wish we could just carve pumpkins forever.

WILL AND CAULDER leave after my mom goes to her room to get ready for her shift. I finish cleaning the kitchen and gather the sacks of pumpkin discards and combine them all into a large trash bag. I take the bag to the curb at the end of the driveway, when Will comes outside with his own bag of trash. He walks to the end of his driveway before he realizes I'm even there. He smiles at me and lifts the lid, throwing the bag inside.

"Hey," he says. He puts his hands in his jacket pockets and walks toward me.

"Hey," I reply.

"Hey," he says again. He walks past me and sits against the bumper of my Jeep.

"Hey," I reply as I lean against the Jeep next to him.

"Hey."

"Stop it," I laugh.

We both wait for the other to talk again, but instead there's just an awkward silence. I hate awkward silences, so I break it.

"I'm sorry I told Eddie. She's just so smart. She figured it out and thought there was more going on between us than there is, so I had to tell her the truth. I didn't want her to think badly of you."

He leans his head back and stares up at the sky. "I trust your judgment, Lake. I even trust Eddie. I just need her to know why this job is so important to me. Or maybe I said all that so *you* would know why it's so important to me."

My brain is too tired to even analyze his comment. "Either way," I say. "I know it was hard for you . . . telling us everything like that. Thank you."

We watch as a car passes by and pulls into the driveway next to us. A woman gets out, followed by two girls. They're all carrying pumpkins.

"You know, I don't know a single person on this whole street other than you and Caulder," I say.

He directs his gaze to the house that the three people just entered. "That's Erica. She's been married to her husband, Gus, for about twenty years, I think. They have two daughters, both teenagers. The older one is who babysits Caulder sometimes.

"The couple to the right of Caulder and me have been here the longest, Bob and Melinda. Their son just joined the military. They were great after my parents died. Melinda cooked for us every day for months. She still brings something over about once a week.

"The house over there?" He points down the street. "He's the one renting your house to you. His name is Scott. He owns six of the houses on this street alone. He's a good guy, but his renters come and go a lot. Those are about the only people I know anymore."

I look at all the houses along the street. They're all so similar, and I can't help trying to imagine the differences of all the families inside the homes. I wonder if any of *them* are hiding secrets? If any of them are falling in love. Or out of love. Are they happy? Sad? Scared? Broke? Lonely? Do they appreciate what they have? Do Gus and Erica appreciate their health? Does Scott appreciate his supplemental rental income? Because every bit of it, every last bit of it, is fleeting. Nothing is permanent. The only thing any of us have in common is the inevitable. We'll all eventually die.

"There was this one girl," Will says. "She moved into a house on the street a while back. I still remember the moment I saw her pull up in the U-Haul. She was so confident in that thing. It was a hundred times bigger than her, yet she backed it right up without even asking for help. I watched as she put it in park and propped her leg up on the dash, like driving a U-Haul was something she did every day. Piece of cake.

"I had to leave for work but Caulder had already run across the street. He was imaginary sword-fighting with the little boy that had been in the U-Haul. I was just going to yell at him to come get in the car, but there was something about that girl. I just had to meet her. I walked across the street, but she never even noticed me. She was watching her brother play with Caulder with this distant look on her face.

"I stood beside the U-Haul, and I just watched her. I stared at her while she looked on with the saddest look in her eyes. I wanted to know what she was thinking about, what was going on in her head. What had made her so sad? I wanted to hug her so bad. When she finally got out of the U-Haul and I introduced myself to her, it took all I had to let go of her hand. I wanted to hold on to it forever. I wanted to let her know that she wasn't alone. Whatever burden it was that she was carrying around, I wanted to carry it *for* her."

I lean my head on his shoulder, and he puts his arm around me.

"I wish I could, Lake. I wish I could take it all away. Unfortunately, that's not how it works. It doesn't just go away. That's what your mom is trying to tell you. She needs you to accept it, and she needs for Kel to know, too. You need to give that to her."

"I know, Will. I just can't. Not yet. I'm not ready to deal with it yet."

He pulls me to him and hugs me. "You'll never be ready for it, Lake. No one ever is." He lets go of me and walks away. And he's right again, but I don't care this time.

"LAKE? CAN I come in?" Mom says from outside the bedroom door.

"It's open," I say.

She walks in and shuts my door behind her. She's got her scrubs on now. She sits on the bed next to me as I continue to write in my notebook.

"What are you writing?" she asks.

"A poem."

"For school?"

"No, for me."

"I didn't know you wrote poetry." She tries to peek over my shoulder at it.

"I don't, really. If we read our poetry at Club N9NE we're exempt from the final. I'm thinking about doing one, but I don't know. The thought of getting up there in front of all those people makes me nervous."

"Push your boundaries, Lake. That's what they're there for."

I flip the poem upside down and sit up. "So, what's up?"

She smiles at me and reaches to my face and tucks my hair behind my ear.

"Not much," she says. "I just had a few minutes before I had to leave for work and thought we could talk. I wanted to let you know that it's my last night. I'm not working anymore after tonight."

I break our stare and lean forward and grab my pen. I put the cap back on it and close my notebook, tucking both the items inside my backpack.

"I'm still carving pumpkins, Mom."

She slowly inhales and stands up, hesitates, then walks back out the door.

15.

Forever I will move like the world that turns
beneath me
And when I lose my direction, I'll look up to the
sky
And when the black cloak drags upon the ground
I'll be ready to surrender, and remember
Well we're all in this together
If I live the life I'm given, I won't be scared to
die.

—THE AVETT BROTHERS,
"ONCE AND FUTURE CARPENTER"

WILL WALKS INTO THE CLASSROOM CARRYING A SMALL projector. He sets it on the desk and begins hooking it up to his laptop.

"What are we doing today, Mr. Cooper?" Gavin asks.

Will continues to prepare the projector as he responds to Gavin. "I want to show you why you should write poetry." He swings the plug around his desk and inserts it into the outlet on the wall.

"I know why people write poetry," Javi says. "Because they're a bunch of emotional saps with nothin' better to do than whine about ex-girlfriends and dead dogs."

"You're wrong, Javi," I say. "That's called country music."

Everyone laughs, including Will. He sits at his desk and turns the laptop on and glances at Javi. "So what? If it makes someone feel better to write a poem about their dead dog, then great. Let them. What if some girl broke your heart, Javi, and you decided to vent with a pen and paper? That's your business."

"That's fair," Javi says. "People are free to write what they want to write about. But the thing that bothers me is, what if the person who writes it doesn't want to relive it? What if a dude performs a slam about a bad breakup, but then he gets over it and moves on? He falls in love with some other chick, but now there's probably this YouTube video floating around on the Internet of him talking all sad about how his heart got broke. That sucks. If you perform it, or even write it down, someday you'll have to relive it."

Will stops fidgeting with the projector and stands up and turns to the board. He grabs a piece of chalk, writes something, and then steps aside.

The Avett Brothers

Will points to the name on the board. "Has anyone heard of them?" He looks at me and gives his head a slight shake, indicating he doesn't want me to speak up.

"Sounds familiar," someone says from the back of the room.

"Well," he says as he paces the room. "They're famous philosophers who speak and write extremely wise, thought-provoking words of wisdom."

I try to stifle my laugh. He's mostly right, though.

"They were asked about this once. I believe they were doing a *reading*. Someone asked them a question about their *poetry*, and whether it was hard having to relive their words each time they performed. Their reply was that although they had ideally moved *beyond* that—from the person or event that inspired their words at that point in time—it doesn't mean someone listening to them wasn't *in* that.

"So? So *what* if the heartache you wrote last year isn't what you're feeling today. It may be exactly what the person in the front row is feeling. What you're feeling now, and the person you may reach with your words five years from now—that's why you write poetry."

He flips on the overhead projector and I immediately recognize the words projected onto the wall. It's the piece he performed at the slam on our date. His piece about death.

"See this? I wrote this piece two years ago, after my parents died. I was angry. I was hurt. I wrote down *exactly* what I was feeling. When I read it now, I don't share those same feelings. Do I regret writing it? No. Because there's a chance that someone in this very room may relate to this. It might mean something to them."

He moves his mouse and the projector zooms in, highlighting one of the lines of his poem.

> People don't like to **talk** about death because
> it makes them **sad**.

"You never know, someone in this very room might relate to this. Does talking about death make you sad? Of course it does. Death sucks. It's not a fun thing to talk about. But sometimes, you *need* to talk about it."

I know what he's doing. I fold my arms across my chest and glare at him as he looks directly at me. He glances back to his computer, highlighting another line.

> If *only* they had been **prepared**, **accepted** the
> **inevitable**, laid out their **plans**,

"What about this one? My parents weren't prepared to *die*. I was *angry* at them for this. I was left with bills, debt, and a *child*. But what if they'd had warning? A chance to discuss it, to lay out their plans? If talking about death wasn't so easy to avoid while they were alive, then maybe I wouldn't have had such a hard time dealing with it after they died."

He's looking directly at me as he zooms in on another line.

understood that it *wasn't* just *their* lives at hand.

"Everyone assumes they have at least one more day. If my parents had any clue what was about to happen to them before it happened, they would have done everything in their *power* to prepare us. *Everything.* It's not that they weren't thinking about *us*, it's that they weren't thinking about *death*."

He highlights the last line of his poem.

Death. The only thing inevitable in *life*.

I look at the phrase and I read it. I read it again. I read it again, and again, and again. I read it until the end of the class period, after everyone around me has left. Everyone but Will.

He's sitting at his desk, watching me. Waiting for me to understand.

"I get it, Will," I finally whisper. "I get it. In the first line, when you said that death was the only thing inevitable in life . . . you emphasized the word *death*. But when you said it again at the end of the poem, you didn't emphasize the word death, you emphasized the word *life*. You put the *emphasis* on *life* at the end. I get it, Will. You're right.

She's not trying to prepare us for her *death*. She's trying to prepare us for her *life*. For what she has left of it."

He leans forward and turns the projector off. I grab my stuff, and I go home.

I SIT ON the edge of my mother's bed. She's asleep in the center of it. She doesn't have a side anymore, now that she sleeps in it alone.

She's still wearing her scrubs. When she wakes up and takes them off, it'll be the last time she takes off a pair of scrubs. I wonder if that's why she's still wearing them: because she realizes this too.

I watch the rhythm of her body as she breathes. With every breath that she inhales, I can hear the struggle of her lungs within her chest. The struggle of lungs that failed her.

I reach over and stroke her hair. When I do, a few of the strands fall off in my fingers. I pull my hand back and slowly wrap them around my finger as I walk to my room and pick my purple hair clip up off the floor. I open the clip and place the strands of hair inside and snap it shut. I place the clip under my bedroom pillow and I go back to my mother's room. I slide into the bed beside her and wrap my arms around her. She finds my hand and we interlock fingers as we talk without saying a single word.

16.

" "

—THE AVETT BROTHERS,

"COMPLAINTE D'UN MATELOT MOURANT"

AFTER MY MOTHER FALLS BACK TO SLEEP, I GO TO THE grocery store. Kel's favorite food is basagna. It's how he used to say lasagna, so we still call it basagna. I gather everything I need for the meal and I go back home and start cooking.

"Smells like basagna," Mom says as she comes out of her bedroom. She's in regular clothes now. She must have taken her scrubs off for the last time.

"Yep. I figured we could make Kel his favorite tonight. He'll need it."

She walks to the sink and washes her hands before she starts helping me layer the noodles. "So, I guess we finally stopped carving pumpkins?" she asks.

"Yep," I reply. "The pumpkins have all been carved."

She laughs.

"Mom? Before he gets here, we need to talk. About what's going to happen to him."

"I *want* to, Lake. I *want* to talk about it."

"Why don't you want him to be with me? Do you not think I'm capable? That I wouldn't make a good mom?"

She layers the last of the noodles as I cover them with sauce.

"Lake, I don't think that at all. I just want you to be able to live your life. I've spent the entire last eighteen years raising you, teaching you everything I know. It's supposed to be time for you to go screw up. Make mistakes. Not raise a child."

"But sometimes life doesn't happen in chronological order," I say. "You're a prime example of that. If it did, you wouldn't die until you were supposed to. Until you were seventy-seven or so, I think. That's the average age of death."

She laughs and shakes her head.

"Seriously, Mom. I want him. I *want* to raise him. He'll want to stay with me—you know he will. You have to give us the choice. We haven't had a choice in any of this. You have to give us this one."

"Okay," she says.

"Okay? Okay you'll think about it? Or *okay*, okay?"

"*Okay*, okay."

I hug her. I hug her tighter than I've ever hugged her before.

"Lake?" she says. "You're getting basagna sauce all over me."

I pull away and realize I'm still holding the spatula and it's dripping all over her back.

"WHY CAN'T HE come over?" Kel asks after I pull in the driveway and send Caulder home.

"I told you already. Mom needs to talk to us."

We walk inside the house and Mom is putting the basagna in the oven.

"Mom, guess what?" Kel says as he runs to the kitchen.

"What, sweetie?"

"Our school is having a costume contest on Halloween. The winner gets fifty bucks!"

"Fifty bucks? Wow. Have you decided what you want to be yet?"

"Not yet." He walks over to the bar and throws his backpack down.

"Did your sister tell you we're all having a talk tonight?"

"Yeah. She didn't have to, though. We're having basagna."

My mother and I both look at him.

"Every time we have basagna it's bad news. Y'all

cooked basagna when Grandpa died. Y'all cooked basagna when y'all told me Dad was dead. Y'all cooked basagna when y'all told me we were moving to Michigan. Y'all are cooking basagna right now. Either someone's dying or we're moving back to Texas."

My mom looks at me wide-eyed, questioning our timing. He seems to have opened it up for an even earlier discussion. She walks over to him and sits down. I follow suit.

"You're very observant, that's for sure," she says.

"So, which one is it?" he asks, looking up at her.

She places her hand on the side of his face and strokes it. "I have lung cancer, Kel."

He immediately throws his arms around her and hugs her. She strokes the back of his head, but he doesn't cry. They are both silent for a while as she waits for him to speak.

"Are you gonna die?" he finally asks. His voice is muffled because his head is buried in her shirt.

"I am, sweetie. But I don't know when. Until then, though, we're going to spend a lot of time together. I quit my job today so that I can spend more time with you."

I wasn't sure how he would react. At only nine years old, he probably won't grasp the true reality of it until after she actually passes away. My father's death was sudden and unexpected, which naturally prompted a more dramatic reaction from him.

"But what about after you die? Who are we gonna go live with?"

"Your sister is an adult now. You're going to live with her."

"But I wanna stay here, by Caulder," he says as he lifts his head from her shirt and looks at me. "Layken, are you gonna make me move back to Texas with you?"

Up until this very second, I had every intention of moving back to Texas.

"No, Kel. We're staying right here."

Kel sighs, soaking in everything he's just been told. "Are you scared, Mom?" he asks her.

"Not anymore," she says. "I've had a lot of time to accept it. In fact, I feel lucky. Unlike your dad, at least I've got warning. Now I get to spend more time with the two of you here at home."

He lets go of my mother and puts his elbows on the bar.

"You have to promise me something, Layken."

"Okay," I respond.

"Don't ever make basagna again."

We all laugh. We all *laugh*. This was the hardest thing my mother and I have ever had to do, and we're *laughing*. Kel is amazing.

AN HOUR LATER, we have a huge spread of basagna, bread sticks, and salad. There's no way we're eating all of this.

"Kel, why don't you go see if Caulder and Will have

eaten yet," my mother says as she eyes the food with me. Kel darts out the door.

She sets two more places at the table while I fill drinks with tea.

"We need to talk to Will about helping out with Kel," I tell her.

"Will? Why?"

"Because I want to take you to your treatments from now on. It's too much for Brenda. I can miss a day of school every now and then, or we can go when I get out."

"Okay." She looks at me and smiles.

Kel and Caulder come running through the front door, followed by Will a moment later.

"Kel said we're having basagna?" Will asks, hesitantly.

"Yes, sir," my mother says as she scoops basagna onto plates.

"What *is* basagna? Bologna lasagna?"

He looks scared.

"It's basagna. And it's the last time we'll ever have it, so you better enjoy it," she says.

Will walks to the table and waits for Mom and I to sit before he takes his seat.

We pass around bread sticks and salad until everyone's plates are filled. And just like last night, Kel is the first one to make it awkward.

"My mom's dying, Caulder."

Will glances at me and I give him a half smile, letting him know we talked.

"When she dies, I'm gonna live with Layken. Just like you live with Will. It's like we'll be the same. All of our parents will be dead, and we'll live with our brother and sister."

"Cool. That's crazy," Caulder says.

"Caulder!" Will yells.

"It's fine, Will," my mom says. "It is kind of crazy if you think about it from the perspective of a nine-year-old."

"Mom," Kel says. "What about your bedroom? Can I have it? It's bigger than mine."

"No," I say. "It's got a bathroom in it. I get her bedroom."

Kel looks defeated. I don't budge, though. I'm getting the bedroom with the bathroom.

"Kel, you can have my computer," my mother says.

"Sweet!"

I look at Will, hoping this conversation isn't weirding him out, but he's laughing. This is exactly what he was hoping would happen. *Acceptance.*

Over dinner, we all discuss what will happen over the next few months and make arrangements for Caulder and Kel while Mom receives her treatments. Will agreed to let Kel come over whenever he needed to and said he'll continue to take them to school. I'll be picking them up on the way home every day, unless I'm at a treatment with

Mom. She made Will agree to let her cook them supper most nights in return for his help. The entire night was a success. I feel like together, we all just punched death square in the face.

"I'm exhausted," my mom says. "I need to take a shower and get to bed."

She walks into the kitchen where Will is washing dishes at the sink. She puts her arms around him and hugs him from behind. "Thanks, Will. For everything."

He turns around and hugs her back.

When she walks past me on her way to her bedroom, she purposefully nudges me with her shoulder. She doesn't speak a word but I know what she's hinting at—she's giving me her approval. Again. Too bad it doesn't count.

I wipe the table off and walk to the sink to rinse out the rag.

"Eddie's birthday is Thursday. I don't know what I should get her."

"Well, I know what you *shouldn't* get her," he says.

"Believe me, I know," I laugh. "I think Gavin's taking her out Thursday night. Maybe I'll do something for her on Friday."

"Oh, speaking of Friday. Do you guys need me to watch Kel? I forgot Caulder and I go to Detroit this weekend."

"No, you're fine. Family stuff?"

"Yeah. We stay with our grandparents one weekend a

month. Kind of a truce we worked out for me stealing him away in the middle of the night."

"That's fair enough," I say. I reach over to the sink and unplug the drain.

"So you won't be at the slam Thursday?" he asks.

"No. We'll watch Caulder that night, though. Just send him over after school."

He puts the last dish in the strainer and dries his hands on the towel. "It's pretty weird, isn't it? How everything worked out? You guys moving here when you did? Kel and Caulder finding each other, right when Kel probably needed a best friend the most? Him taking your mother's news so well? It just all worked out."

He turns toward me and smiles. "I'm proud of you, Lake. You did good today." He plants one of his lingering kisses on my forehead, then walks to the living room.

"Caulder still needs to take a shower; I guess we need to go. I'll see you tomorrow," he says.

"Yeah. See ya."

I sigh as I think about the one thing that *isn't* on his mind. The one incredibly huge thing that *didn't* work out: us.

I'm starting to accept it. That we won't be together. That we *can't* be together. Especially the last two nights he's been here. It really feels like we've finally transitioned. There are definitely still moments, but none we're not able to overcome. It's only October, and he'll be my teacher until June. That's still eight long months. When I look at the shift my life has made in the past eight months, I can't fathom what my life will be eight months from now. When I lie down and close my eyes, I make a resolution. Will is not going to be my first priority anymore. I'm putting my mother first, Kel second, and *life* third.

Finally. He no longer has a hold on me.

"EDDIE, WILL YOU go grab me a chocolate milk, babe? I forgot to get one." Gavin is giving Eddie puppy-dog eyes. Eddie rolls her eyes and gets up. As soon as she leaves the table, he turns toward us and starts whispering.

"Tomorrow night. Getty's. Six o'clock. Bring a pink balloon. And we're going to the slam afterward."

"Gavin, are you crazy? That's not funny; she'll be pissed," I whisper.

"Just trust me."

She's back at the table with the chocolate milk. "Here. You owe me fifty cents."

"I owe you my heart," Gavin says as he takes the milk.

She slaps him lightly across the head. "Oh, grow a pair! You're such a sap," she says, right before she kisses his cheek.

I RELUCTANTLY WALK into Getty's Pizza with a pink balloon in my hand. Gavin and Nick are gathered in the back of the room at a booth. He motions for me to join them. There are so many pink balloons. She's going to be pissed.

Gavin grabs my balloon and writes something on it with a big marker. "Here," Gavin says as he hands me the fistful of balloons. "Take all these and go to the back by the bathrooms. I'll come get you when it's time; she'll be here soon."

He shoves me toward the bathroom before I have a chance to object. I stand in a corner in the hallway between the men's room and the janitor's closet. I look up at all the balloons, and that's when I notice there are names written on each one of them.

Moments later, an older gentleman walks down the hall toward me.

"Are you Layken?" he asks.

"Yes," I reply.

"I'm Joel, Eddie's foster dad."

"Oh, hey."

"Gavin wants you out front; I'll take the balloons now. Eddie's out there. She thinks I went to the bathroom, so don't say anything about the balloons."

"Uh, okay." I hand him the balloons and walk back to the table.

"Layken! You came! Guys, this is so sweet," Eddie says. She starts to sit at the booth, when Gavin pulls her back up.

"We're not eating yet. We need to go outside."

"Outside? But it's cold out there."

"Come on," he says, pulling her toward the door.

We all follow Gavin outside and stand next to Eddie. I look at Nick but he shrugs, implying he doesn't know what's going on, either. Gavin pulls a piece of paper out of his pocket and stands in front of Eddie.

"I didn't write this letter, Eddie. But I was told to read it."

Eddie looks at us and smiles, trying to gain hints from our expressions. We can't give her any, because we don't know.

It was July 4th when you came to me. Independence Day. You were fourteen. You burst in the door and went straight to the refrigerator, telling me you needed a Sprite. I didn't have any Sprite. You told me it was okay, and you grabbed a Dr Pepper instead. You freaked me out. I told the caseworker there was no way I could keep you. I'd never fostered a teenager before. She told me she would find you somewhere to go the next day, that she just needed me to keep you for the night.

I was so nervous. I didn't know what to say to a fourteen-year-old girl. I didn't know what kinds of things they liked, what shows they watched. I was clueless. But you made it so easy. You were so worried about making me feel comfortable.

Later that night, when it was dark outside—we

heard fireworks. You grabbed my hand and pulled
me off the couch and dragged me outside. We lay
on the grass in the front yard, and we watched the
sky. You didn't shut up. You told me all about the
family you just came from, the family before that,
and the family before that. The whole time you were
talking, I was listening. Listening to this little girl,
so full of life. So full and enthralled with a life that
tried so hard to knock her down.

Eddie gasps when she sees Joel in the window of the
restaurant with dozens of pink balloons. He walks outside and stands beside Gavin. Gavin continues reading
the letter.

I've never been able to give you much. Other
than eventually teaching you how to park, I've
never even taught you very much. But you've
taught me more than you will ever know. And on
this very special birthday, your eighteenth birthday,
you no longer belong to the state of Michigan. And
as of right now, you legally no longer belong to me.
You no longer belong to any of the following people
that once held claim to you and your past.

Joel starts reading names out loud as he releases balloons one by one. Eddie is crying as we all watch the

balloons slowly disappear into the darkness. He continues releasing them, until all twenty-nine siblings' and all thirteen parents' names have been read and released.

He still has one pink balloon remaining in his hand. Across the front of it, in big black letters, it says DAD.

Gavin folds the paper up and takes a step back as Joel walks toward Eddie.

"I hope for your birthday you'll accept this gift," Joel says as he hands her the pink balloon. "I want to be your dad, Eddie. I want to be your family for the rest of your life."

Eddie hugs him and they cry. The rest of us slowly walk back inside Getty's so they can have their moment.

"Oh my god, I need a napkin," I sniff as I search for something to wipe my eyes. I grab some napkins off the counter when I look at Nick and Gavin. They're both crying. I grab a few more napkins for them and we walk back to our booth.

17.

If I get murdered in the city
don't go revengin' in my name
One person dead from such is plenty
No need to go get locked away.

—THE AVETT BROTHERS,
"MURDER IN THE CITY"

I CAN HONESTLY SAY I FEEL LIKE I'VE MOVED THROUGH the five stages of grief in every aspect of my life.

I have accepted my father's death. I accepted his death months before we even moved to Michigan. I've accepted my mother's fate. I realize she hasn't died yet, and that the stages of grief will recommence when she does. But I know it won't be as hard.

I've accepted living in Michigan. The song I listened to on repeat at Will's house was called "Weight of Lies." A portion of the lyrics say,

The weight of lies will bring you down, follow you to every town 'cause

nothing happens here that doesn't happen there.

Every time the song looped, all I heard was the part about the lies—and how they weigh you down. Tonight, as I drive toward Detroit in my Jeep, I know what those words really mean. It's not just *lies* they're referring to. It's *life*. You can't run to another town, another place, another state. Whatever it is you're running from—it goes with you. It stays with you until you find out how to confront it.

Whatever it is I was hoping to run back to Texas from, it would eventually make its way back to me. So here I am in Ypsilanti, Michigan—where I'll stay. And I'm okay with that.

I've accepted the situation with Will. I don't blame him at all for what he chose. Sure, I had fantasies of him sweeping me off my feet, telling me he doesn't need a *career* when he has *love*. The reality of it is, if he had put his feelings for me first, it would've been hard to accept that he could so easily throw away the things that are the most important to him. It would have said a lot less for his character. So I don't blame him, I respect him. And someday, when I'm ready, I'll thank him.

I PULL UP to the club a little after eight o'clock. Gavin had a surprise for Eddie, so they took a detour, said they'd be here late. The parking lot is unusually crowded, so I have to take a spot in the back of the building. When I get out of the car, I take a deep breath and prepare myself. I'm not sure when it was that I decided I was going to perform tonight, but I'm having second thoughts.

My mother's words linger in my head as I make my way to the front door. *"Push your boundaries, Lake, that's what they're there for."*

I can do this. They're just words. Repeat them and you're done. It's that simple.

I walk in the door a few minutes late. I can tell the sac is about to perform, because you could hear a pin drop. I sneak in and quietly make my way to the back of the room. I don't want to draw attention to myself, so I slide into an empty booth. I take my phone out to turn the volume down and text Eddie letting her know where I'm sitting. That's when it happens; I hear him.

Will is standing in front of the microphone on the stage, performing a piece as the sacrifice.

I used to *love* the ocean.

Everything about her.

Her coral *reefs*, her white *caps*, her roaring *waves*, the *rocks* they *lap*, her *pirate* legends and *mermaid* tails,

Treasures *lost* and treasures *held* . . .

And *ALL*

Of her *fish*

In the *sea*.

Yes, I used to *love* the ocean,

Everything about her.

The way she would *sing* me to *sleep* as I *lay* in my *bed*

then *wake* me with a *force*

That I *soon* came to *dread*.

Her *fables*, her *lies*, her *misleading* eyes,

I'd drain her *dry*

If I *cared* enough to.

I used to *love* the ocean,

Everything about her.

Her coral *reefs*, her *whitecaps*, her roaring *waves*, the

rocks they *lap*, her *pirate* legends and *mermaid* tails,

treasures *lost* and treasures *held*.

And *ALL*

Of her *fish*

In the *sea*.

Well, if you've ever tried *navigating* your *sailboat*

through her stormy *seas*, you would *realize* that

her *whitecaps* are your *enemies*. If you've ever tried

swimming ashore when your *leg* gets a *cramp* and

you just had a *huge meal* of *In-N-Out* burgers that's

weighing you down, and her *roaring waves* are

knocking the *wind* out of you, filling your *lungs* with

water as you *flail* your arms, trying to get *someone's*

attention, but your friends

just

wave

back at you?

And if you've ever grown up with *dreams* in your *head*

about *life*, and how one of these days you would pirate

your *own* ship and have your *own* crew and that *all* of

the mermaids

would *love*

only

you?

Well, you would *realize* . . .

As I eventually realized . . .

That all the *good* things about her?

All the *beautiful?*

It's not *real.*

It's *fake.*

So you *keep* your *ocean,*

I'll take the *Lake.*

Air. Or water. I don't know which one I need. I slide out of the booth and head toward the front door but make a beeline for the bathroom. I just need silence.

When I open the door to the bathroom, the stalls are empty. There's a girl washing her hands at the only available sink, so I decide to wait on the water. I pick the big stall. I lock it behind me and lean up against the door.

Did that just really happen? Does he know I'm even here? No, he doesn't. I told him I wasn't coming. He didn't intend for me to hear it. Even so, he *wrote* it. He said himself that he writes what he's feeling. Oh my god, he *loves* me. Will Cooper is *in love* with me.

I've known all along how he feels about me. I can see it in the way he looks at me. But to hear his words and the emotions behind them—how he said my name. How am I supposed to face him? I'm not. He still doesn't know I'm here. I just have to leave. I need to leave before he sees me.

I open the bathroom door and scan the area, but I don't see him. Luckily, another performer is onstage, so most of the eyes are glued to the front of the room. I slip through the entryway and out the front door.

"Layken! Look what Gavin got me!" Eddie is making her way inside, holding her hair back, wanting me to look at her ears.

"Eddie, I've got to go."

Her smile fades.

"I'll call you later." I brush past her without looking at the earrings. "You didn't see me!" I yell behind me as I go.

I make my way around the building and smash into Javi as he's rounding the corner. *Good grief!* Is the whole class here? Someone's going to let it slip that I was here. I don't want Will to know I saw him.

"Hey, what's the hurry?" he asks as I slip between him and the wall.

"I gotta go. I'll see you tomorrow." I quickly walk away. I don't have time for chitchat. I just want to get in my Jeep and pull out of this parking lot as soon as I can.

"Wait, I'll walk you to your car," he says as he catches up to me.

"I'm fine, Javi. Go ahead and go inside, they've already started."

"Layken, we're in Detroit. You're parked behind a club. I'm walking you to your car."

"Fine. But walk fast."

"What's your hurry?" he asks as we make our way to the rear of the building.

"I'm just tired. I need sleep." I slow down, feeling confident that Will didn't see me.

"There's a café down the road. Want to go grab some coffee?" he asks.

"No, thanks. I don't need caffeine, I need my bed."

When we get to my Jeep, I reach down to grab my keys out of my—shit! My purse. I left my purse in the booth.

"Shit!" I say. I kick at the gravel in front of me. My shoe loosens a piece of rock and it flicks against the door of my Jeep.

"What's wrong?" he asks.

"My purse. I left my keys and my purse inside." I fold my arms across my chest and lean against the Jeep.

"It's not that big a deal. We'll go back inside and get them."

"No, I don't want to. Would you mind getting them for me?" I smile at him, hoping it will be enough.

"Layken, you don't need to stay back here by yourself."

"Fine. I'll just text Eddie to bring it out. Do you have your phone?"

He pats his pockets. "No, it's in my truck. Come on, you can use it." Javi says this as he reaches down and takes my hand, leading me toward his truck. He unlocks his door and reaches inside for his phone. "It's dead." He plugs it into the charger. "Give it a couple minutes to get a charge, then you can call her."

"Thanks," I say as I lean against his truck and wait.

He stands next to me while we wait for the phone to charge. "It's snowing again," Javi says as he wipes something off my arm.

I look up and see the falling flakes contrasted against the black sky. I guess we're finally about to see what a Michigan winter really looks like.

I turn to face Javi. I was about to ask him something about snow tires, or plows, but it slips my mind as soon as his hands grasp my face and his tongue makes its way into my mouth. I turn my face and push against his chest with my hands. When he feels my resistance, his face backs away from mine, but his body is still pressed against me, pushing me against the cold metal of his truck.

"What?" he says. "I thought you wanted me to kiss you."

"No, Javi!" I'm still pushing against him with my hands but he doesn't budge.

"Come on," he says with a smug grin on his face. "You didn't leave your *keys* inside. You *want* this." His mouth encircles mine again, and my pulse starts to race in my chest. It's not the same reaction I get when Will makes my pulse race. This time it's more like fight-or-flight mode. I try to scream at him, but his hands are pulling my face into his so hard that I can't catch a breath. I try to move, but he's using his body to pin me against his truck, making it impossible for me to break free.

I close my eyes. *Think*, Layken. *Think*.

Just as I'm about to bite down on his lip, Javi pulls away from me. But he keeps going backward. Someone is dragging him away from me. He falls to the ground, and Will straddles him, grabs hold of his shirt, and sends a blow straight to Javi's jaw. Javi falls back to the ground but turns over and pushes off against it, causing Will to stumble backward.

"Stop!" I scream.

Will is knocked to the ground when Javi returns the punch. I'm afraid Javi is going to hit him a second time, so I throw myself between them just as Javi swings a punch intended for Will—straight into my back. I fall forward and land on Will. I try to catch a breath, but I have none. I can't inhale.

"Lake," Will says, rolling me onto the ground next to him. His worry is fleeting, however, and rage fills his eyes. He grabs the door handle of the car next to us and starts to pull himself up.

"I didn't mean to hit you, Layken," Javi says, walking toward me.

I'm on the ground so I don't see what happens next, but I hear a smack, and I can see Javi's feet are no longer planted on the ground. I look up just as Will leans over Javi and delivers another punch.

"Will, get off him!" Gavin yells. Gavin is pulling Will back and they both fall to the ground.

Eddie rushes to my side and pulls me upright. "Layken, what happened?" She has her arms around me, and I'm clutching my chest. I know I was hit in the back, but it feels like my lungs are concrete. I'm gasping for air, and I can't answer her.

Will rustles out of Gavin's grip and stands up. He walks to me and takes my hand as Eddie scoots out of his way. He pulls me up and puts my arm around his shoulder, wraps his other arm around my waist, and starts walking me forward.

"I'm taking you home," is all he says.

"Wait," Eddie yells as she circles to the front of us. "I found your purse."

I reach out and take it from her and attempt to smile. Her hand goes up to her ear in the shape of a phone and she mouths, "Call me."

Will assists me into his car and I lean back against the seat. My lungs have refilled with air, but every breath I take feels like I've got a knife protruding from my back. I close my eyes and focus on inhaling and exhaling through my nose as we drive away.

Neither one of us speaks. Me, because I can't. Will

because—I don't know why. We drive in silence until we're almost to the Ypsilanti city limits.

Will jerks the car to the side of the road and throws it in Park. He punches the steering wheel before he gets out of the car and slams the door. His figure is illuminated by the headlights of the car as he walks away from the vehicle, sporadically kicking at the ground and cursing obscenities. He finally stops and stands with his hands on his hips. His head is leaned back and he's looking up at the sky, letting the snow fall on his face. He stands like this for a while until he finally makes his way back to the car, sits down, and calmly shuts his door. He puts the car in gear, and we continue to drive in silence.

I'm able to walk, my breathing has returned to normal, and the knife in my back feels more like a lump now. Regardless, he still assists me into his house.

"Lie down on the couch, I'll get some ice," he says.

I do as he says. I ease myself stomach first onto the couch and close my eyes, wondering what in the world just happened to tonight.

I feel his hand on the couch when he kneels down next to me. "Will!" I gasp when I open my eyes and actually see his face. "Your eye." There's a trail of blood running down his neck from a gash above his eye.

"It's fine. I'll be fine," he says, leaning over me. "Do you mind?" His hands grasp the bottom edge of my shirt.

I shake my head.

He pulls my shirt up over my back and I feel something cold compress against my skin. He positions the ice pack on top of the injury, then stands and opens the front door, shutting it behind him when he leaves.

He *left*. He just left without saying a word. I lie there for a few more minutes, expecting him to return right away, but he doesn't. I roll onto my side and let the pack of ice fall onto the couch. I ease my shirt back down and prepare myself to stand up just as the door bursts open and my mother runs in.

"Lake? Sweetie, are you okay?" She throws her arms around me. Will walks in behind her.

"Mom," I say weakly. I return her hug and cry.

"IT'S FINE, MOM, really." She's tucking me into my bed, asking me how my back feels for the one hundredth time in the ten minutes that I've been home. She smiles and strokes my hair. That's what I'm going to miss the most about her. The way she strokes my hair and looks at me with so much love in her eyes.

"Will says you got hit in the back. Who hit you?"

I wince as I push myself up against my pillow. "Javi. He's in my class. He was trying to punch Will, but I got in the way."

"Why was he trying to punch Will?"

"Because Will punched *him*. Javi walked me to my Jeep when I left the club. He thought I wanted him to kiss me. I was trying to push him off of me—I couldn't get him to stop. The next thing I know Will's on top of him, punching him."

"That's awful, Lake. I'm so sorry." She leans forward and kisses my forehead.

"It's fine, Mom. I'm fine. I just need some sleep."

She strokes my head again before she stands up and flicks the lights off. "What about Will? What's he going to do?" she asks before she closes the door.

"I don't know," I reply. Because at first I think her question is referring to what he's going to do about Javi. But after she shuts the door, I realize she's asking what he's going to do about his *job*.

I lie awake for hours after that, dissecting the situation. We weren't on school grounds. He was defending me. Maybe Javi won't say anything. Will *did* throw the first punch, though. And the third. And the fourth. And probably would have thrown the fifth if Gavin hadn't walked up when he did. I try to recall every small detail of the entire night, in case I'm asked to defend his actions tomorrow.

THE NEXT DAY, I wake up to find Caulder eating cereal in my kitchen with Kel.

"Hey. My brother can't take us today. Says he has something he has to do."

"What does he have to do?"

Caulder shrugs. "I dunno. He brought your Jeep

home this morning. Then he left again." A spoonful of Froot Loops goes into his mouth.

I CAN BARELY sit through my first two classes. Eddie and I spend second period writing notes back and forth. I told her everything that happened last night. Everything except for Will's poem.

I feel like I'm floating when we walk to third period. Almost like in my dreams when I'm hovering above myself, watching myself walk. I feel like I'm not in control of my actions, I'm just observing them as they are carried out. Eddie opens the door and walks in first. I follow slowly behind her and make my way through the classroom. Will isn't here yet. Neither is Javi. I inhale and I take my seat. The bustling of the conversation among the other classmates is briefly interrupted by a crackling over the intercom.

"Layken Cohen, please report to administration."

I immediately swing around and look at Eddie. She gives me a half-hearted smile and a thumbs-up. She's just as nervous as I am.

There are several people in the office when I walk in. I recognize the principal, Mr. Murphy, speaking with two men I don't recognize. When he notices me walk in, he nods and motions for me to follow him through the door. When I enter the room, Will is seated with his arms folded at the table. He doesn't look up at me. This doesn't look good.

"Ms. Cohen, please take a seat," Mr. Murphy says. He seats himself at the head, opposite Will.

I choose the chair closest to me.

"This is Mr. Cruz, Javier's father," says Mr. Murphy, motioning toward one of the men I didn't recognize.

Mr. Cruz is sitting across from me. He stands slightly and reaches across the table and shakes my hand.

"This is Officer Venturelli," he says of the other man.

He follows suit and leans across the table, shaking my hand.

"I'm sure you know why you're here. It is our understanding that there was an incident involving Mr. Cooper that occurred off of school grounds," he says, pausing in case I need to object. I don't.

"We would appreciate it if you could tell us your version of events."

I glance toward Will and he gives me an ever so slight nod, letting me know he wants me to tell the truth. So I do. For ten minutes I explain in honest detail everything that happened last night. Everything except for Will's poem.

When I'm finished with the details, and the questions have all been asked, I'm released to return to class. As I get up to leave, Mr. Cruz calls after me.

"Ms. Cohen?"

I turn and look at him.

"I just want to say I'm sorry. I apologize for my son's behavior."

"Thank you," I say. I turn and make my way back to the classroom.

A substitute is filling in for Will. She's an older lady whom I've seen in the halls before, so she must also be a teacher here. I quietly take my seat. I can't think about anything other than Will, and if I'm about to be the reason he loses his job.

When the bell rings, the class begins to file out, and I turn to Eddie.

"What happened?" she says.

I tell her what happened, and that I still don't know anything. I linger outside the classroom door for a while, waiting for Will to return, but he never does. During fourth period, I realize I'm not in the state of mind to learn anything, so I give myself the rest of the day off.

When I turn onto our street, Will's car is in his driveway. I pull my Jeep up to the curb and don't even bother pulling into the driveway. I throw it in park and quickly run across the street. As soon as I'm about to knock on the door, it swings open and Will is standing there with his satchel slung across his shoulder and his jacket on.

"What are you doing here?" he says with a surprised look on his face.

"I saw your car. What happened?"

He doesn't invite me in. Instead, he walks outside and locks the door behind him. "I resigned. They withdrew my contract." He continues walking toward his car.

"But you only have eight weeks left of student teaching. It wasn't your fault, Will. They can't do that!"

He shakes his head. "No, it's not like that. I wasn't fired. We just all thought it was best if I finished my student teaching at a different school, away from Javier. I've got a meeting with my faculty advisor in half an hour; that's where I'm headed." He opens his door and removes his jacket and satchel, throwing them into the passenger seat.

"But what about your job?" I ask as I hold on to the door, not wanting him to shut it. I have so many questions. "So you're saying you don't have an income now? What are you going to do?"

He smiles at me and emerges back out of the car and places his hands on my shoulders. "Layken, calm down. I'll figure it out. But right now, I've got to go." He gets back inside, shuts his door, and rolls down his window.

"If I'm not home in time, can Caulder stay with you guys after school?"

"Sure," I say.

"We're leaving pretty early to go to my grandparents' tomorrow. Can you make sure he doesn't eat any sugar? He needs to get to bed early," he says as he slowly backs out of the driveway.

"Sure," I say.

"And Layken? Calm down."

"Sure," I say again.

And he's gone. Just like that.

18.

I SPEND THE REST OF THE AFTERNOON HELPING MY mother clean. It keeps my mind occupied. She never once asks why I'm not at school. I guess she's leaving the mundane things up to me now. When it's time to pick Caulder and Kel up, Will still isn't home. I bring both of the boys back to the house, and we begin another discussion of Halloween costumes.

"I know what I want to be now," Kel says to my mother.

She is folding clothes in the living room. She lays a towel on the back of the couch and looks at Kel, "What are you going to be, sweetie?"

He smiles at her. "Your lung cancer," he says.

She is so used to the things that come out of Kel's mouth, she doesn't skip a beat. "Oh yeah? Do they sell those at Walmart?"

"I don't think so," he says, grabbing a drink out of the refrigerator. "Maybe you could make it. I want to be a lung."

"Hey," Caulder says. "Can I be the other lung?"

My mom laughs as she grabs a pen and paper off the bar and sits down. "Well, I guess we better figure out how to sew a pair of cancerous lungs."

Kel and Caulder flock to her and start spitting out ideas.

"Mom," I say flatly. "You're not."

She looks up from her sketch at me and smiles. "Lake, if my baby boy wants to be a cancerous lung for Halloween, then I'm going to make sure he's the best cancerous, tumor-ridden lung there is."

I roll my eyes and join them at the bar, writing down a list of the supplies we'll need.

AFTER WE RETURN from the store with the supplies and materials needed for the cancerous lung costumes, Will pulls up in his driveway.

"Will!" Caulder runs across the street and grabs his hand, pulling him toward our house. "Wait till you see this!"

Will helps my mother and me grab the supplies out of the trunk, and we all head inside.

"Guess what we're going to be? For Halloween?" Caulder is beaming as he stands in the kitchen, pointing at the supplies on the floor.

"Uh—"

"Julia's cancer!" Caulder says, excitedly.

Will raises his eyebrows and glances at my mother, who has just returned from her bedroom with a sewing machine. "You only live once, right?" She places the sewing machine on the bar.

"She's letting us make the tumors for the lungs," Kel says. "You wanna make one? I'll let you make the big one."

"Uh—"

"Kel," I say. "Will and Caulder can't help, they'll be out of town all weekend." I carry two of the sacks to the bar and start unpacking them.

"Actually," Will replies as he grabs the other sacks off the floor, "that was before I found out we were making lung cancer. I think we'll have to reschedule our trip."

Caulder runs over to Will and hugs him. "Thanks, Will. They're gonna need to measure me while they're making it anyway. I've been growing a lot."

And once again, for the third time this week, we're one big happy family.

WE HAVE MOST of the design worked out and need to take measurements for the pattern. "Where's your measuring tape?" I ask my mother.

"I don't know," she says. "I don't know if I have one, actually."

"Will has one; we can use his," I say. "Will, do you mind getting it?"

"I have measuring tape?" he asks.

"Yes, it's in your sewing kit," I say.

"I have a sewing kit?"

"It's in your laundry room." I can't believe he doesn't know this. I clean his house once, and I can tell him where everything is better than he can? "It's next to the sewing machine on the shelf behind your mother's patterns. I put them in chronological order according to pattern nu— never mind," I say as I stand up. "I'll just show you."

"You put his patterns in chronological order?" my mother asks, perplexed.

I turn back to her as we're headed to the door. "I was having a bad day."

Will and I head across the street and I use the opportunity to ask him about what happened with his internship. I didn't want to ask him in front of Caulder, because I wasn't sure if he had said anything to him.

"I got a slap on the wrist," he says as we walk inside.

"They told me since I was defending another student, they couldn't really hold it against me."

"That's good. What about your internship?" I say as I walk through the kitchen and into the laundry room, where I grab the sewing kit.

"Well, it's a little tricky. The only available ones they had are here in Ypsilanti, but they were all primary. My major is secondary, so I've been placed at a school in Detroit."

I pause what I'm doing and look at him.

"What's that mean? Are y'all moving?"

He sees the worry cross my face, and he laughs. "No, Lake, we're not moving. It's just for eight weeks. I'll be doing a lot of driving, though. I was actually going to talk to you and your mom about it later. I'm not going to be able to take the boys to school, or pick them up, either. I'll be gone a lot. I know this isn't a good time to ask for your help—"

"Stop it." I grab the tape measure and return the contents into the box. "You know we'll help."

Will follows me as I walk back to the laundry room and replace the sewing kit next to the sewing machine. My hand brushes against the patterns that are neatly stacked in chronological order as I recall all the cleaning and alphabetizing I did the previous weekend. Is it possible that I had a momentary lapse of sanity? I shake my head and reach over and flick off the light switch, when I run into

Will. He's leaning against the door frame with his head resting against the wall, watching me. It's dark now, but his face is slightly illuminated by the glow from the kitchen behind him.

A warm sensation flows through me, and I try not to get my hopes up. He's got that look in his eyes again.

"Last night," he whispers. "When I saw Javi kissing you—" His voice trails off, and he's silent for a moment. "I thought you were kissing him back."

It's hard when he's in such close proximity, but I do my best to focus and process his confession. If he thought I was allowing it to happen, then why did he pull Javi off of me? Why did he punch him? Then it hits me. Will wasn't *defending* me last night. He was *jealous*.

"Oh," is all I can say.

"I didn't know the whole story until this morning, when you told your version," he says as he continues to block my way, making me stand in the dark. He runs his hands through his hair and sighs.

"God, Lake. I can't tell you how pissed I was. I wanted to hurt him so bad. And now? Now that I know he really *was* hurting you? I want to *kill* him." He turns away from me and rests his back against the door frame.

I think back on last night and the emotions Will must have been experiencing. To be professing his love for me onstage one minute and then thinking I was making out with Javi the next? No wonder he was so pissed on the drive home.

He's still blocking my way. Not that I plan on running anywhere. My entire body becomes tense, not knowing what he's about to say or do. I slowly exhale and try to calm my nerves. My breathing has increased so rapidly in the last minute, my lungs are starting to ache again as the knot in my back reminds me of its presence.

"How did you—" I stammer. "How'd you know I was there?"

He turns and faces me, placing both hands on either side of the door frame. His height and the way he has me blocked in are intimidating, but in a very good way.

"I saw you. When I finished my piece, I saw you leaving."

My knees start to fail me, so I place my hand on the dryer behind me for support. He knows I saw him perform? Why is he telling me this? I do my best not to get my hopes up, but maybe since he's no longer my teacher, we can finally be together. Maybe that's what he's trying to tell me.

"Will, does this mean—"

He takes a step toward me, leaving no space between us. His fingers brush against my cheek, and he studies my face with his eyes. I place my hands against his chest, and he wraps his arms around me, pulling me to him. I try to take a step away from him so I can finish my question, but his body presses me against the dryer.

Just as I try to ask him again, he brings his lips to mine, rendering me speechless. I immediately stop resisting, and I let him kiss me. *Of course* I let him kiss me. My entire body becomes weak. My arms fall to my side, and I drop the measuring tape on the floor.

He grabs me by the waist and lifts me up, setting me down on top of the dryer. Our faces are at the same height now. He kisses me like he's making up for an entire month of stolen kisses. I can't tell where my hands end and his begin as we both frantically pull at each other. I wrap my legs around him and pull his mouth to my neck so I can catch my breath. All the feelings I have for him come rushing back. I try to hold back tears as I realize just how much I really do love him. Oh my god, I *love* him. I'm in love with Will Cooper.

I no longer try to control my breathing; it would be pointless.

"Will," I whisper. He continues exploring my neck with his lips. "Does this mean . . . does it mean we don't have to pretend . . . anymore?" I'm breathing so heavily I can barely form a cohesive sentence. "We can be . . . together? Since you're not . . . since you're not my teacher?"

His hands soften their hold on my back, and his lips slowly close and pull away from my neck. I try to pull him back into me, but he resists. He puts his hands on my calves and unlocks my legs from around his waist as he backs up and leans against the wall behind him, avoiding my eyes.

My hands grip the edges of the dryer and I slide off with a jerk. "Will?" I say as I take a step toward him.

The light from the kitchen casts a shadow across his

face, but I can see his jaw—it's clenched. His eyes are full of shame as he looks at me apologetically.

"Will? Tell me. Do the rules still apply?"

He doesn't have to answer me—I can tell by his reaction that they do.

"Lake," he says quietly. "I had a weak moment. I'm sorry."

I shove my hands into his chest. "A weak *moment*? That's what you call this? A weak *moment*?" I yell. "What were you gonna *do*, Will? When were you gonna stop making out with me and kick me out of your house *this* time?" I spin and turn out of the laundry room and make my way through the kitchen.

"Lake, don't. I'm sorry. I'm so sorry. It won't happen again, I swear."

I stop and turn toward him. "You're damn right it won't! I finally accepted it, Will! After an entire month of torture, I was finally able to be *around* you again. Then you go and do *this*! I can't do it anymore," I cry. "The way you consume my mind when we aren't together? I don't have time for it anymore. I've got more important things to think about now than your little *weak moments*."

I cross the living room and open the front door and pause. "Get me the measuring tape," I say calmly.

"Wh—what?" he says.

"It's on the damn floor! Get me the measuring tape!"

His footsteps fade as he walks to the laundry room. He retrieves the measuring tape and brings it back to me.

When he places it in my grasp, he squeezes my hand and looks me intently in the eyes.

"Don't make me the bad guy, Lake. *Please.*"

I pull my hand away from his. "Well, you're certainly not the martyr anymore." I turn and walk out, slamming the door behind me. I cross the street and don't look back to see if he's watching me. I don't care anymore.

I pause at our entryway and take a deep breath as I wipe my eyes. I open the front door to our *home*, put a smile across my face, and help my mother make her very last Halloween costumes.

19.

Ain't it like most people
I'm no different
We love to talk on things
We don't know about.

—THE AVETT BROTHERS,
"TEN THOUSAND WORDS"

WILL AND CAULDER END UP GOING OUT OF TOWN AFTER all. Mom and I spend most of Saturday and Sunday putting the finishing touches on the costumes. I let my mother know about Will's schedule and how we'll be helping them out more. As pissed as I am, I don't want Caulder and Kel to have to suffer. Sunday night, when Will gets home, I don't even notice because I don't even care.

* * *

"KEL, CALL CAULDER and tell him he can come over and put his costume on," I say as I drag Kel out of bed. "Will has to leave early anyway. Caulder can get ready over here."

It's Halloween, day of the cancerous lungs. Kel runs to the kitchen and grabs the phone.

I take a shower and finish getting ready, then wake my mother up so she can see the results. After she's dressed, Kel and Caulder instruct her to close her eyes. I walk her into the living room and position her in front of the two boys.

"Wait!" Caulder says. "What about Will? He needs to see us, too."

I usher my mother back into the hallway and I run to the front door, throw on my boots, and go outside. Will is pulling out of his driveway so I flag him down. I can see by the look on his face that he's hoping I've forgiven him. I immediately cease any false hope.

"You're still an asshole, but your brother wants you to see his costume. Come in for a second." I return to the house.

When Will walks in, I position him and my mother in front of the boys, and tell them to open their eyes.

Kel is the right lung; Caulder is the left. The stuffed material is shaped so that their arms and head fit through small openings, and the bottom is open to their waist and legs. We dyed the material so that it would reflect dead spots here and there. There are larger lumps protruding from the lungs in various places—the tumors. There is a long pause before Will and my mother react.

"It's disgusting," Will says.

"Repulsive," my mother adds.

"Hideous," I say.

The boys high-five. Or rather, the lungs high-five. After we take pictures, I load them up in the Jeep, and I drop the pair of lungs off at school.

I'M NOT EVEN halfway through second period when my phone starts vibrating. I pull it out of my pocket and look at the number. It's Will. Will *never* calls me. I assume he's trying to apologize, so I put the phone back in my jacket. It vibrates again. I turn and look at Eddie.

"Will keeps calling me—should I answer?" I say. I don't know why I'm asking her. Maybe she's got some great advice.

"I dunno," she says.

Maybe not.

On his third attempt, I press the Accept button and put the phone to my ear. "Hello?" I whisper.

"Layken, it's me. Look, you've got to get to the elementary school. There's been an incident, and I can't get through to your mom. I'm in Detroit—I can't go."

"What? With who?" I whisper.

"Both of them, I guess. They aren't hurt; they just need someone to pick them up. Go! Call me back."

I quietly excuse myself from the classroom. Eddie follows me.

"What is it?" she says as we walk into the hallway.

"I don't know. Something with Kel and Caulder," I say.

"I'm going with you," she says.

WHEN WE ARRIVE at the school, I sprint inside. I'm out of breath and on the verge of hysteria when we find the office. Kel and Caulder are both sitting in the lobby.

My feet won't move fast enough as I run to them and hug them.

"Are y'all okay? What happened?"

They both shrug.

"We don't know," Kel says. "They just told us we had to sit here until our parents came."

"Ms. Cohen?" someone says from behind me. I turn around and am face-to-face with a tall, slender redhead. She's wearing a black pencil skirt that meets her knees and a white dress shirt tucked in at the waist. Observing her, I can't help but hope she isn't as uptight as her wardrobe portrays her to be. She gestures toward her office, and Eddie and I follow her.

She takes a seat at her desk, nodding to the chairs in front of her. Eddie and I both sit.

"I'm Mrs. Brill. I'm the principal here at Chapman Elementary. Principal Brill."

The curt way she's speaking to me and her hoity-toity posture have immediately turned me off. I already don't like her.

"Are Caulder's parents joining us?" she asks.

"Caulder's parents are dead," I reply.

She gasps, then attempts to control her reaction by sitting up even straighter. "Oh, that's right. I'm sorry," she says. "Is it his brother? He lives with his brother, right?"

I nod. "He's in Detroit; he can't make it. I'm Kel's sister. What's the problem?"

She laughs. "Well, isn't it obvious?" She gestures out her office window to them.

I look at the boys. They're playing rock-paper-scissors and laughing. I know she's referring to their costumes, but she's already lost my respect with her attitude, so I continue to act oblivious.

"Is rock-paper-scissors against school policy?" I ask. Eddie laughs.

"Ms. Cohen," Principal Brill says. "They're dressed as cancerous lungs!" She shakes her head in disbelief.

"I thought they were rotten kidney beans," Eddie says. We both laugh.

"I don't think this is funny," Principal Brill says. "They're causing a distraction among the students! Those are very offensive and crude costumes! Not to mention disgusting. I don't know who thought it was a good idea, but you need to take them home and change their clothes."

My focus returns to Principal Brill. I lean forward and place my arms on her desk.

"Principal Brill," I say calmly. "Those costumes were made by my mother. My mother, who has stage-four small-cell lung cancer. My mother, who will never watch her little boy celebrate another Halloween again. My mother, who will more than likely experience a year of 'lasts.' Last Christmas. Last birthday. Last Easter. And if God is willing, her last Mother's Day. My mother, who when asked by her nine-year-old son if he could be her cancer for Halloween, had no choice but to make him the best cancerous-tumor-ridden-lung costume she could. So if you think it's so offensive, I suggest you drive them home yourself, and tell my mother to her face. Do you need my address?"

Principal Brill's mouth gapes open and she shakes her head. She fidgets in her seat, but doesn't respond. I stand up, and Eddie follows me out the door. I stop short and spin around and walk back into her office.

"And one more thing. The costume contest? I hope it's *fairly* judged."

Eddie laughs as I shut the door behind us.

"What's going on?" Kel asks.

"Nothing," I say. "Y'all can go back to class. She just wanted to know where we got the materials for your costume so she can be a hemorrhoid next year."

Eddie and I try to contain our laughter after the boys

make their way back to class. We head outside, and as soon as we open the doors, we explode. We laugh so hard, we cry.

When we get back in the Jeep, I have six missed calls from my mother and two from Will. I return their calls and assure them, without sparing any details, that the situation has been resolved.

Later that afternoon, when I pick the boys up from school, they sprint to the car.

"We won!" Caulder yells when he climbs into the backseat. "We both won! Fifty dollars each!"

20.

Well I've been locking myself up in my house for some
time now
Reading and writing and reading and thinking
and searching for reasons and missing the seasons
The Autumn, the Spring, the Summer, the snow
The record will stop and the record will go
Latches latched the windows down,
the dog coming in and the dog going out
Up with caffeine and down with the shot
Constantly worried about what I've got
Distracted by work but I can't make it stop
and my confidence on and my confidence off
And I sink to the bottom I rise to the top
and I think to myself that I do this a lot
World outside just goes it goes it goes it goes it goes

. . .

—THE AVETT BROTHERS, "TALK ON INDOLENCE"

THE NEXT FEW WEEKS COME AND GO. EDDIE HELPS OUT with watching the boys until Will gets home on the days I take my mother to her treatments. Will leaves every morning at six thirty and doesn't return home until after five thirty. We don't see each other. I make sure we don't see each other. We've resorted to texting and phone calls when it comes to Kel and Caulder. My mother has been pressing me for information, wanting to know why he doesn't come around anymore. I lie and tell her he's just busy with his new internship.

He's only been to the house once in the past two months. It was the only time we've really spoken since the incident in the laundry room. He came to tell me he was offered a job at a junior high that starts in January, just over two weeks from now.

I'm happy for him, but it's bittersweet. I know how much the job means for him and Caulder, but I know what it means for Will and me, too. Deep down there was a part of me silently counting down the days until his last day of the internship. It's finally here, and he's already signed another contract. It solidifies things for us, really. Solidifies that they're over.

We finally put the house in Texas up for sale. Mom has managed to save almost $180,000 from life insurance Dad actually *had*. The house isn't paid off yet, but we should get another check from the sale. Mom and I spent most of November focusing on our finances. We set aside more for our college funds, and she opened a savings account for Kel. She paid off all the outstanding credit cards and charge cards that are in her name, and instructed me to never open any in my own name. Said she would *haunt* me if I did.

TODAY IS THURSDAY. It's the final day of school for all the districts, including Will's. We have early release today, so I bring Caulder home with us. He usually spends the night on Thursdays, while Will goes to the slam.

I haven't been back to Club N9NE since the night Will read his poem. I understand what Javi meant in class now—about having to relive heartache. That's why I don't go. I've relived it enough for a lifetime.

I feed the boys and send them to their bedroom and then head to my mother's room for what has become our nightly chat.

"Shut the door; these are Kel's," she whispers.

She's wrapping Christmas gifts. I shut the door behind me and sit on the bed with her and help her wrap.

"What are your plans for Christmas break?" she asks.

She's lost all of her hair now. She chose not to go with a wig—said it felt like a ferret was taking a nap on her head. She's still beautiful, nonetheless.

I shrug. "Whatever yours are, I guess."

She frowns. "Are you going to Will's graduation with us tomorrow?"

He sent us an invite two weeks ago. I think each graduate gets a certain number of guests, and his grandparents are the only other people he invited besides us.

"I don't know; I haven't decided yet," I say.

She secures a box with a bow and sets it aside. "You should go. Whatever happened between the two of you, you should still go. He's been there for us, Lake."

I don't want to admit to her that I don't want to go because I don't know how to be around him anymore. That night in his laundry room when I thought for a brief moment that we could finally be together, I had never felt so elated. It was the most amazing feeling I've ever experienced, to finally be free to love him. But it wasn't real. That one minute of pure happiness I felt and the heartache that came moments later is something I never want to experience again. I'm tired of grieving.

My mother moves the wrapping paper from her lap and reaches out and hugs me. I didn't realize I was wearing my emotions on my sleeve.

"I'm sorry, but I think I may have given you some terrible advice," she says.

I pull away from her and laugh. "That's impossible, Mom. You don't know how to do terrible." I take a box from the floor and pull it onto my lap as I grab a sheet of cut paper and begin to wrap it.

"I did, though. Your whole life, I've been telling you to think with your head, not your heart," she says.

I meticulously fold the edges up and grab the roll of tape. "That's not good advice, Mom. That's *great* advice.

That same advice is what has gotten me through these past few months." I tear a piece of tape and secure the edge of the package.

My mother grabs the box out of my hand before I'm finished wrapping it and sets it beside her. She takes my hands and turns me toward her.

"I'm serious, Lake. You've been doing so much thinking with your head that you're ignoring your heart completely. There has to be a balance. The fact that both of you are letting other things consume you is about to ruin any chance you'll ever have at being happy."

I shake my head in confusion. "Nothing is consuming me, Mom."

She shakes my hands like I'm not getting it. "*I* am, Lake. *I'm* consuming you. You've got to stop worrying so much about *me*. Go live your life. I'm not dead yet, you know."

I stare down at our hands as her words soak in. I *have* been focusing on her a lot. But that's what she needs. It's what we both need. She doesn't have that much time left, and I want to be there for every second of it.

"Mom, you need me. You need me more than I need Will. Besides, Will has made his choice."

She darts her eyes away and lets go of my hands. "No he hasn't, Lake. He made what he *thought* was the best choice, but he's wrong. You're both wrong."

I know she wants to see me happy. I don't have the heart to tell her that it's over between us. He made his choice that night in the laundry room when he let me go. He has his priorities, and right now I'm not one of them.

She takes the box I was wrapping and returns it in front of her and starts wrapping it again. "That night I told you I had cancer, and you ran to Will's house?" Her voice softens. She clears her throat, still avoiding my eyes. "I need to tell you what he said to me . . . at the door."

I remember the conversation she's referring to, but I couldn't hear what they were saying.

"When he answered the door I told him you needed to come home. That we needed to talk about it. He looked at me with heartache in his eyes. He said, 'Let her stay, Julia. She needs me right now.'

"Lake, you broke my heart. It broke my heart that you needed *him* more than you needed *me*. As soon as the words came out of his mouth, I realized that you were grown up . . . that I wasn't your whole life anymore. Will could see that. He saw how bad his words hurt me. When I turned away to walk back to the house, he followed me into the yard and hugged me. He told me he would never take you from me. He said he was going to let you go . . . let you focus on me and on the time I had left."

She places the wrapped gift on the bed. She scoots toward me and takes my hands in hers again. "Lake, he didn't move on. He didn't choose this new job over you . . . he chose *us* over you. He wanted you to have more time with *me*."

I take a deep breath as I absorb everything my mother

just revealed. Is she right? Does he love me enough that he would be willing to let me go?

"Mom?" My voice is weak. "What if you're wrong?"

"What if I'm *not* wrong, Lake? Question *everything*. What if he *wants* to choose you? You'll never know if you don't tell him how you feel. You've completely shut him out. You haven't given him the *chance* to pick you."

She's right, I haven't. I've been completely closed off since that night in the laundry room.

"It's seven thirty, Lake. You know where he is. Go tell him how you feel."

I don't move. My legs feel like Jell-O.

"Go!" she laughs.

I jump off the bed and run to my room. My hands are shaking and my thoughts are all jumbled together while I change my pants. I put on the purple shirt that I wore on our first and only date. I go to the bathroom and inspect my reflection.

There's something missing. I run to my room and reach under my pillow and pull out the purple clip. I snap it open and remove my mother's strands of hair and place them in my jewelry box. I go back to the bathroom and brush my bangs to the side of my head and snap the clip in place.

21.

Don't say it's over
'Cause that's the worst news I
could hear I swear that I will
Do my best to be here
just the way you like it
Even though it's hard to hide
Push my feelings all aside
I will rearrange my plans and
change for you.

—THE AVETT BROTHERS,
"IF IT'S THE BEACHES"

WHEN I WALK INTO THE CLUB, I DON'T STOP TO LOOK FOR him. I know he's here. I don't give myself time to second-guess myself as I walk with false confidence toward the front of the room. The emcee is announcing scores for the previous performer when I walk onto the stage. He's apprehensive as I grab the microphone from him and turn toward the audience. The lights are so bright, I can't see anyone's faces. I can't see Will.

"I would like to perform a piece I wrote," I say into the microphone. My voice is steady, but my heart is about to jump out of my chest. I can't turn back now. I have to do this. "I know this isn't standard protocol, but it's an emergency," I say.

Laughter overcomes the audience. The rumble of the crowd is loud, causing me to freeze at the thought of what I'm about to do. I start to have second thoughts and turn around to the emcee, but he nudges me back and gives me the go-ahead.

I place the microphone in the stand and lower it to my height. I close my eyes and take a deep breath before I begin.

"Three dollars!" someone yells from the audience.

I open my eyes and realize I haven't paid my fee yet. I frantically dig my hands in my pockets and pull out a five-dollar bill and walk it over to the emcee.

I return to the microphone and close my eyes.

"My piece is called—"

Someone's tapping me on the shoulder. I open my eyes and turn around to see the emcee holding up two one-dollar bills.

"Your change," he says.

I take the money and put it back in my pocket. He's still standing there.

"Go!" I whisper through clenched teeth.

He stammers and walks off the stage.

Once again, I turn toward the microphone and begin to speak. "My piece is called 'Schooled,'" I say into the microphone. My voice is shaking, so I take a few deep breaths. I just hope I can remember it: I rewrote a few lines on the way here. I inhale one last time and begin.

I got *schooled* this year.

By *everyone*.

By my little brother . . .

by the *Avett* Brothers . . .

by my *mother*, my *best friend*, my *teacher*, my *father*,

and

by

a

boy.

A boy that I'm *seriously*, *deeply*, *madly*, *incredibly*,

and undeniably in *love* with.

I got *so schooled* this year.

By a *nine*-year-old.

He taught me that it's *okay* to live *life*

a little *backward*.

And how to *laugh*

At what you would *think*

is *unlaughable*.

I got *schooled* this year

By a *band*!

They taught me how to find that *feeling* of *feeling*
again.
They taught me how to *decide* what to *be*
And go *be* it.
I got *schooled* this year.
By a *cancer* patient.
She taught me *so* much. She's *still* teaching me so
much.
She taught me to *question*.
To *never* regret.
She taught me to *push* my boundaries,
Because *that's* what they're *there* for.
She told me to find a *balance* between **head** and **heart**
And then
she taught me **how** . . .
I got *schooled* this year
By a *foster kid*.
She taught me to *respect* the hand that I was *dealt*.
And to be *grateful* I was even dealt a *hand*.
She taught me that *family*
Doesn't have to be *blood*.
Sometimes your *family*
are your *friends*.
I got *schooled* this year
By my *teacher*
He taught me
That the *points* are not the *point*,

The *point* is *poetry* . . .
I got *schooled* this year
By my *father*.
He taught me that *heroes* aren't always *invincible*
And that the *magic*
is *within* me.
I got schooled this year
by
a
boy.
A boy that I'm *seriously, deeply, madly, incredibly,*
and undeniably in *love* with.
And he taught me the most important thing of *all*—
To put the *emphasis*
On *life*.

    The feeling that comes over you, when you're in front of an audience? All those people craving for your words, yearning to see a glimpse into your soul . . . it's exhilarating. I thrust the microphone back into the emcee's hands and run off the stage. I look around but don't see him anywhere. I look at the booth we sat in on our first date, but it's empty. I realize, after standing there, waiting to be swept off of my feet—that he's not even here. I spin around in a circle, scanning the room a second time. A third time. He's not here.

    The same glorious feeling I had on that stage . . . on

his dryer . . . in the booth in the back of the room—it's gone. I can't do it again. I want to run. I need air. I need to feel the Michigan air against my face.

I throw open the door and take a step outside when a voice, amplified through the speakers, stops me in my tracks.

"That's not a good idea," it says. I recognize that voice *and* that phrase. I slowly turn around and face the stage. Will is standing there, holding the microphone between his hands, looking directly at me.

"You shouldn't leave before you get your scores," he says, motioning to the judges' table. I follow his gaze to the judges, who are all turned around in their seats. All four of them have their eyes locked on me; the fifth seat is empty. I gasp when I realize *Will* was the fifth judge.

I sense that I'm floating again as I make my way to the center of the room. Everyone is quiet. I look around, and all eyes are on me. No one understands what's happening. I'm not sure even *I* understand what's happening.

Will looks at the emcee standing next to him. "I'd like to perform a piece. It's an *emergency*," he says.

The emcee backs away and gives Will the go-ahead. Will turns back to face me.

"Three dollars," someone yells from the crowd.

Will darts a look at the emcee. "I don't have any cash," he says.

I immediately pull the two dollars out of my pocket

and run to the stage, smacking them down in front of the emcee's feet. He inspects the money I lay before him.

"Still a dollar short," he says.

The silence in the room is interrupted as several chairs slide from under their tables. There is a faint rumble as people walk toward me. I'm surrounded, being pushed and shoved in different directions as the crowd grows thicker. It begins to disperse just as fast and the silence slowly returns as everyone makes their way back to their seats. I return my gaze to the stage, where dozens of dollar bills are haphazardly thrown at the emcee's feet. My eyes follow along as a quarter rolls off the edge of the stage and falls onto the floor. It wiggles and spins as it comes to rest at my foot.

The emcee is focused on the pile of money before him. "*Okay*," he says. "I guess that covers it. What's the name of your piece, Will?"

Will brings the microphone to his mouth and smiles at me. " 'Better Than Third,' " he says. I take a few steps back from the stage and he begins.

I met a girl.

A *beautiful* girl

And I fell for her.

I fell *hard*.

Unfortunately, sometimes *life* gets in the *way*.

Life *definitely* got in *my* way.

It got *all up* in my damn way,
Life *blocked* the *door* with a stack of wooden *two-by-fours* nailed together and *attached* to a fifteen inch
concrete wall behind a *row* of solid steel *bars*, *bolted* to
a *titanium frame* that *no matter* how *hard* I shoved
against it—

It

wouldn't

budge.

Sometimes *life* doesn't *budge.*

It just gets *all up* in your *damn* way.

It blocked my *plans*, my *dreams*, my *desires*, my
wishes, my *wants*, my *needs.*

It blocked out that *beautiful* girl

That I *fell* so *hard* for.

Life tries to tell you what's *best* for you.

What should be most *important* to you.

What should come *first*

Or *second*

Or *third.*

I tried *so hard* to keep it all *organized*, *alphabetized*,
stacked in *chronological order*, everything in its
perfect space, its *perfect place.*

I thought that's what life *wanted* me to do.

This is what life *needed* for me to do.

Right?

Keep it *all* in *sequence*?

Sometimes life gets in your *way.*

It gets all up in your damn *way*.

But it doesn't get all up in your damn way because it wants you to just *give up* and let it *take control*. Life doesn't get all up in your damn way because it just wants you to *hand* it all *over* and be *carried along*.

Life wants you to *fight* it.

Learn how to make it your *own*.

It wants you to grab an *ax* and *hack* through the *wood*.

It wants you to get a *sledgehammer* and *break* through the *concrete*.

It wants you to grab a *torch* and *burn* through the *metal* and *steel* until you can reach through and *grab* it.

Life wants you to *grab* all the *organized*, the *alphabetized*, the *chronological*, the *sequenced*. It wants you to mix it all *together*,

stir it up,

blend it.

Life doesn't want you to let it *tell* you that your little *brother* should be the *only* thing that comes *first*.

Life doesn't want you to let it *tell* you that your *career* and your *education* should be the *only* thing that comes in *second*.

And life *definitely* doesn't want *me*

To just let it *tell* me

that the *girl* I met—

The *beautiful, strong, amazing, resilient girl*

That I fell *so hard* for—

Should *only* come in *third*.

Life *knows*.

Life is trying to *tell* me

That the *girl* I *love*?

The girl I fell

So *hard* for?

There's room for her in *first*.

I'm putting *her* first.

Will sets the microphone down and jumps off the stage. I've gone so long teaching myself how to let go of him, to break the hold he has on me. It hasn't worked. It hasn't worked a damn bit.

He takes my face in his hands and wipes my tears away with his thumbs. "I love you, Lake." He smiles and presses his forehead against mine. "You deserve to come first."

Everyone and everything else in the entire room fades; the only sound I hear is the crash of the walls I've built up around me as they crumble to the ground.

"I love you, too. I love you so much."

He brings his lips to mine, and I throw my arms around him and kiss him back. *Of course* I kiss him back.

epilogue

My parents taught me to learn
When I miss
Just do your best
Just do your best.

—THE AVETT BROTHERS, "WHEN I DRINK"

I WALK AROUND THE LIVING ROOM, TAKING LONG LEAPS over mounds of toys as I gather wrapping paper and stuff it into the sack. "Did y'all like your presents?" I ask.

"Yes!" Kel and Caulder yell in unison. I gather the last of the wrapping paper and tie the ends of the trash bag together and head outside to throw it away.

As I'm walking to the curb, Will emerges from his house and jogs toward me.

"Let me get that, babe," he says as he takes the bag out of my hands and carries it to the curb. He walks back to where I'm standing and puts his arms around me, nuzzling his face in my neck.

"Merry Christmas," he says.

"Merry Christmas," I reply.

313

It's our second Christmas together. The first without my mother. She passed away in September this year, almost a year to the day after we moved to Michigan. It was hard. It was *extremely* hard.

When someone close to you dies, the memories of them are painful. It isn't until the fifth stage of grief that the memories of them stop hurting as much—when the recollections become positive. When you stop thinking about the person's death and remember all of the wonderful things about their *life*.

Having Will by my side has made it bearable. After graduation, he applied to get his master's in education. He didn't take the job at the junior high after all. Instead, he lived off of student loans for another semester, until I graduated.

Will takes my hand as we walk back inside the house. The number of toys that are piled in my living room floor is astonishing.

"I'll be back—last load," Will says as he takes a stack of Caulder's things and walks back out the front door. This is his third trip across the street, transferring all of Caulder's new toys to their house.

"Kel, these can't all be yours," I say, scanning the living room. "Y'all start gathering them up and take them to the spare bedroom. I need to vacuum." There are small remnants of gift chaos all over the living-room floor. After I finish vacuuming, I wrap up the cord and return the vacuum to the hallway closet. Will walks in the front door with two gift sacks in hand.

"Uh-oh. How'd we forget those?" I ask, just before I call the boys into the living room.

"These aren't for the boys. These are for you and Kel." He walks to the couch and motions for Kel and me to take a seat.

"Will, you didn't have to do this. You already got me concert tickets," I say as I settle into the sofa.

He hands the sacks to us and kisses me on the forehead. "I didn't. They aren't *from* me." He takes Caulder's hand, and they quietly slip out the front door. I look at Kel, and he just shrugs.

We simultaneously rip the tissue out of the sacks and pull out envelopes. "Lake" is sprawled across the front in my mother's handwriting. My hands are weak as I slide the paper out of the envelope. I run my arm across my eyes and wipe away my tears as I unfold my letter.

To my babies,

Merry Christmas. I'm sorry if these letters have caught you both by surprise. There is just so much more I have to say. I know you thought I was done giving advice, but I couldn't leave without reiterating a few things in writing. You may not relate to these things now, but someday you will. I wasn't able to be around forever, but I hope that my words can be.

—Don't stop making basagna. Basagna is good. Wait until a day when there is no bad news, and bake a damn basagna.

—*Find a balance between head and heart. Hopefully you've found that, Lake, and you can help Kel sort it out when he gets to that point.*

—*Push your boundaries, that's what they're there for.*

—*I'm stealing this snippet from your favorite band, Lake. "Always remember there is nothing worth sharing like the love that let us share our name."*

—*Don't take life too seriously. Punch it in the face when it needs a good hit. Laugh at it.*

—*And laugh a lot. Never go a day without laughing at least once.*

—*Never judge others. You both know good and well how unexpected events can change who a person is. Always keep that in mind. You never know what someone else is experiencing within their own life.*

—*Question everything. Your love, your religion, your passions. If you don't have questions, you'll never find answers.*

—*Be accepting. Of everything. People's differences, their similarities, their choices, their personalities. Sometimes it takes a variety to make a good collection. The same goes for people.*

—*Choose your battles, but don't choose very many.*

—*Keep an open mind; it's the only way new things can get in.*

—And last but not least, not the tiniest *bit least.* Never *regret.*

Thank you both for giving me the best *years of* my life.

Especially *the last one.*

Love,

Mom

acknowledgments

To Abigail Ehn with *Poetry Slam, Inc.* for answering all of my questions with lightning speed. To my sisters, Lin and Murphy, for equally sharing all of the awesome components of our father's DNA. To my mother, Vannoy, for loving "Mystery Bob" and encouraging my passion. To my amazing husband and children for not complaining about four weeks' worth of laundry and dishes that piled up while I locked myself in my bedroom. To Jessica Benson Sparks for her kind heart and willingness to help me succeed. And last but certainly not least, to my "life coach" Stephanie Cohen for being so butterflying bemazing!

about the author

Colleen Hoover is the *New York Times* bestselling author of two novels: *Slammed* and *Point of Retreat*. She lives in Texas with her husband and their three boys.

To read more about this author, visit her website at www.colleenhoover.com.

In the second book in the Slammed series by *New York Times* bestselling author Colleen Hoover, Layken and Will's relationship has endured through hardships, heartache, and a cruel twist of fate, further solidifying the fact that they belong together. But the two lovers could not have expected that the things that brought them together may ultimately be the things that tear them apart. Their connection is on the brink of being destroyed forever and it will take an extraordinary amount of willpower to keep their love afloat.

Layken is left questioning the very foundation on which her relationship with Will was built. Will is left questioning how he can prove his love for a girl who can't seem to stop "carving pumpkins." Upon finding the answers that may bring peace back into their relationship, the couple comes across an even greater challenge—one that could change not only their lives but the lives of everyone who depend on them.

Read on for a look at Colleen Hoover's
Point of Retreat.

1.

THURSDAY, JANUARY 5

I registered for classes today. Didn't get the days I wanted, but I only have two semesters left, so it's getting harder to be picky about my schedule. I'm thinking about applying to local schools for another teaching job after next semester. Hopefully, by this time next year, I'll be teaching again. For right now, though, I'm living off student loans. Luckily, my grandparents have been supportive while I work on my master's degree. I wouldn't be able to do it without them, that's for sure.

We're having dinner with Gavin and Eddie tonight. I think I'll make cheeseburgers. Cheeseburgers sound good. That's all I really have to say right now . . .

"IS LAYKEN OVER HERE OR OVER THERE?" EDDIE ASKS, peering in the front door.

"Over there," I say from the kitchen.

Is there a sign on my house instructing people *not* to

knock? Lake never knocks anymore, but her comfort here apparently extends to Eddie as well. Eddie heads across the street to Lake's house, and Gavin walks inside, tapping his knuckles against the front door. It's not an official knock, but at least he's making an attempt.

"What are we eating?" he asks. He slips his shoes off at the door and makes his way into the kitchen.

"Burgers." I hand him a spatula and point to the stove, instructing him to flip the burgers while I pull the fries out of the oven.

"Will, do you ever notice how we somehow always get stuck cooking?"

"It's probably not a bad thing," I say as I loosen the fries from the pan. "Remember Eddie's Alfredo?"

He grimaces when he remembers the Alfredo. "Good point," he says.

I call Kel and Caulder into the kitchen to have them set the table. For the past year, since Lake and I have been together, Gavin and Eddie have been eating with us at least twice a week. I finally had to invest in a dining room table because the bar was getting a little too crowded.

"Hey, Gavin," Kel says. He walks into the kitchen and grabs a stack of cups out of the cabinet.

"Hey," Gavin responds. "You decide where we're having your party next week?"

Kel shrugs. "I don't know. Maybe bowling. Or we could just do something here."

Caulder walks into the kitchen and starts setting

places at the table. I glance behind me and notice them setting an extra place. "We expecting company?" I ask.

"Kel invited Kiersten," Caulder says teasingly.

Kiersten moved into a house on our street about a month ago, and Kel seems to have developed a slight crush on her. He won't admit it. He's just now about to turn eleven, so Lake and I expected this to happen. Kiersten's a few months older than he is, and a lot taller. Girls hit puberty faster than boys, so maybe he'll eventually catch up.

"Next time you guys invite someone else, let me know. Now I need to make another burger." I walk to the refrigerator and take out one of the extra patties.

"She doesn't eat meat," Kel says. "She's a vegetarian."

Figures. I put the meat back in the fridge. "I don't have any fake meat. What's she gonna do? Eat bread?"

"Bread's fine," Kiersten says as she walks through the front door—without knocking. "I like bread. French fries, too. I just don't eat things that are a result of unjustified animal homicide." Kiersten walks to the table and grabs the roll of paper towels and starts tearing them off, laying one beside each plate. Her self-assurance reminds me a little of Eddie's.

"Who's she?" Gavin asks, watching Kiersten make herself at home. She's never eaten with us before, but you wouldn't know that by how she's taking command.

"She's the eleven-year-old neighbor I was telling you about. The one I think is an imposter based on the things that come out of her mouth. I'm beginning to suspect she's really a tiny adult posing as a little redheaded child."

"Oh, the one Kel's crushing on?" Gavin smiles, and I can see his wheels turning. He's already thinking of ways to embarrass Kel at dinner. Tonight should be interesting.

Gavin and I have become pretty close this past year. It's good, I guess, considering how close Eddie and Lake are. Kel and Caulder really like them, too. It's nice. I like the setup we all have. I hope it stays this way.

Eddie and Lake finally walk in as we're all sitting down at the table. Lake has her wet hair pulled up in a knot on top of her head. She's wearing house shoes, sweatpants, and a T-shirt. I love that about her, the fact that she's so comfortable here. She takes the seat next to mine and leans in and kisses me on the cheek.

"Thanks, babe. Sorry it took me so long. I was trying to register online for Statistics, but the class is full. Guess I'll have to go sweet-talk someone at the admin office tomorrow."

"Why are you taking Statistics?" Gavin asks. He grabs the ketchup and squirts it on his plate.

"I took Algebra Two in the winter mini-mester. I'm trying to knock out all my math in the first year, since I hate it so much." Lake grabs the ketchup out of Gavin's hands and squirts some on my plate, then on her own.

"What's your hurry? You've already got more credits than Eddie and I do, put together," he says. Eddie nods in agreement as she takes a bite of her burger.

Lake nudges her head toward Kel and Caulder. "I've already got more *kids* than you and Eddie put together. *That's* my hurry."

"What's your major?" Kiersten asks Lake.

Eddie glances toward Kiersten, finally noticing the extra person seated at the table. "Who are you?"

Kiersten looks at Eddie and smiles. "I'm Kiersten. I live diagonal to Will and Caulder, parallel to Layken and Kel. We moved here from Detroit right before Christmas. Mom says we needed to get out of the city before the city got out of us . . . whatever that means. I'm eleven. I've been eleven since eleven-eleven-eleven. It was a pretty big day, you know. Not many people can say they turned eleven on eleven-eleven-eleven. I'm a little bummed that I was born at three o'clock in the afternoon. If I would have been born at eleven-eleven, I'm pretty sure I could have got on the news or something. I could have recorded the segment and used it someday for my portfolio. I'm gonna be an actress when I grow up."

Eddie, along with the rest of us, stares at Kiersten without responding. Kiersten is oblivious, turning to Lake to repeat her question. "What's your major, Layken?"

Lake lays her burger down on her plate and clears her throat. I know how much she hates this question. She tries to answer confidently. "I haven't decided yet."

Kiersten looks at her with pity. "I see. The proverbial undecided. My oldest brother has been a sophomore in college for three years. He's got enough credits to have five majors by now. I think he stays undecided because he'd rather sleep until noon every day, sit in class for three hours, and go out every night, than actually graduate and get a real job. Mom says that's not true—she says it's because he's trying to 'discover his full potential' by examining all of his interests. If you ask me, I think it's bullshit."

I cough when the sip I just swallowed tries to make its way back up with my laugh.

"You just said 'bullshit'!" Kel says.

"Kel, don't say 'bullshit'!" Lake says.

"But she said 'bullshit' first," Caulder says, defending Kel.

"Caulder, don't say 'bullshit'!" I yell.

"Sorry," Kiersten says to Lake and me. "Mom says the FCC is responsible for inventing cuss words just for media shock value. She says if everyone would just use them enough, they wouldn't be considered cuss words anymore, and no one would ever be offended by them."

This kid is hard to keep up with!

"Your mother *encourages* you to cuss?" Gavin says.

Kiersten nods. "I don't see it that way. It's more like she's encouraging us to undermine a system flawed through overuse of words that are made out to be harmful, when in fact they're just letters, mixed together like every other word. That's all they are, mixed-up letters. Like, take the word 'butterfly,' for example. What if someone decided one day that 'butterfly' is a cuss word? People would eventually start using the word 'butterfly' as an insult and to emphasize things in a negative way. The actual *word* doesn't mean anything. It's the negative association people give these words that make them cuss words. So, if we all just decided to keep saying 'butterfly' all the time, people would stop caring. The shock value would subside, and it would become just another word again. Same with every other so-called bad word. If we would all start saying them all the time, they wouldn't be bad anymore. That's what my mom says, anyway." She smiles and takes a french fry and dips it in ketchup.

I often wonder, when Kiersten's visiting, how she turned out the way she did. I have yet to meet her mother, but from what I've gathered, she's definitely not ordinary. Kiersten is obviously smarter than most kids her age, even if it is in a strange way. The things that come out of her mouth make Kel and Caulder seem somewhat normal.

"Kiersten?" Eddie says. "Will you be my new best friend?"

Lake grabs a french fry off her plate and throws it at Eddie, hitting her in the face with it. "That's bullshit," Lake says.

"Oh, go *butterfly* yourself," Eddie says. She returns a fry in Lake's direction.

I intercept the french fry, hoping it won't result in another food fight, like last week. I'm still finding broccoli everywhere. "Stop," I say, dropping the french fry on the table. "If you two have another food fight in my house, I'm kicking *both* of your butterflies!"

Lake can see I'm serious. She squeezes my leg under the table and changes the subject. "Suck-and-sweet time," she says.

"Suck-and-sweet time?" Kiersten asks, confused.

Kel fills her in. "It's where you have to say your suck and your sweet of the day. The good and the bad. The high and the low. We do it every night at supper."

Kiersten nods as though she understands.

"I'll go first," Eddie says. "My suck today was registration. I got stuck in Monday, Wednesday, Friday classes. Tuesday and Thursdays were full."

Everyone wants the Tuesday/Thursday schedules. The classes are longer, but it's a fair trade, having to go only twice a week rather than three times.

"My *sweet* is meeting Kiersten, my new best friend," Eddie says, glaring at Lake.

Lake grabs another french fry and throws it at Eddie. Eddie ducks, and the fry goes over her head. I take Lake's plate and scoot it to the other side of me, out of her reach.

Lake shrugs and smiles at me. "Sorry." She grabs a fry off my plate and puts it in her mouth.

"Your turn, Mr. Cooper," Eddie says. She still calls me that, usually when she's trying to point out that I'm being a "bore."

"My suck was definitely registration, too. I got Monday, Wednesday, Friday."

Lake turns to me, upset. "What? I thought we were both doing Tuesday/Thursday classes."

"I tried, babe. They don't offer my level of courses on those days. I texted you."

She pouts. "Man, that really is a suck," she says. "And I didn't get your text. I can't find my phone again."

She's always losing her phone.

"What's your sweet?" Eddie asks me.

That's easy. "My sweet is right now," I say as I kiss Lake on the forehead.

Kel and Caulder both groan. "Will, that's your sweet *every* night," Caulder says, annoyed.

"My turn," Lake says. "Registration was actually my sweet. I haven't figured out Statistics yet, but my other four classes were exactly what I wanted." She looks at Eddie and continues. "My suck was losing my best friend to an eleven-year-old."

Eddie laughs.

"I wanna go," Kiersten says. No one objects. "My suck was having bread for dinner," she says, eyeing her plate.

She's ballsy. I toss another slice of bread on her plate. "Maybe next time you show up uninvited to a carnivore's house, you should bring your own fake meat."

She ignores my comment. "My sweet was three o'clock."

"What happened at three o'clock?" Gavin asks.

Kiersten shrugs. "School let out. I butterflying *hate* school."

All three kids glance at one another, as if there's

an unspoken agreement. I make a mental note to talk to Caulder about it later. Lake nudges me with her elbow and shoots me a questioning glance, letting me know she's thinking the same thing.

"Your turn, whatever your name is," Kiersten says to Gavin.

"It's Gavin. And my suck would have to be the fact that an eleven-year-old has a larger vocabulary than me," he says, smiling at Kiersten. "My sweet today is sort of a surprise." He looks at Eddie and waits for her response.

"What?" Eddie says.

"Yeah, what?" Lake adds.

I'm curious, too. Gavin just leans back in his seat with a smile, waiting for us to guess.

Eddie gives him a shove. "Tell us!" she says.

He leans forward in his chair and slaps his hands on the table. "I got a job! At Getty's, delivering pizza!" He looks happy, for some reason.

"*That's* your sweet? You're a pizza delivery guy?" Eddie asks. "That's more like a suck."

"You know I've been looking for a job. And it's Getty's. We love Getty's!"

Eddie rolls her eyes. "Well, congratulations," she says unconvincingly.

"Do we get free pizza?" Kel asks.

"No, but we get a discount," Gavin replies.

"That's my sweet, then," Kel says. "Cheap pizza!"

Gavin looks pleased that someone is excited for him. "My suck today was Principal Brill," Kel says.

"Oh Lord, what'd she do?" Lake asks him. "Or better yet, what did *you* do?"

"It wasn't just me," Kel says.

Caulder puts his elbow on the table and tries to hide his face from my line of sight.

"What did you do, Caulder?" I ask him. He brings his hand down and looks up at Gavin. Gavin puts his elbow on the table and shields his face from my line of sight as well. He continues to eat as he ignores my glare. "Gavin? What prank did you tell them about this time?"

Gavin grabs two fries and throws them at Kel and Caulder. "No more! I'm not telling you any more stories. You two get me in trouble every time!" Kel and Caulder laugh and throw the fries back at him.

"I'll tell on them, I don't mind," Kiersten says. "They got in trouble at lunch. Mrs. Brill was on the other side of the cafeteria, and they were thinking of a way to get her to run. Everyone says she waddles like a duck when she runs, and we wanted to see it. So Kel pretended he was choking, and Caulder made a huge spectacle and got behind him and started beating on his back, pretending to give him the Heimlich maneuver. It freaked Mrs. Brill out! When she got to our table, Kel said he was all better. He told Mrs. Brill that Caulder saved his life. It would have been fine, but she had already told someone to call 911. Within minutes, two ambulances and a fire truck showed up at the school. One of the boys at the next table told Mrs. Brill they were faking the whole thing, so Kel got called to the office."

Lake leans forward and glares at Kel. "Please tell me this is a joke."

Kel looks up with an innocent expression. "It was a joke. I really didn't think anyone would call 911. Now I have to spend all next week in detention."

"Why didn't Mrs. Brill call me?" Lake asks him.

"I'm pretty sure she did," he says. "You can't find your phone, remember?"

"Ugh! If she calls me in for another conference, you're grounded!"

I look at Caulder, who's attempting to avoid my gaze. "Caulder, what about you? Why didn't Mrs. Brill try to call me?"

He turns toward me and gives me a mischievous grin. "Kel lied for me. He told her that I really thought he was choking and I was trying to save his life," he says. "Which brings me to my sweet for the day. I was rewarded for my heroic behavior. Mrs. Brill gave me two free study hall passes."

Only Caulder could find a way to avoid detention and get rewarded instead. "You two need to cut that crap out," I say to them. "And Gavin, no more prank stories."

"Yes, Mr. Cooper," Gavin says sarcastically. "But I have to know," he says, looking at the kids, "does she really waddle?"

"Yeah." Kiersten laughs. "She's a waddler, all right." She looks at Caulder. "What was your suck, Caulder?"

Caulder gets serious. "My best friend almost choked to death today. He could have *died*."

We all laugh. As much as Lake and I try to do the responsible thing, sometimes it's hard to draw the line between being the rule enforcer and being the sibling. We choose which battles to pick with the boys, and Lake says it's important that we don't choose very many. I look at her and see she's laughing, so I assume this isn't one she wants to fight.

"Can I finish my food now?" Lake says, pointing to her plate, still on the other side of me, out of her reach. I scoot the plate back in front of her. "Thank you, Mr. Cooper," she says.

I knee her under the table. She knows I hate it when she calls me that. I don't know why it bothers me so much. Probably because when I actually was her teacher, it was absolute torture. Our connection progressed so quickly that first night I took her out. I'd never met anyone I had so much fun just being myself with. I spent the entire weekend thinking about her. The moment I walked around the corner and saw her standing in the hallway in front of my classroom, I felt like my heart had been ripped right out of my chest. I knew immediately what she was doing there, even though it took her a little longer to figure it out. When she realized I was a teacher, the look in her eyes absolutely devastated me. She was hurt. Heartbroken. Just like me. One thing I know for sure, I never want to see that look in her eyes again.

Kiersten stands up and takes her plate to the sink. "I have to go. Thanks for the bread, Will," she says sarcastically. "It was delicious."

"I'm leaving, too. I'll walk you home," Kel says. He jumps out of his seat and follows her to the door. I look at Lake, and she rolls her eyes. It bothers her that Kel has developed his first crush. Lake doesn't like to think that we're about to have to deal with teenage hormones.

Caulder gets up from the table. "I'm gonna watch TV in my room," he says. "See you later, Kel. Bye, Kiersten." They both tell him goodbye as they leave.

"I really like that girl," Eddie says after Kiersten leaves. "I hope Kel asks her to be his girlfriend. I hope they grow up and get married and have lots of weird babies. I hope she's in our family forever."

"Shut up, Eddie," Lake says. "He's only ten. He's too young for a girlfriend."

"Not really, he'll be eleven in eight days," Gavin says. "Eleven is the prime age for first girlfriends."

Lake takes an entire handful of fries and throws them toward Gavin's face.

I just sigh. She's impossible to control. "You're cleaning up tonight," I say to her. "You, too," I say to Eddie. "Gavin, let's go watch some football, like real men, while the women do their job."

"Let's go," Eddie says as she pulls Gavin up off the couch. "Thanks for supper, Will. Joel wants you guys to come over next weekend. He said he'd make tamales."

I don't turn down tamales. "We're there," I say.

After Eddie and Gavin leave, Lake comes to the living room and sits on the couch, curling her legs under her as she snuggles against me. I put my arm around her and pull her closer.

"I'm bummed," she says. "I was hoping we'd at least get the same days this semester. We never get any alone time with all these butterflying kids running around."

You would think, with our living across the street from each other, that we would have all the time in the world together. That's not the case. Last semester she went to school Monday, Wednesday, and Friday, and I went all five days. Weekends we spent a lot of time doing homework but mostly stayed busy with Kel's and Caulder's sports. When Julia passed away in September, that put even more on Lake's plate. It's been an adjustment, to say the least. The only place we seem to be lacking is getting quality alone time. It's kind of awkward, if the boys are at one house, to go to the other house to be alone. They almost always seem to follow us whenever we do.

"We'll get through it," I say. "We always do."

She pulls my face toward hers and kisses me. I've been kissing her every day for over a year, and it somehow gets better every time.

"I better go," she says at last. "I have to get up early

Gavin scoots his glass toward Eddie. "Refill this glass, woman. I'm watching some football."

While Eddie and Lake clean the kitchen, I take the opportunity to ask Gavin for a favor. Lake and I haven't had any alone time in weeks due to always having the boys. I really need alone time with her.

"Do you think you and Eddie could take Kel and Caulder to a movie tomorrow night?"

He doesn't answer right away, which makes me feel guilty for even asking. Maybe they had plans already.

"It depends," he finally responds. "Do we have to take Kiersten, too?"

I laugh. "That's up to your girl. She's her new best friend."

Gavin rolls his eyes at the thought. "It's fine; we had plans to watch a movie anyway. What time? How long do you want us to keep them?"

"Doesn't matter. We aren't going anywhere. I just need a couple of hours alone with Lake. There's something I need to give her."

"Oh . . . I see," he says. "Just text me when you're through 'giving it to her,' and we'll bring the boys home."

I shake my head at his assumption and laugh. I like Gavin. What I hate, however, is the fact that everything that happens between me and Lake, and Gavin and Eddie . . . we all seem to *know* about. That's the drawback of dating best friends: there are no secrets.

and go to the college to finish registration. I also need to make sure Kel's not outside making out with Kiersten."

We laugh about it now, but in a matter of years it'll be our reality. We won't even be twenty-five, and we'll be raising teenagers. It's a scary thought.

"Hold on. Before you leave . . . what are your plans tomorrow night?"

She rolls her eyes. "What kind of question is that? You're my plan. You're always my only plan."

"Good. Eddie and Gavin are taking the boys. Meet me at seven?"

She perks up and smiles. "Are you asking me out on a real, live date?"

I nod.

"Well, you suck at it, you know. You always have. Sometimes girls like to be *asked* and not *told*."

She's trying to play hard to get, which is pointless, since I've already got her. I play her game anyway. I kneel on the floor in front of her and look into her eyes. "Lake, will you do me the honor of accompanying me on a date tomorrow night?"

She leans back into the couch and looks away. "I don't know, I'm sort of busy," she says. "I'll check my schedule and let you know." She tries to look put out, but a smile breaks out on her face. She leans forward and hugs me; I lose my balance, and we end up on the floor. I roll her onto her back, and she stares up at me and laughs. "Fine. Pick me up at seven."

I brush her hair out of her eyes and run my finger along the edge of her cheek. "I love you, Lake."

"Say it again," she says.

I kiss her forehead and repeat, "I love you, Lake."

"One more time."

"I." I kiss her lips. "And love." I kiss them again. "And you."

"I love you, too."

I ease my body on top of hers and interlock my fingers with hers. I bring our hands above her head and press them into the floor, then lean in as if I'm going to kiss her, but I don't. I like to tease her when we're in this position. I barely touch my lips to hers until she closes her eyes, then I slowly pull away. She opens her eyes, and I smile at her, then lean in again. As soon as her eyes are closed, I pull away again.

"Dammit, Will! Butterflying kiss me already!"

She grabs my face and pulls my mouth to hers. We continue kissing until we get to the "point of retreat," as Lake likes to call it. She climbs out from under me and sits up on her knees as I roll onto my back and remain on the floor. We don't like to get carried away when we aren't alone in the house. It's so easy to do. When we catch ourselves taking things too far, one of us always calls retreat.

Before Julia passed away, we made the mistake of taking things too far, too soon—a crucial mistake on my part. It was just two weeks after we started officially dating, and Caulder was spending the night at Kel's house. Lake and I came back to my place after a movie. We started making out on the couch, and one thing led to another, neither of us willing to stop it. We weren't having sex, but we would have eventually if Julia hadn't walked in when she did. She completely flipped out. We were mortified. She grounded Lake and wouldn't let me see her for two weeks. I apologized probably a million times in those two weeks.

Julia sat us down together and made us swear we would wait at least a year. She made Lake get on the pill and made me look her in the eyes and give her my word. She wasn't upset about the fact that her eighteen-year-old daughter almost had sex. Julia was fairly reasonable and knew it would happen at some point. What hurt her was that I was so willing to take that from Lake after only two weeks of dating. It made me feel incredibly guilty, so I agreed to the promise. She also wanted us to set a good example for Kel and Caulder; she asked us not to spend the night at each other's houses during that year, either. After Julia passed away, we've stuck to our word. More out of respect for Julia than anything. Lord knows it's difficult sometimes. A lot of times.

We haven't discussed it, but last week was exactly a year since we made that promise to Julia. I don't want to rush Lake into anything; I want it to be completely up to her, so I haven't brought it up. Neither has she. Then again, we haven't really been alone.

"Point of retreat," she says, and stands up. "I'll see you tomorrow night. Seven o'clock. Don't be late."

"Go find your phone and text me good night," I tell her.

She opens the door and faces me as she backs out of the house, slowly pulling the door shut. "One more time?" she says.

"I love you, Lake."

Continue Layken and Will's journey in *Point of Retreat*, the second book in the series.

New York Times **Bestseller**
COLLEEN HOOVER

POINT *of* RETREAT

a novel

"As brilliant and entertaining as *Slammed*, *Point of Retreat* is absolute poetry."

—Jamie McGuire,
New York Times
bestselling author
of *Beautiful Disaster*

"Buy the sequel (which is out now—lucky you!), because you're gonna want it. As. Soon. As. You. Finish. Reading."

—Tammara Webber, *New York Times* bestselling author of *Easy*

POINT OF RETREAT

by *New York Times* bestselling author Colleen Hoover

Pick up or download your copy now!

ATRIA
PAPERBACK
A Division of Simon & Schuster